CITY GIRLS TO FRAME

DIANE WINTERS

Diane

First published in 2023 by Blossom Spring Publishing
City Girls To Prairie Girls © 2023 Diane Winters
ISBN 978-1-7392326-9-6
E: admin@blossomspringpublishing.com
W: www.blossomspringpublishing.com

Dedicated to Beth – For remembering the past, the generations before us, our current generation, and the generations to come. Thank you for making me stretch my imagination a little further.

PART ONE

THE ADVENTURES BEGIN

LIST OF CHARACTERS
PART ONE

Ada Paring – daughter of Cecily Paring – from the East Coast.

Alan Beemer – good friend of Herbert Ray and promised to Maude Ray.

Bea and Noreen – sisters who moved to Hastings to become nursemaids.

Cecily Paring – mother of Ada Paring – from the East Coast.

Crystal – owner of the seamstress shop in Omaha.

Dr. Johnson – the only doctor in the Hastings territory.

George Carsten – banker in Hastings.

Greg Walker – good friend to the Turner brothers – rancher.

Harriett Ray – wife of Herbert Ray – mother of Maude Ray – lives on the East Coast.

Herbert Ray – husband of Harriett Ray – father of Maude Ray – lives on the East Coast.

Jackson Turner – younger brother of William Turner – rancher.

Jane Peterson – owner of the women's boarding house in Omaha.

Jesse May Brown – raised by her grandparents in Flat River Missouri.

Maude Ray – daughter of Harriett and Herbert Ray – from the East Coast.

Miss Anderson – country schoolteacher in Hastings.

William Turner – older brother of Jackson Turner – rancher.

JESSE MAY BROWN

Jesse May watched as her grandfather checked the wagon loaded down with their belongings, making sure that the traces were hooked up right to the horses. The old horses were hitched and ready to go, pawing the ground in anticipation. They had made many a trip for their owners, though they had no idea this trip would entail a longer and more arduous excursion. Jesse May's grandmother was already sitting on the hard bench, trying not to cry. She reached up and took her grandmother's hand. They both knew, without saying it, that they might never see each other again. Before climbing into the wagon beside his wife, her grandfather gave Jesse May a quick hug. That hug meant a lot to Jesse May. Her grandfather seldom demonstrated affection. It was just his way.

The horses moved off with a flick of her grandfather's wrist, struggling with the heavy load until the wagon finally began rolling. The trip to St. Louis would be several days of traveling. Her grandparents had located a small home in which to retire to. Their farm had sold for a hefty price. Grandpa had been a good farmer and rancher, having bought several acres near his original homestead. There was no one to leave it to, and it was too much for him to handle any longer. Jesse May's parents had been gone for years.

Now, there was a little money in the bank for her future, whatever that entailed. She watched her grandparents move away from her until they rounded a corner out of sight. Shaking off her sudden loneliness, Jesse May walked back inside the house to retrieve her own trunk. Her grandmother had helped her pack, ensuring she had new dresses and shoes. The neighbor boy would take her to the nearest place to catch a stage. Jesse May walked around the empty house once more before shoving her trunk out the door.

The barnyard was empty of animals now, and the silence was deafening. She heard the wagon long before seeing it. Jesse May paced on the porch until Jimmy pulled up alongside the house. Then, hopping down, he deftly placed her trunk in the back and helped her up to the bench seat. They were a couple of miles down the road before Jimmy broke the silence.

"I wish you would change your mind. Please stay here and marry me."

"I can't, Jimmy. We've been over this before. You know I care for you, but just as a friend. You're more like a brother to me."

Jimmy mumbled to himself and kept quiet. The stage depot was in sight, and, judging by the way the dust was billowing on the horizon, it wouldn't be long before it arrived. Jimmy helped Jesse May down and then retrieved her trunk. Not able to bear watching her get on the stagecoach, he grabbed Jesse May into a bear hug and then jumped into the wagon. Turning the horses, he left in a hurry, riding away from what he considered a big mistake on Jesse May's part.

Several minutes later, Jesse May was on the stage and bouncing around the rough riding carriage. She would have to get used to the ride, as it would be a long trip.

There were still marauders around, and Jesse May didn't wear jewelry or carry cash, except for a few coins. However, her grandmother had sewn a pocket into her dress for a few bills, and there was another secret pocket in her trunk for her jewelry. Not that she had very much, but her grandmother had passed down all her brooches and necklaces, which had been passed down to her, also. The heirlooms were more for sentimental value than being worth anything.

A couple of hours into the trip, Jesse May considered changing course and heading to St. Louis to be with her grandparents. She dozed off somewhere in the middle of that thought and was jerked awake at the next stop. Jesse May took a few moments to orient herself and then got out to stretch her legs. They would soon be at Jefferson City. Jesse May planned to stay one day and take the next stage to Kansas City. She planned to visit each big city for at least a day and decide if she wanted to stay or not.

A woman on her own wasn't safe, so she needed to be exceptionally careful while she explored. It was no wonder her grandparents were worried about her. Even Jesse May herself didn't know what she was looking for.

After her arrival in Jefferson City and Kansas City, she immediately disliked both towns. Kansas City was way too rowdy for her liking, and she took the next stage North. Her destination this time was Omaha. If she didn't like it, she had no idea where to go from there. St. Louis and the safety of her grandparents were beginning to sound like a better idea all the time.

Jesse May had ridden with a variety of passengers. Most of them had been polite. She was on the last leg of her journey before anyone attempted to bother her. It was just her and a man for the long trip between stops, and he was becoming quite obnoxious. Jesse May wasn't sure what she could do to protect herself. She didn't even have an umbrella to hit the man.

She was just getting ready to scream for one of the men on top for assistance when she felt the carriage begin to slow, pulling up to a small stream. The driver and guard got down, and the driver opened the door.

"We need to give the horses a breather and some water. So, please, feel free to stretch your legs."

Jesse May rushed to the door and pulled the driver aside as soon as he assisted her down. "This passenger

5

won't leave me alone. I need you to keep him away from me and not let him talk to me. It's awful some of the things he is saying."

The passenger looked as innocent as could be. "I haven't touched her."

"Please," Jesse May pleaded with the driver.

The driver looked at Jesse May's face and could see the fear in her eyes. "Yes, Ma'am. I'll take care of it. You get some fresh air, and we'll be ready to go pretty soon."

"Thank you." Jesse May walked under a shade tree, carefully watching from the corner of her eye where the obnoxious man was. He apparently thought her shade tree was perfect, so the man headed her way. Jesse May yelled at him:" Stay away from me. You can go over there." Jesse May pointed to another tree.

"Now, Ma'am, I see no reason we can't share the same shade tree." He continued to leer at her and walked closer.

Just then, the guard walked over with his shotgun pointed at the man. "Get your tail end up on top of the coach."

"Now, see here. I'm not doing anything wrong."

"Move."

The guard shoved the shotgun barrel into the man's chest, so he had no choice but to do as he was told. With one last look at Jesse May, the man pulled himself into the guard's spot. The driver had finished watering the horses and had checked the harnesses. Jesse May was helped back into the carriage, and the guard jumped in and sat across from her.

"We'll let him sit in the hot sun for a few miles. We should be fine. Now that so many people are riding the train, the bad fellas have gotten pretty scarce along this route. And we never carry strong boxes anymore. I suppose I'll be out of a job, pretty soon. Now. I'll sit back and take a nap. Feel free to take one yourself."

"Thank you. I might just do that."

The guard stretched out his legs, tipped his hat over his face, crossed his arms, and was soon snoring. Jesse May smiled and relaxed. Occasionally, the wind blew the words inside from the top of the carriage. That awful man was constantly complaining about sitting in the sun. Jesse May smiled before dropping into a fitful sleep.

At the next stop, the guard hopped out, and once the man was down from his perch, the driver told him he had to wait for the next stage. A couple more people got on, and the rest of Jesse May's trip to Omaha went without incident. The man they left behind strung out several sentences with words Jesse May had never heard before, but she knew they weren't good. She made sure she thanked the guard for his kindness.

After what seemed like forever, Jesse May was ready for a break from traveling. She was directed to a woman's boarding house and planned to stay for several days. The first order of business was a bath, followed by a good night's sleep in a real bed. Then she would send her grandparents a letter to let them know she had arrived safely. It was too soon to know what she would do from here, but she'd had enough traveling around in a stagecoach.

MAUDE RAY AND ADA PARING

Maude Ray left Boston in a huff. Her parents had demanded she marry some upstart. Alan Beemer gave Maude a terrible feeling when he came anywhere close to her, and lately, that had been several times since he had been invited repeatedly to the house for meetings with her father. Those were followed by supper, where the slimy man would sit as close to her as possible. If Maude moved her chair away even an inch or two, he eventually moved his closer to her. As a result, Maude frequently received glares from her mother and was sternly lectured after the meal. But, no matter what Maude said, there was no way out of the soon-to-be wedding.

Once the fittings for her dowry began, Maude knew she had to do something brash. Her first stop was to talk to her best friend, Ada Paring. She, too, was being pushed to get married, but in Ada's case, her parents would be happy with anyone Ada chose.

The two met for a walk in the park and sat by themselves to discuss their futures. Neither one felt like they could go through with a wedding to anyone at this point. Both felt stifled, but for different reasons. Together they plotted a way to escape their situations. More so, Maude. Ada wasn't under any time constraints like her best friend. Ideas were bandied about, but they couldn't find any way to fix their problems. Promising to meet back in the same place in two days, they hugged, and Maude trudged home, feeling defeated.

A couple of days later, Ada met Maude with a huge smile. "I have the answer for both of us."

Maude felt her stomach flutter and quickly sat beside her friend. "Tell me, quick. My parents have set a date for the wedding."

Ada's mouth fell open. "Oh, no!" She picked up the newspaper and handed it to Maude. "Look at this."

Maude looked to see mail-order bride ads. She looked at Ada. "I don't have time to do all of that. Too bad we didn't think of it sooner."

Smiling, Ada took the paper and folded it tight. "We need to hop the train and head off to one of these states. We can hunt for a husband once we get there."

"You're crazy; you know that?"

"I know, but I'll be with you."

The two sat quietly in thought, pondering their situation. Finally, Maude spoke in a whisper. "What about money and our clothes? We can't pack a trunk without our parents knowing about it."

"Just a satchel or something with a few things. You'll have to get some money from your parents somehow. I can check out the train schedule, and we can plan from there. I'm unsure how far to take the train or how much it will cost."

"It's so daring, Ada. My stomach is in knots just thinking about how to get away."

"I'll do some investigating, and we will meet back here. It's easier for me to check things out. Your parents keep too close of an eye on you."

"Oh, Ada." Maude took her hand in hers. "Do you really think we can get away?"

"The bigger question is, can you marry Mr. Creeper?"

Maude laughed at the new nickname. "No. I can't. We have to find a way to leave. And soon."

"Alright. I'll meet you back here in a couple of days, and we will finalize our plan."

Maude spent her evenings looking at her clothes, trying to decide what would be the easiest to pack. Finally, she realized with stark realization that all her fine belongings would remain behind. Only a couple of day dresses would be appropriate to roll up and stuff in a valise.

Maude finally found a small valise and packed it with a couple of dresses and a few other personal items then pushed it under her bed. After a moment, she pulled it back out and placed it in the bottom of her wardrobe. Still not feeling right, she took her clothes out of the bag and hung them back up but left her personal items in the valise. Feeling better about not being found out, Maude now had to figure out how to get money.

In the meantime, Ada went on an errand for her mother and detoured by the train station. She took down several dates and times and asked how much different trips would cost. Then, armed with her new information, Ada remembered to run her mother's errand before going home.

Feeling excited, Ada rushed into her room and began pacing the floor. Finally, she looked at her scribbled notes and formulated a plan. By the time she met up with Maude the following day, Ada was ready to leave town.

Maude rushed to meet Ada. She was late because her mother had insisted on another fitting. Ada was pacing by the park bench and was happy to see Maude rushing toward her.

"I thought you might have forgotten about our meeting."

"Mother kept me busy. I thought I would never get away." Maude took some deep breaths and looked around before sitting. "You look like the cat that ate the canary with that grin on your face. Do tell me you have good news."

"Wonderful news. Look." Ada drew out a rewritten list and showed it to her best friend. "We can go across the country to the other side, but I vote we stop halfway."

"Why halfway?"

"Most of the men looking for wives are out there. Men trying to make an honest living, and we can have our pick of the litter."

Maude laughed. "Ada. You are so funny. Let me look at that list again." The two checked out the dates and times again. "Look, Ada. See this? The train leaves around the same time as we usually get together." Maude put the paper down and looked across the park. "I need to find a way to get some money." Maude turned to her friend. "Did you get some, yet?"

"I did. Do you want me to find a bit more for you?"

Maude shook her head. "No. I must do it. Invite me for tea three days from now. We will leave from your house. I'll try to bring my valise, but no promises. If I get enough money, I'll just leave it behind and buy my things later."

"Maude, I'm so excited that we're going to really do this. We have to save you from a terrible future."

Maude nodded. "I'll do what I can."

She got up to head for home. Grabbing Ada into a big hug, she took a deep breath and hurried on her way. She just had to find some money without her father finding out. Just thinking of marrying someone she loathed firmed her resolve to leave with Ada. Her best friend was much braver, and, over the years, she had gotten into trouble with her parents more than once for some stunts she had pulled.

The following day, Maude received her Invitation for tea at Ada's house. Her mother tried to change the plans, but Maude put her foot down. She explained to her mother that with little time left before she married, she wanted to spend as much time as possible with her friends. Finally, her mother gave in but made it well known that Maude's circle of friends would change immediately once she married. And that meant that Ada would no longer be accessible.

Finally, the day arrived for what Ada called 'escape day'. Maude sneaked into the kitchen and took the house money from its box while the cook stepped outside. Then, rushing back to her room, she pulled out her valise. She carefully packed a nice simple dress on the bottom, then followed that with three of her garden dresses. Finally, Maude put a couple of extra layers under her own dress before heading toward the front door.

Ada only lived six blocks away, and Maude tried to get out the door before her mother saw her. No such luck.

"What are you doing with your valise?"

Maude jumped. Her hand was on the doorknob, and she gripped it tightly. "Oh! You scared me." Maude tried to swallow, but her mouth was dry with fear. "Didn't I tell you? We are donating some of our clothes to the poor house. I thought, with my new wardrobe almost ready, you wouldn't mind me donating my garden dresses. This was the easiest way to carry them." Maude set down the valise and opened it to show her mother what was packed.

"I see. Well, that's a lovely thing to do, dear." Her mother eyed her daughter warily and had a frown on her face as she looked Maude over head to toe. "Come home soon. We have things to do before Mr. Beemer attends supper with us this evening."

Maude grimaced at her fiancée's name. "Yes, Mother. I'm going to be late, so I need to leave now. Goodbye, Mother."

Maude rushed out the door before she broke down. She was shaking from head to toe. Relieved when she arrived at her accomplice's place, they went directly to Ada's room so she could remove the extra layers. She changed into one of the garden dresses and left her fancy silk dress on Ada's bed.

Ada grabbed her valise, and the two rushed out the back door, away from all they knew. It was several minutes before they arrived at the train station, but they were relieved that their train had not yet arrived. The young women bought tickets to Omaha and then sat waiting impatiently for the train. It hadn't occurred to them to bring any food until they noticed someone eating.

Ada jumped up and rushed out the door to a small deli nearby. The deli served many a train passenger and knew just what she needed to buy for the trip. She purchased a few food items and hurried back. Maude laughed nervously as she paid Ada for her share. Soon, they could hear the train's mournful whistle as it neared the station. Maude and Ada held hands tightly as the two young women headed out on their own. Neither one wanted to let go of the other, fearing that one of them would change their mind. But, together, they were stronger.

The next thing they knew, the girls were on the train and headed to parts beyond. It was too late to change their minds now. Tears fell down the cheeks of both girls. Some tears were for what they left behind, but many of Maude's were from knowing she wouldn't have to get married to that awful man. Their lives would be forever changed by the decisions they had just made.

The bench seat across from the girls remained empty, so Maude moved over to face Ada. The noise of the train made it almost impossible to talk to each other, but they watched the ever-changing view from the window. A couple of hours later, the sun was hanging low in the sky. Maude moved next to Ada, and they dug out a few provisions. They were both starving by then, as neither one had eaten since breakfast. Their stomachs had been tied in knots most of the day.

Looking at the large chunk of cheese, they both laughed and joked about how they would need to take bites like a mouse since they didn't have anything to cut it with. Finally, a kind gentleman sitting across the aisle from them noticed the girl's dilemma and offered to slice the cheese for them. Ada had him cut the hard bread while he was at it. The girls offered him a slice, and he gladly took the food. The gentleman pointed out a water barrel strapped in the corner so they could wash the food down when they were done.

Rationing their food was a must, so they only ate enough to satisfy their hunger pangs. The girls drank a generous amount of water. They then suddenly realized they had no idea where they would be able to relieve themselves. It had been a long day, and neither one had realized how unprepared they were for this trek.

It was pitch black outside when the train finally made a stop. Everyone was invited to get off the train and walk a bit. The stopover was not only for the passengers but also for the train to add water and wood for fuel. The girls readily hopped off the steps and found a privy. After a short walk, the girls felt like they were ready to continue. They were learning as they went.

By the time they returned to their seats, a few more people were on board, but their seats were still available. Grateful, Maude took the other bench. The girls got their bags down and used them for pillows. Finally, they curled up on the hard benches and tried to sleep.

Several days later, the girls got off the train in Omaha. They had long since had anything to talk about and were both grumpy, filthy, and exhausted from their excursion. The girls paid to have someone take them to a hotel for the night. All they wanted was a bath and a bed. They would figure everything else out in the morning. They were so tired that they got into bed and skipped the bath.

After breakfast, the girls inquired about a place they could stay for a month or so. They were told about a woman's boarding house several blocks away, but since this part of town could be a little rowdy at times, the clerk suggested they hire someone to take them. Not wanting to have any trouble now that they had got to their destination, they hired a driver. By mid-morning, the girls had a room with two beds. They sorted out their belongings and arranged for a bath. Still tired, all they wanted to do was rest before exploring their new surroundings. It was at supper when they met Jesse May Brown. The three young women got on quite easily. They planned to get together again the following morning at breakfast. Still tired, Ada and Maude turned in early, anxious to awaken to their new life.

MAUDE, ADA, AND JESSE MAY

Jane Peterson ran the boarding house. She was a comely woman, rarely smiled, and worked hard to keep her boarding house clean and inviting.

After Jesse May recovered from her lengthy trip, she offered to help Jane but refused to be paid. She began by helping to clean off the table and help with the dishes. Jane adamantly refused help with the laundry and cooking. Jesse May grabbed a broom and tidied up around the place. Then she did a little exploring in the neighborhood stores. She was still contemplating what to do or where to go when Maude and Ada arrived.

Breakfast was a pleasant affair now that the girls were rested and even Jane had a slight smile on her face. Everyone helped clear the dishes without question before heading down the street. Maude mentioned they needed to find the telegraph office first thing. Jane directed them to the right area, and the girls began their walk.

It was a gorgeous day. Not quite spring and not still winter; they enjoyed the walk. The trio took their time, window shopping as they went. Omaha was definitely a cow town, and the men outnumbered women ten to one. Ada spent most of her time flirting as the men passed by. More than once, Maude jerked Ada's arm to get her attention away from the cowboys. When they finally arrived at the telegraph office, Maude was disgusted by Ada's behavior. Jesse May laughed at her antics.

Ada tried to look innocent. "What? I've never seen so many good-looking men in one place before."

Maude shook her head. "Okay, but you don't need to act like a hussy. You'll get us all in trouble."

Jesse May finally got into the conversation. "Ada, some of these men will take your flirting as an invitation and won't take no for an answer later. As fun as it's been to watch you, Maude is right. This isn't like where you're from. These men will take liberties if given a chance. There will be plenty of time to meet men in a safer setting than a street corner. Church, barn dances, socials, and places like that."

Ada huffed but also noticed the telegraph operator nodding his head in agreement with Jesse May. "I suppose. I'll try not to be so obvious." Maude and Jesse May both shook their heads. Ada picked up some paper. "Let's get our wires sent."

Maude picked up a piece of paper and thought about what to write. She had been dreading this moment the whole trip. Ada quickly jotted down a few lines. Maude looked at it before Ada handed it off to the operator. All it said was: *Headed West with Maude. We are safe. Looking for a man.* Maude shook her head. Ada's parents were so much different from her own. They would be thrilled by her telegraph. While Ada paid for her message and watched it being sent, Maude finally wrote: *Went West with Ada. Safe. Could not marry Alan.* Ada looked at her note and nodded her approval. Maude handed it over and paid her fee. She didn't want to hang around to watch it being sent. She grabbed Ada and headed out the door. Jesse May followed but didn't question either one. As the girls walked down the street, Ada spotted a *HELP WANTED* sign in the window of a mercantile.

"Let's go in here." They entered, and Ada immediately questioned the owner about the job. His wife came out from the back room, and she introduced herself.

"As you can see, my wife is expecting soon, and I'll need someone to do everything she has helped me with. That includes some cleaning and straightening around the store."

Ada and the couple talked for several minutes, and before the two knew it, Ada was hired for a few hours a week, starting the following day. They were all excited about the job, but not nearly as much as Ada was.

As they walked down the street, she practically burst at the seams. "And think about how many single men walk through the store every day!"

There was a pause before Jesse May and Maude both cracked up laughing. Then, they each tucked an arm through one of Ada's and headed back to the boardinghouse. By the time they were back, Maude had realized Ada's job had meant they were staying in Omaha and not going any farther. At least for now. There was no way she would leave Ada behind, either. All these men wouldn't know what hit them.

Jane was reading the paper, a cup of coffee beside her. She heard the girls coming long before she saw them. Laying her paper aside, she waited for them to come through the door. There would be no reading with all the noise those girls were making. Jane suddenly realized it was something she enjoyed. Her days had all been fairly bland up until this group joined her. Ada announced her job as soon as she saw Jane. Jane assured the group that the Jacksons were good people to work for.

"So, I guess you will stay in Omaha after all?" Both Maude and Ada nodded. "What about you, Miss Jesse May?"

"I suppose I better be looking for a job, too. I just made some new friends."

Jane pushed the paper toward Jesse May. "My break is over. There is a job or two listed in here."

Jane left the girls scanning the paper as she took her coffee to the back porch. Jane stood there looking toward the horizon. The town was growing all around her, and she knew that people would keep coming, just like those three girls. She didn't know how she felt about it all, but for now, she had some permanent boarders who weren't afraid of hard work. She put her empty coffee mug down and started work on the laundry again.

Jesse May exclaimed. "Look. The school needs a teacher. That's what I want to do. I'll go talk to this person tomorrow. What about you, Maude? What do you want to do?"

Sighing, Maude answered, "I have no idea. I was supposed to get married and run a house." Ada and Jesse May looked at each other and then back to Maude. Maude followed her response by whispering, "But absolutely not with Alan." She shuddered. "I just couldn't do it. He was abhorrent."

Ada and Jesse May hugged Maude as the tears flowed. Maude was led to a chair in the parlor, and they all sat down. It was the first time Maude had cried that much over leaving home because of Alan Beemer. She didn't count the emotional tears when they left home. These tears were for the disappointment in her parents not listening to her concerns and how she had to uproot herself to save her life.

Jesse May went back and retrieved the paper. Seeing only a couple of ads, she shook her head. "There is really nothing here, but something will come up. Look at Ada. She found her job when we walked by a store."

Maude felt better once she had shed a few tears. It was time to decide her future. Whatever it held, it would start in Omaha which meant not getting married to Alan Beemer. That, at least, was good news.

MAUDE

Ada went off to work, Jesse May headed out to talk to someone about the teaching job, and Maude stayed at the boarding house and helped Jane. Maude worked diligently from room to room, dusting and sweeping. The place always seemed to have travelers staying over, so there was always laundry to be done. Jane never let anyone help her with the laundry as it was nasty, back-breaking work. Maude wandered out the back door and watched as Jane finished hanging up the last sheet.

Jane walked to the porch and took Maude by the arm. "Let's take a well-deserved break."

They poured themselves a coffee, and Jane pulled out a few cookies. They sat at the table, and both sighed at the same time. They chuckled and then started to eat their cookies and drink the coffee, surrounded by a pleasant silence.

Maude was much more reserved than her friend, Ada. Her flaming red hair was managed by tying it up in a severe bun and after all her hard work this morning, strands were poking out all over and curling around her face. Jane noted how the loose curls had softened Maude's look.

"You should always wear your hair like that."

"Like what?" Maude tried to tuck some curls away.

"With the curls floating around like that. You're prettier that way than that tight bun. In fact, you should let it all down."

"Let it down?"

"Yes."

"It gets so out of control, I can't seem to manage it all."

Jane got up and took the matter into her own hands. Maude's hair not only tumbled loose and down her back, but the curls bounced and jumped around until her hair settled. Jane sat back and smiled. "Much better."

Maude blushed. "Are you sure?" She patted her head.

"Definitely. Just tie it back when you're working. You aren't back East anymore. We're just average country folk around here."

Maude soon excused herself when she couldn't wait any longer. She ran up to her room to look in the mirror. She always brushed her hair and braided it before going to bed, but Maude hadn't ever considered leaving it down. Maybe she would leave it in a braid until she was used to it being free. The longer she looked at herself, the more she realized Jane was right. Finding a ribbon, she tied it back. The hair fell in ringlets, and smaller curls flew around her face. Smiling, she headed back to the parlor to read a book. Jane had a shelf with several titles she hadn't read before. Until she knew what to do for a job, she might as well enjoy herself. Her money certainly wouldn't last much longer than a day or two.

Jane saw Maude walk through to the parlor and smiled when she noticed Maude's hair. Jane realized she hadn't smiled as much in the last few years as she had in the last few days. She shook her head and busied herself with the supper meal.

Ada arrived home just before Jesse May came flying inside. Jesse May had spent the day visiting with several people about the teaching position. She had to be approved by them all. She couldn't wait to tell everyone all about it. Ada had had a full day, and loved every minute of her new job. Still, she only wanted to talk about the good-looking men that walked around Jackson's Mercantile instead of her actual work.

All this chatter happened over supper. Ada stopped suddenly and looked at Maude. "What happened to you?"

Maude looked puzzled. "What do you mean?"

"Your hair. You never wear it down."

"Oh." Maude patted it and gave a quick glance at Jane. "I've decided to wear it down. Mother isn't here to criticize me."

The girls complimented her and gushed over how it made her look so pretty. Maude gave Jane a look and mouthed a thank you. Jane returned a brief nod and went on with her meal.

Jesse May wouldn't begin teaching until fall. Before school started, she would be able to move into the small home located behind the school building, but she needed an income in the meantime. One of the families she talked to offered to have Jesse May come to their house for a few hours a week and tutor the children over the summer. Having recently moved to town, they hadn't been able to offer any formal education to their children for the last couple of years.

With Ada and Jesse May out of the house several days a week, Jane hired Maude to help around the boarding house to pay for her room and board. It was a win-win for them both.

One day, Maude began to make herself a dress. As she stitched and sewed, Jane watched the dress come together. It was a simple design, but the color and print were perfect for Maude's coloring.

"You do beautiful work, Maude." Jane looked closely at the detailed work. "I love the design, too. Maybe you should do this for a living."

"I never considered it. My mother made sure I could sew but was always critical of my choices of color and style."

"Apparently, your mother was critical of everything you did. You have a wonderful talent. You need to go see a friend of mine. And wear this when you do. In fact, I'll go with you."

"Who is your friend?"

"She's a seamstress." Jane smiled. "You'll like her. She sews for all the rich people living on the other side of town. I believe you will fit right in and be able to handle their needs."

Maude fidgeted with the last button she needed to sew on. "You think I could do that? I love to sew."

"I'm sure of it. We'll go tomorrow."

True to her word, Jane hooked up her buggy, and the two were soon on their way across town. These were parts of Omaha Maude and the girls had never seen. Maude was surprised at the shops and large homes.

"I didn't know this area existed."

"Well, we live in the original town. As the big whigs moved in, they wanted to be as far away from the riff-raff as they could. They didn't want to have to associate with people like me."

"Oh, Jane. That's awful." Maude paused. "But I understand it. I'm afraid my parents are like that. They barely tolerated Ada. Her family wasn't rich like my own, but they were well enough to live in the same neighborhood."

Jane maneuvered her buggy to a side street and stopped. "We'll stop here and walk to the shop. My buggy isn't up to their standards, either."

Jane smiled at Maude to let her know it didn't bother her in the least. She tied the horses to the railing, and the women walked down the fancy walkway. Maude glanced in a few windows and thought of home. On any given day, Ada and Maude would go shopping in a store very similar to these.

"Here we are."

Maude pulled up short, almost running into Jane. "Sorry. I was daydreaming, I guess."

Jane smiled. "Come on."

As they entered the shop, Maude heard a little tinkle of a bell over the door. Then they heard someone say, "Be right there." Before long, a woman strode out from behind a curtain. "Jane! It's so good to see you again. It's been so long." The two women hugged.

"Crystal, I wanted you to meet Maude Ray. She and her friends have been staying at my place for a few weeks. This gal can sew up a storm, and I thought you might need a little help around the shop."

"Oh my." Crystal turned to Maude and did a quick check of her dress. "Are you wearing something you made?"

Maude shyly nodded and said, "Yes, Ma'am."

"Come into the back so I can take a closer look."

The three went into a room behind the curtain. It was filled with dresses in various stages of completion. Crystal began to look at all of Maude's stitching and fancy work while Maude looked around the room. The store front was filled with bolts of fabric, thread, buttons, and lace. It was all laid out in an orderly fashion. In contrast, the back room looked like an explosion had occurred. Done inspecting the dress, Crystal and Jane chatted about life in general while Maude spent her time eyeing all the projects.

"Well, Maude. I do love this dress you are wearing. And your stitching is perfection. I'd love to have you work for me. I pay by the finished project."

Maude blinked a few times and couldn't believe her ears. "Really?" Jane laughed, and Maude looked at her in surprise. She had never heard Jane laugh before. "Can I take something back with me, or do I need to work from here?"

"Hmmm. It is a long drive over. How about you take a couple of projects with you today, and when you bring them back, we can discuss additional work after I look at the final product."

"That's wonderful. Thank you."

The women looked at different dresses, and Maude picked out two formal gowns that needed a lot of sewing completed.

"Are you sure you want to start with those?"

Maude nodded. "Yes. But I think we need to add some fancy piecework to dress it up a bit." Crystal frowned. "Once I get them together and bring them back, I'll show you what I mean. I believe you will be pleased with the finished product."

The material was bundled up, and while Crystal and Maude talked, Jane went to get the carriage. They were soon on their way back to the boarding house. Jane helped Maude take her large packages to the parlor, and Maude was soon busy preparing to work on the first dress. Unfortunately, due to the waning light, she would have to wait until the following morning to start. So instead of sewing, she helped Jane get supper ready. Several guests were staying right now, so Maude shut the sliding doors to the parlor to prevent anyone from touching the material.

After supper, Maude, Ada, and Jesse May helped clean up the table and do the dishes. Then the three girls went into the parlor and shut the door behind them. Maude couldn't wait to show them what she would be working on to pay her own way. After all, the few dollars she had come with were gone now. The girls chatted well into the late evening before turning in. They were all excited about their futures.

CHANGES COMING

The summer sky shone hot almost every day. Everyone began to be short-tempered due to the lingering heat. Crops dried up, and farmers began to worry about how or if they could survive another year. Gardens were given as much water as a person could carry to keep the plants alive. But even then, the heat managed to kill off a good portion of the produce. Jane was grateful that the travelers had all but stopped for a few weeks. Her food supply was dangerously low, and her garden was pathetic.

Ada came home discouraged in the middle of the day. She announced that the Jacksons had had to let her go. Business was slow, and now that Mrs. Jackson was up and around and the baby was doing well, she was helping out in the store once again.

Jesse May came home early, too. The heat was too much, and the children too crabby. The parents had agreed that everyone could wait until school started in the fall, so for now, Jesse May was out of a job, too.

The girls watched as Maude put on the finishing touches to her most recent project. It was a lovely gown made to be worn at a fancy dance or dinner. On occasion, Maude had twinges of jealousy since she had, at one time, been the one to wear such a fine dress. Maude gathered the dress and hung it over the mannequin to ensure it hung right and that she hadn't missed anything. She checked all the seams, the buttons, and the lace, followed by the hemline. Noting it all looked perfect, she stood back.

"What do you think, girls?"

Ada clapped her hands. "It's gorgeous, as usual. I'm glad I don't have to wear all of that frip-frap anymore."

"You are?" Maude was surprised.

Ada nodded. "I was never comfortable in any of those fancy dresses. They itched and choked me. I'm much happier in my day dresses that don't have a bunch of layers under the folds."

Jesse May nodded. "I've never worn anything that fine, but I would hate to have myself all corseted up in this heat."

The girls laughed, and Maude sat back down. "So, what are you two going to do now that you don't have jobs?"

Jesse May smiled. "I'll get settled into the little house the school provided for me. I've earned enough to get by until the school starts to pay me. And I have my savings if I absolutely need some money." Then, she whispered, "I think Jane needs us to get out of here. I'm afraid we eat more than she can afford, and we certainly aren't paying her very much to stay here." The girls nodded in agreement.

Maude looked at Ada. "What about you?"

Ada blushed. "Well..." Clearing her throat, she hesitated before blurting out her answer. "Greg Walker asked me to marry him and move West."

"What?" both Maude and Jesse May exclaimed at the same time.

"I didn't want to leave the Jacksons in a lurch or Maude behind."

Maude shook her head. "Oh, Ada. Why didn't you tell me? I knew you two were sparking."

"I just felt bad that you hadn't met anyone yet, and you spend all of your time with those darn dresses."

Maude got up and moved next to Ada. "You're my best friend and saved me from that awful man. But all you've ever wanted was a good man and a simple way of life. It will be adventurous for you, and I think you should do it. In fact, I'll get started on your wedding dress immediately."

"Really? We aren't planning anything big. We will have it at the church, of course. And I want my parents to come. So, if they agree, I'll wait until they get here."

Jesse May stood up and walked over to the fancy dress. "Will your dress be something like this?"

Ada frowned. "Oh! Heavens no! Something simple I can wear to church on Sundays on the prairie. I'll have to have a few more day dresses, too, but I can get them at Jackson's Mercantile."

The girls were chattering away incessantly about their future plans when Jane walked into the room. "What is going on in here? I could hear you clear outside."

Jesse May grinned and shouted, "Ada's getting married!"

Jane gasped. "Already? Let me guess. Greg Walker." Everyone laughed.

Ada walked over and hugged Jane. "I guess we've been pretty obvious, haven't we? We're moving West, and I'd like to stay at the boarding house until I get married."

"Of course. You are welcome to stay as long as you want." Jane looked around the room. "What about you two? Anything to surprise me with?"

Jesse May spoke up. "I'll be moving into the house by the school soon. It needs to be cleaned up a bit first."

Maude looked at the floor, embarrassed to talk about her plans. "There's a room above Crystal's boutique that I will be moving into. But I'm not leaving until Ada gets married. If that's okay, that is."

Jane gathered the three girls in her arms. With a little sniff to keep the tears at bay, she hugged them all tightly. Then, pulling back, she asked them to sit down.

"You girls arrived at a terrible time in my life. My husband died a couple of years ago in an accident at work, and my only child died a few months later from some illness. We don't know what it was, and the doctor didn't know how to treat something he had never seen before. I had all but given up and was ready to join them when you three arrived. You have all brought me joy and meaning to my life in your own special ways. If I can survive this blasted heat, I plan on helping other girls just like you three."

With no other boarders, the four women put together a light meal and sat outside on the back porch, trying to catch what little breeze they could. The humidity was always high since they lived right along the Missouri River. They sat there long into the evening, chattering about their lives and futures.

As they began to head into the house, a far-off rumble of thunder could be heard. Hoping for a break in the weather, they headed toward their rooms. Jane watched the girls go to their rooms before moving outside to the front porch. It was almost dark, but the clouds looked dark and sinister. Frowning, she worried about what the storm could bring. Closing up the house to the sudden wind became a priority. As she shut the parlor windows, she looked at the beautiful dress that Maude had just completed. Jane quickly folded it up and placed it in the box Maude had for transporting the finery. She slid it under a heavy table and finished closing up the house.

Returning to the front porch, her worries were proven correct. The air had chilled, and Jane could see a wall of hail and rain headed their way. She ran inside and yelled for the girls. They came out of their rooms and stood at the upstairs railing. Jane told them about the terrible storm raging toward them. She also said to gather some clothes and come downstairs immediately.

Already in their night clothes, the girls grabbed the clothing and shoes they had just removed. As soon as they were downstairs, Jane took them to the root cellar. The wind was blowing hard by then, and she had a bit of a problem getting the cellar doors shut and latched. The girls huddled together as Jane found her lantern and finally got the match to light the wick. The warm glow helped comfort the group.

Jane told them to get dressed again. They struggled in the small space, but with a bit of help from each other and Jane holding the lamp, they managed. The noise from the hail was so loud no one could hear each other without shouting.

When the noise died down, Jane waited and listened to the rainfall. They would be drenched if they tried to leave the cellar too soon; it might be close to the back porch, but there wasn't any shelter between the two. Neither Maude nor Ada knew much about these types of storms, so Jane explained what she had seen and heard, and what could happen. Jesse May had experienced all kinds of storms, including tornadoes, when she was on the farm in Missouri. Jane wasn't sure if there was a tornado or not, but the hail was fierce, and she was afraid of the damage they would find.

When the rain finally slowed down, and the wind backed off a little, Jane peeked out the door. She could see that the house looked intact, but the ground was piled with hail. Since it was still raining, she told the girls to scurry to the kitchen and wait for her before going any further. Once they were all inside, Jane led them single file into the rest of the house. The only damage they could see was a couple of broken windows on the main floor. Heading upstairs, every window on one side was broken, and the rain blew in with the wind. There was hail scattered across the floor, along with the broken glass. It would be sometime before Jane could repair all the damage.

The next day, Jane looked at the damage outside. The hail had wiped out the small garden plot, but Jesse May and Jane gathered what they could of the produce that was left. The root vegetables were left in the ground, and Jane hoped they wouldn't rot before she harvested them.

Ada borrowed a rig from Jane and rode out to find Greg Walker. She told him the good news that she was ready to get married and move West with him. When she told him about the broken windows from the storm, he returned to town with her to do the repairs. Greg was a hired man at a ranch, and when he told his boss he would be getting married, the man knew Greg would be moving on soon. So, he not only let Greg go to town with Ada, but he also sent some spare supplies to help board up the windows. Once Ada's wagon was full of supplies, Greg got on his horse and rode to Jane's house alongside Ada.

Maude was happy to find the finished dress carefully wrapped under a table; the mannequin had been close to a window to provide the light she needed. Unfortunately, that window had splintered from the hail, and the rain had blown inside. The storm would have ruined the dress. When Ada returned with the buggy, Maude told Jane she would take the dress to Crystal's shop. She also wanted to check and see if the boutique had sustained any damage. Thankfully, the dress shop had fared well.

While Maude was there, she told Crystal that Ada was getting married and that she would move into the room above the shop once Ada had moved West. Crystal was thrilled, and Maude was glad not to worry about bad weather to transport her finished products. Each finished project was precious to her. And now, Maude would be right there and have all the supplies she needed.

THE WEDDING

Everyone was busy canning produce or cleaning and repairing the house for the next few days. Greg was welcomed like an old friend, and he handled the teasing like a pro. Ada heard back from her parents and was thrilled they would be coming for the wedding.

Greg had repaired one of the big rooms first to make sure his new in-laws-to-be would be comfortable. Ada worried about leaving Maude in Omaha, but with Jane and Jesse May around, she knew that Maude would be in good hands.

Maude made Ada's wedding dress. Ada had picked out the material at Jackson's Mercantile, along with a couple of new day dresses. Greg had gone ahead to make sure that the land he had heard about was still available and would work for a small herd of cattle. He didn't want to buy anything until Ada had agreed to get married. Greg wanted a partner when he moved to the prairie and knew he had found one in Ada. He promised to return as soon as possible and took the train to save time.

Ada's parents arrived, and she picked them up from the station. Hugs and kisses all around, they slowly made their way back to Jane's house. Ada's parents took in their surroundings along the way, but more importantly, they were happy with how their daughter looked. So happy. After they arrived at the boarding house, they were also impressed with Maude's new demeanor. Relaxed and smiling, Maude hugged Mr. and Mrs. Paring. During that brief moment, Maude had a feeling of homesickness. But it soon passed, knowing that if this had been her parents, they would be scolding her for the choices she had been making lately, and then drag her away to a miserable life.

It was only a few days before Ada's wedding.

Everywhere you looked, the boarding house was busy with preparations. Ada and Greg would have a small reception before they left on the evening train. Ada had packed and repacked several times, trying to decide what she needed to take with her. The Parings had bought more items for her new home than she could count. Greg finished purchasing the property, which had a small home already built. It needed work, but he felt up to the job. With help from his current boss, Greg purchased a half-dozen steers, a milk cow, and some chickens. All would be loaded on the train just before leaving.

Mrs. Paring took Maude aside one evening, a couple of days before the wedding. They took a stroll to have a moment to themselves. After a few minutes of silence, Mrs. Paring stopped to look at someone's flowers. Considering all the recent hail, Maude was surprised anything was left to bloom.

"Maude, your parents are worried sick about you. Your mother says they have only received one telegram, but you never said where you were. All I would tell her was that Ada's letters have said you were just fine and that you girls had made some new friends. I must say, Jesse May and Jane appear to be lovely people, and I'm glad to see you look so healthy and vibrant. In fact, I'm not sure I've ever seen you look so happy."

Maude smiled. "I'm very happy, Mrs. Paring. I could never have married that awful man. Ada saved me, and I'll always be grateful."

"I know, dear. I've received some very detailed letters from Ada. She also demanded I not tell your parents where you were. Ada even reminded us not to tell your parents we were coming here for the wedding. That is why I needed to talk to you tonight. You see, when we get home, we will be posting Ada's wedding in the paper. Then you realize everyone, including your parents, will know your whereabouts."

Maude nodded and continued the walk. She was thoughtful in her response. "I want all of our friends to know Ada is happily married. Greg is a wonderful man, and he has settled her down. I will miss her terribly, but we knew the changes in our lives could eventually split us up. If I had married Alan, I would never have been able to see Ada or any of my other friends again. But it's different with Ada and Greg. She is happy, and we can mail letters to each other. Maybe someday I'll find someone, but I won't return home."

Mrs. Paring agreed. "Your parents are hard people, Maude. You are of age now, and you can make your own decisions. Even if they come to get you, you don't have to return with them. What I would suggest is to write a letter, and I'll take it to your parents. Tell them the truth. You've made a life for yourself here, and if you go home, it should be on your terms, not theirs." Mrs. Paring chuckled. "It's independent ideas like that that drive your parents crazy, you know. That's why they disapproved of Ada and how we brought her up."

"I know," Maude laughed. "My parents had a hard time with my relationship with Ada." Maude sighed as they climbed the steps of the boarding house. Then, turning to Mrs. Paring, she hugged her tight. "Thank you for being so understanding. I promise to write that letter, and I'm so glad you decided to come to Omaha for the wedding."

"I wouldn't have missed it for anything, my dear. And if you let me know when you're getting married, I'll try to show up for yours, too." After another hug, the two walked back into the chaos together. The decorations were almost done, and Jane and Jesse May giggled like schoolgirls. Ada was sitting at the table with Greg, holding hands.

Everyone met at the church on Saturday morning, and the ceremony went off without a problem. Ada's dress was simple but beautiful. She made a lovely bride. Mr. Paring had tears in his eyes as he gave away his little girl. The reception was lively, and soon Greg, his boss, and a few friends went to the railroad station to load all the animals and Ada's belongings onto the evening train. Several chests of goods were waiting to be loaded, too, thanks to Mrs. Paring. Greg had rented his own train car due to the animals. He hoped there would be plenty of space in the baggage car for all their other items. When the train arrived, it would take some time to hook up his cattle car.

Ada said goodbye to everyone, and her parents took her to the train station, along with the smaller luggage that she would keep with her. It was a tearful send-off. Not a dry eye could be found. Mr. Paring finally put his foot down and made Ada get in the carriage, saying the train would leave without her if they didn't get going. The train was huffing and puffing, getting ready to leave as Mr. Paring pulled up. Greg helped his new wife down from the carriage and grabbed the luggage. They rushed to the passenger car, and he helped Ada climb the stairs. He threw the luggage onto the small platform and jumped up beside her. With no time to spare, the train began moving. Ada and Greg waved at her parents until they were out of sight. Greg took his wife inside, found a comfortable spot, and stowed the luggage. It was going to be a few hours before their stop, and Greg told Ada to try to get a little rest. She was still keyed up and didn't think that was possible, but soon, the rocking train lulled her to sleep.

Back at the station, Mr. Paring stood with tears in his eyes as he watched his little girl leave him behind. Of course, he was happy for her, but it didn't make it any easier for him. Mrs. Paring gently turned her husband back to the awaiting carriage. They would take their own train back home in the next day or two.

THE MOVE

Jesse May and Maude spent the next week cleaning and preparing the little house behind the school for Jesse May to move into. It was a cute little place, and by the end of the week, Jesse May was all moved in.

Jesse May, in kind, helped Maude move into her room located above Crystal's shop. It was only a few weeks before school began, and Maude was already helping Crystal with several orders for young girls. The two had been so busy sewing that Maude had forgotten all about the letter she had sent with Mrs. Paring to give to her parents, so it took Maude by surprise when Jane showed up at the shop with a letter from her mother.

After several minutes, Maude excused herself and went to her room to read the letter. She left Crystal and Jane visiting over tea. Maude sat for several minutes, fingering the envelope before she was brave enough to open the letter. Thirty minutes later, she was still sitting on the window seat staring out into the street. That's where Jane found her. She sat down beside Maude and reached out to grasp a hand. Maude turned her head, looked at Jane, and then burst into tears. Jane gathered Maude in a bear hug and let her bawl her eyes out.

Several minutes went by before Maude got herself under control. Finally, she handed Jane the letter to read while she washed her face and blew her nose.

"Well. I see your parents haven't changed their minds about your life."

"I don't understand. I thought my letter would make them understand how I felt about everything and how happy I am now. I can't believe they think I would hop on a train and come home to marry Alan. Did they even read my letter?" Maude was becoming angry now. "I love my life now. I love working for Crystal. I love you and

Jesse May. I miss Ada terribly, but I'm so happy for her. If it weren't for Ada, I wouldn't be here, and I'll always be grateful for her." Maude looked at Jane and pointed at her. "You have helped me feel better about myself and be secure in my decisions. If it weren't for you, I wouldn't have this job. First Ada, then you, Jane. You've been a much better mother than my own in supporting my dreams and helping me develop my talents while working with Crystal. Thank you."

Jane walked over and enveloped Maude in another hug. "You are very welcome." Then, leaning back, she put her hands on Maude's shoulders. "And thank you, Ada, and Jesse May, for making me happy again."

The two walked back downstairs to the shop, and Maude poured herself some tea. A few minutes later, Jane left. She planned to stop and see Jesse May on her way home. Smiling, she felt like a mother again. Maude was right. She looked after the girls and encouraged them. When she got home, a new boarder named Sally was going to need her now. Jane was looking forward to helping another young woman find her way.

JESSE MAY

The school year had finally begun. Jesse May had prepared the school room, straightened the desks several times, gone over her list of students multiple times, and now, she could hear them arrive outside. It was time to open the door. The butterflies wouldn't settle down, either. Taking a deep breath and putting a smile on her face, Jesse May opened the door and rang the bell. The children ran for the door and rushed to their desks.

Jesse May closed the door and looked at the rambunctious children settling in for their first day of school. It was always exciting when she would return for her first day, and she knew these children felt the same way. She continued to smile as she made her way to the front. Her name was boldly printed on the large chalkboard at the front of the class. Turning, she got everyone's attention.

"Good morning, class. My name is Miss Brown."

Everyone said, "Good morning, Miss Brown."

Jesse May smiled broadly. "I'll need to learn everyone's names, and I need to make sure you are sitting in the right group."

She spent the next several minutes marking down names according to where the child was sitting and only had to shuffle a couple of children to the correct age group. The morning went well, and soon it was lunchtime. Everyone grabbed their lunch pails and headed outside. After the meals were consumed, the boys ran around and the girls got together and giggled. Jesse May sat on the school steps and watched the activities.

It was soon time to head back inside. By the end of the day, she was exhausted. She said goodbye to the last child, straightened up the room for the following day, and walked the short distance to her home. Jesse May sat down and put her feet up. Supper was the last thing on her mind right then.

The school term flew by. Before Jesse May knew it, the weather was turning cold at night, and she knew the first frost would arrive soon. Her weekends were spent catching up on the laundry and other errands, which left her little time to see friends. However, she was grateful for the time spent at church and was frequently a guest for lunch at Jane's. Maude and Crystal usually joined them, too.

At least monthly, Jesse May wrote her grandparents. She was grateful they were still doing well and promised to see them once school was out in the spring. Maude and Jesse May received letters from Ada and were pleased she was happy. A little one would be joining their family in a few months.

Ada's parents had decided to move closer to their only daughter and planned to be moved before their grandchild arrived. Maude was so pleased, even though she was a little jealous of Ada's great relationship with her parents. Jesse May couldn't fathom not having the love from her grandparents and expressed disdain for the whole thing with Maude's parents. Continuing to be grateful for Jane's guidance, Maude responded to her parents' last response with a short response of her own. She was not giving up her life to return home and marry Alan Beemer.

Jesse May spent a little time watching Maude one Sunday. From a quiet, prim, and proper young lady, Maude had turned into a happy, beautiful woman. There was a fall barn dance coming up, and Jesse May figured Maude would be asked to dance all night, what with her flaming red hair. She sighed and glanced at herself in the hall mirror before leaving Jane's. She was tired, her hair was flying everywhere, and her plain dress was nothing to look at. She mumbled to herself as they walked to the carriage. Jane would be taking them both home today, after their lunch.

Jane looked over at Jesse May as they got into the carriage. "What was that?"

Jesse May sighed again and shrugged her shoulders. "Just feeling sorry for myself."

"Why?"

"I look like an old maid. A tired one, at that." She knew what she looked like, and no one could tell her otherwise.

Jane made a *hmmm* sound. "I see."

No one said a thing for several minutes. Jesse began to feel worse the longer they stayed quiet. Jane pulled up to Jesse May's house first and turned to her.

"So, you're feeling sorry for yourself?"

Jesse May shrugged. "I guess so. I spend all my days with the children, and then all my free time is spent catching up with work around the house. There isn't a moment of peace in my life. Except for a few hours on Sunday, of course. I'm tired and grouchy."

"As the young girl that wanted to be a teacher whines, I'm not sure what you expected. So, are you going to the dance?"

"I was, but now I'm not so sure."

Maude gasped. "But you promised! You must go. I won't go if you don't. I can't go by myself."

Jesse May was surprised. "Why? You'll dance all night and have a great time. I'll be the wallflower."

Jane put a hand on Jesse's shoulder. "Enough. I'll take Maude home and be back to talk to you. But, in the meantime, go take a nap. I mean it."

Jesse May hung her head. "I've got some mending to do."

"It will keep, and I can help you when I get back. Scoot."

Jesse May slowly walked into her house and did as she was told. She felt like a little girl in trouble with her mother. Ashamed of her outburst, Jesse May lay down and was sound asleep as soon as her head hit the pillow. She was surprised when Jane arrived and couldn't believe she had even gone to sleep to begin with.

"Feel better?"

"I do. Thank you for making me take a nap."

"Now. What's the real problem?"

Jesse May fixed the tea, which gave her time to collect her thoughts. "I guess I'm just tired. My wardrobe is rather drab, too. It's fine for being a teacher, or my one nice dress for church. I guess that's why I was hired. They wanted someone plain, and I fit the bill for that. You know the rules."

"Jesse May Brown. No one said you had to be an old maid. Just because you have this job right now doesn't mean you will have it forever. Someone will come along."

"Not when I look like this."

Jane looked Jesse May over. "What happened to your good dresses?"

Jesse got up and walked to the window. "See these curtains? That's where they went."

Jane cracked up laughing. "Oh, goodness. And your tablecloth is another one, isn't it?" Jesse May nodded. "I thought they looked familiar." Jane laughed long and hard, and even Jesse May had to chuckle. "Oh, my. That's a good one. So tomorrow after school, you get down to Jackson's and get yourself a pretty dress."

"I can't."

"Why not?"

"I don't get paid much, and it's all I can do to buy my food and necessities. So that's why I used my dresses to pretty up the place."

Jane frowned. "Ridiculous." She pondered the problem. "Okay. On the day of the dance, you come over to my place early, and you can wear one of my dresses. We will make sure it fits right, and then I'll fix up your hair. Maude plans to come over, so we can go together."

"You're coming, too?"

"Of course. I told you girls that you have helped me more than you know. I can't let you two have all the fun. Besides, I wanted Maude to go. You know she wouldn't have gone otherwise."

"I know. Are you sure about the dress? I mean, we'll have to do some alterations. We aren't even the same height."

"Maude will help. She's quick with a needle and thread."

Jesse May smiled. "Okay. I'll be there. What time?"

"Come for lunch, and we'll get busy right afterward. And we will take Sally with us, if she agrees. She needs to get out from under my feet and have some fun, too."

"She certainly is quiet when we visit."

"I'm working on it." Jane got up to leave. "See you soon."

A quick hug and Jane flew out the door. Jesse May sat back down and poured herself another tea. She had forgotten all about the mending. She prepared a light supper, cleaned the kitchen, washed, and went to bed early. She needed sleep more than getting the mending done.

There was a cold snap, and the children stayed inside instead of going out for their breaks. After a couple of days behind the four walls, the children became restless, and Andrew wouldn't leave the girls alone. He pulled pigtails and tried tripping them. After a few reprimands, Jesse May snapped. She grabbed Andrew by his collar and pulled him to the corner.

"You will stand there and not move until I tell you otherwise. Do you understand me?"

"Yes, Ma'am."

Jesse May looked around the room at the shocked faces. "Anyone else want to try my patience?" The room was quiet, and she saw many students shake their heads. "Alright, then. Sarah, start reading where we left off."

The room remained quiet as Sarah began reading. Jesse May moved from child to child, having them take turns with the assignment. Finally, when it came time to work on their numbers, Jesse May walked over to Andrew and whispered in his ear.

"Have you learned your lesson, or do you need to stand here another hour?" She heard a sniffle and a mumble. "What?"

"I'll behave, Miss Brown."

"You're sure?"

"Yes, Ma'am. My dad will have my hide for this."

"Go sit down and do your numbers."

"Yes, Miss Brown."

Jesse May spent the rest of the day helping her students and was happy when the day was done. She helped the little ones put on their heavy coats, gloves, and hats, and shut the door behind them. She was surprised to see Andrew and his sister still inside.

"I'm sorry, Miss Brown. Please don't tell my Pa. I promise to behave."

His sister nodded her head. "He promises."

"I see. Andrew, I know you have a lot of energy, but you can't pick on girls. Or boys, either. You need to be helpful and polite. You won't have any friends when you get older if you continue to act this way."

"Yes, Ma'am."

Jesse May smiled. "I won't tell your Pa this time.

Andrew smiled back. "Thank you, Miss Brown."

"Now get home. It's too cold to be hanging around the school building." The two took off running and slammed the door behind them.

Andrew and his sister had held a special place in Jesse May's heart since she had tutored them for a few weeks earlier that summer. She knew Andrew could be onery but had hoped to teach him to put that energy into something good instead of picking on other children.

She tidied up the room, banked the fire, and hurried over to her house to get her heating stove going. Thankfully, since her home was so small, it took very little time to ward off the chill.

One more day stood between her and the barn dance. She hoped the weather held and didn't snow. Jesse May let school out a little early on Friday. Everyone was restless, and it was difficult for even Jesse May to stay on task. She decided then and there that no matter the weather, the children would go outside and run around to burn off some energy each day. It would do them all a world of good.

THE DANCE

The day of the dance turned out to be a beautiful fall day. The sun came out and stayed, taking the terrible chill out of the air. Jesse May appreciated the warmth as she rushed over to Jane's. She arrived shortly after Maude. Crystal had lent her the fancy carriage for the day, wanting to help the girls get to their dance in style. Maude had tried to talk Crystal into coming, too, but she chose to stay home instead.

Lunch was consumed quickly, as they all wanted to get busy preparing Jesse May's dress. After carefully sorting through an old chest she had kept locked up, Jane laid out four dresses. The dresses had been worn a few times, then locked away after she lost her husband. Jesse May *'oohed'* and *'awed'* over the material, and Maude made some quick assessments to update the style. Holding each one up in front of Jesse May while she stood in front of a long mirror, they all decided on a dress. Maude quickly got to work updating the dress. Soon, Jesse May found herself standing on a box while Maude pinned and mumbled to herself. Jane had tears she refused to shed while watching her dress altered for a new life.

Once the dress was removed, Maude headed to the parlor where the light was the best and began stitching away, her needle flying. Jane started working on Jesse May's hair and brushed it forever to make it shine and behave itself. Jesse May relaxed as Jane worked miracles; she almost nodded off.

"Jane, is Sally going?"

"No. She isn't interested. I think she has been hurt pretty badly in the past, so I didn't push it."

"I'm glad she is here to help you, though."

"Me, too. Business has been pretty good lately, and

Sally is a good cook."

"Really?"

"Surprised me, too. I was under the weather one day, so she took care of things for me. Since then, I let her do what she wants in the kitchen."

Jesse May looked surprised. "Your kitchen? The one you wouldn't let us girls get near?"

Jane laughed. "Yes, my kitchen." To change the subject, Jane handed Jesse May a mirror. "Here. Take a look."

Jesse May couldn't believe it. Her hair was tamed and framed her face perfectly. The ribbons laced through her long mane matched the dress Maude was working on. "I can't believe that is really me."

"Believe it."

Jesse May got up and hugged Jane. Then she looked at the other dresses still lying on the bed. "By the way, you never mentioned where you got these."

Jane shrugged. "I brought them with me when we came West. Totally inappropriate for a boarding house, or even church. Back then, anyway."

"It wasn't that long ago."

"Long enough. Come on. Let's see how your dress is coming along."

Maude had the dress spread out on a table and was finishing up some trimmings. "Almost done." Maude turned from the dress. "Your hair is gorgeous!"

Jesse May blushed to her roots. "Thank you." She looked at the dress. "What do you mean it's almost done? You can't have done all that already."

"There wasn't much to do. A few tucks here and there. I know all the shortcuts." Maude finished tying a knot and bit off the thread. "Let's get this on you and see how it looks."

The girls giggled, and soon Jesse May was adorned in

a beautiful dress. "It's perfect, Maude. Thank you."

"Don't thank me. It's Jane's dress. You'll be the belle of the ball tonight."

Jesse May blushed again. "You think so?"

"I know so," Jane agreed.

Maude had brought her gown with her, and once Jesse May was ready, she also changed. The girls giggled and laughed like old times. They missed Ada's craziness and reminisced while putting on the finishing touches. Jane had arranged for the girls to spend the night. It would be much safer for them all to travel together, too. It was going to be too cold to go much farther, anyway. Jane packed several layers of blankets in the carriage before they left. Sally promised to keep their rooms warm for their arrival.

Jane looked lovely herself. In fact, the girls had never seen Jane look so nice. Now that she smiled easily, Jane no longer had a dour look about her. The three took off in the fancy carriage, heavy blankets over their legs. They were glad the sun was still out for their trip to the dance.

The barn belonged to a prominent rancher just outside of Omaha. He grew a lot of hay, and his barn was huge. Much of the hay had already been sold, but there was plenty along the walls and floor to keep the chill out. Once the dancing started, the place would be warm enough.

Food and drink covered one side of the barn, set up on big planks. The women said their hellos to several acquaintances as they made their way to the area where the coats were stacked high. Then, they walked over to the food table. Glancing around, they saw several men watching them. They all three giggled and filled their plates.

The band tuned up and played a short tune or two as people continued to arrive. Jane noticed some friends and promised to meet up with the girls later in the night. The music began in earnest, and soon the floor was bustling. The girls took their dirty plates over to a tub and then got themselves a drink. It was only a couple of minutes before they were both on the floor dancing. Men were scrambling over who got to ask the girls to dance next. The whole night went like that, and the girls were exhausted when Jane gathered them together to go home. The dance was still going strong when they left, but over half of the crowd had left before them. Jane was concerned that the men that were left were having a little too much fun, as someone had brought in the alcohol, and the men were getting a little loud and obnoxious.

It was midnight by the time they were back at the boarding house. They put the horses in the barn, rubbed them down, and gave them a little grain. The girls tried to be as quiet as possible as they went upstairs to their room. Buried deep under the covers, they had barely laid their heads on their pillows before fallingasleep. Sally had kept the fires burning as promised, and their room was nice and toasty warm.

The following morning, both girls complained of sore feet, but they thought it was all worth the fun they had. They asked Jane how her evening went, and she blushed. Jesse May smiled.

"I thought I saw you were dancing with someone, but I was so busy I couldn't tell who it was."

"A couple of gentlemen. I had a lovely time. I'm glad you girls did, too. You never stopped talking about all the men on the trip back to town. It reminded me of Ada." They all laughed but had to agree.

Everyone went to church, had lunch, and then Maude dropped Jesse May off at her house before returning to her own apartment. Crystal's buggy had been a blessing. It had been much more comfortable than Jane's small rig.

Jesse May sat in front of her stove with her feet soaking in a tub of hot water. She had blisters on blisters, but it was worth every minute. It had been months since she had had so much fun. She thought back to the night before. She and Maude tried to stay together the best they could and often smiled across the room at each other when they couldn't. It was nice to have a good friend like Maude. Someone she could count on. Of course, Jane, too. But Maude was her age.

She tried to keep count of how many dances she had and with whom, but as the evening wore on, she gave up. Later in the evening, it was mostly between two men, and it didn't look like they were happy with each other. Maude had been in a similar situation. As the evening wore on, the two girls took a moment to themselves and compared notes. It had been a fabulous, if not exhausting, night.

Although her feet were sore on Monday morning, Jesse May headed to the school and got ready to start the day. The week went well, and Andrew was behaving exceptionally. He stayed after school everyday and cleaned the chalkboard and erasers before taking his sister home. The following week, one of the other older students asked if he could help do something, so Jesse May had him straighten the desks as she banked the fire. Her evening began much sooner with a bit of help from her students, and she was grateful for the assistance. Before long, other students offered to do a variety of things for their teacher. Some got the wood inside, and others helped the younger students with their studies.

By the time Christmas arrived, snow was falling, and everyone was ready for their break, Jesse May included. She had forgotten all about the dance by then, as she was so busy with school. Jane had invited Maude and Jesse May to stay at her house over the holiday and celebrate

Christmas together. Naturally, they both jumped at the chance to be with friends.

Sally joined the trio as they cut down a small tree and put it up in the parlor. Trimming it was fun for them all, and Sally appeared to have broken out of her shell a bit. They each had a small present under the tree from Jane, and Maude and Jesse May had gone shopping to buy Jane and Sally something. Ada had sent gifts of her own, which surprised everyone. They felt bad they hadn't thought to do the same. Everyone decided to buy something for her baby and send the packages with some trinkets for Ada, too.

A couple of days after Christmas, Maude and Jesse May were getting ready to return home when someone knocked on the door. Sally came running up the stairs and into the girl's room.

"You two have visitors."

"Who is it?"

"I don't know. Men." Sally spat out the word like it was poison and left as quickly as she came.

The girls did a little primping before leaving their room. Sure enough, two gentlemen stood just inside the front door, hats in their hands.

"Good afternoon, gentleman. What can we do for you?"

Fidgeting, one of the men finally answered after the other elbowed him in the ribs. "Hello. We've had a little difficulty finding you. Our boss suggested we stop here since he knew Jane had brought a couple of girls with her to the barn dance."

"I see." Jesse May looked at Maude, who seemed very nervous. "Well, we don't actually live here, and we were just leaving to go home."

"Oh." The man looked over at the other, then cleared his throat. "Yes, Ma'am. I mean…"

The other man interrupted. "Excuse us. We didn't introduce ourselves properly. You may not remember we danced with you. I'm sure you wouldn't remember our names. I'm Jackson Turner. Everyone calls me Jack. And this is my older brother, William. We would like to call on you sometime."

Jane walked into the room about then. She had been eavesdropping since Sally told her there were men at the door. "Hello. Girls, why don't you take these gentlemen to the parlor so you can get acquainted instead of standing by the front door. I'll bring them a nice hot cup of coffee to warm them up."

Maude blushed. "Of course. Sorry. This way."

Everyone settled in, and Jane brought refreshments as the four began to get to know each other better. The men actually worked for the man that put on the barn dance, and because they had specific duties that night, they both missed seeing the girls leave. It was a couple of weeks before they had gotten up the nerve to ask their boss about them. After narrowing down the women that were there, the boss stumbled across the idea that the girls the Turner boys might be looking for came with Jane Peterson. Unfortunately, the holidays were busy, and they had to wait to check it out until after their visits home.

Maude and Jesse May remembered the men as polite and fun to be around, but they had only seen them occasionally. After an hour of chatting, Jane returned and suggested the boys take Jesse May and Maude home, so they knew where they lived.

"Oh, but Ma'am, all we have are our horses."

That's okay. I had my rig ready to go for the girls anyway, so you can leave your horses here and then come back for them after you drop off the girls."

"You're sure?" They looked at the girls, seeking permission.

They both shrugged. "If Jane thinks it's alright, then that's fine."

Jane shooed the girls upstairs to retrieve their small valises and sent the men out back to bring the rig around to the front. She had it layered in blankets for everyone. Then, grinning from ear to ear, she returned to the kitchen and joined a very nervous Sally. The girls had gone upstairs and giggled as they quickly finished their packing. They whispered as they put on their coats and gloves, and yelled goodbye to Jane as they went through the door. The boys were standing by the rig, waiting for them.

They headed to Maude's first, so it gave them all more time to visit. Jesse May was soon dropped off. The men had promised to stop by in two days to take them out again. The men returned to Jane's to drop off the rig and retrieve their horses.

Jesse May smiled as she started the fire in her stove. She didn't even notice how cold it was in the house. It would take quite some time to get a blaze going long enough to warm up the place since there hadn't been heat in it for several days. She danced around the small space as she waited for the warmth to surround her.

Two days later, the four of them were sitting in a café having a lovely meal. William and Jesse May, Maude and Jackson. Thankfully, the girls were as attracted to the same boys as they were to the girls. Otherwise, that wouldn't have worked out at all. Jack was more serious and quieter than William, matching Maude's personality. William was more effusive, and Jesse May had always been more outgoing.

Due to the cold weather, they had a luncheon meal instead of waiting for the evening's freezing temperatures. They stayed in the warm café as long as possible, then took the girls home. The men made separate dates for the following week. It seemed as if everyone was getting along just fine.

JESSE MAY

The holiday break had ended, but a bad storm hit just as school was going to restart. Jesse May made her way to the school and checked to make sure everything was okay. There was a rope between the two buildings, and Jesse used it for a clothesline when the weather was good. However, its actual use had been for a case just like this – a bad storm.

Seeing that the doors and windows were secure against the driving wind, Jesse returned home and brought in an overabundance of firewood. Thankfully, the families kept her stocked. It was kept in a lean-to at the back of the house. The last load of wood brought in, she brushed the snow off her coat and stamped her feet. The wood spilled out of the box and onto the floor, but she didn't care because she didn't want to go back out there until the storm had let up.

In this case, it was two days. It would be a couple more days before the first of the children came to school. It was several more days before the children that lived in the country could make it back to class. It didn't matter to Jesse May. She worked with whoever arrived to learn.

It was more than two weeks before William stopped by to see her after school. He promised to stop by the next day, since it would be Saturday. He didn't stay long, but long enough for Jesse May to get tingly all over. Saturday couldn't come soon enough.

Three months later, one of the school board members who had initially interviewed her stopped to see her after school. She had just sent the last child home and was heading out the back door.

"Mr. Raymond. What can I do for you?"

"I understand you are seeing someone."

Jesse May dropped the smile. "Yes. Why?"

"I thought you understood that there was to be no dating."

"I understood that I couldn't be married."

"You have to be above reproach. No dating."

Jesse May took a deep breath. "Are you giving me an ultimatum?"

"I suppose I am."

Jesse May did something she would never have done in the past, but something about this man didn't sit right with her. "No."

Mr. Raymond gasped. "What?"

"I said no. I'm not married. That was our agreement. I'll pack my things tonight and return to Jane's if you don't like my behavior. You can teach the children for the rest of the school year. If you'll excuse me, I have things to do."

She grabbed her wrap, walked out the back door, and kept going. She was so upset that she didn't stop until she had walked clear over to see Jane.

"Jane? Are you home?" Jesse May stormed inside the house. She was still shaking.

Sally came out from the kitchen. "Jane went to Jackson's, but she should be home soon."

"Thanks. I'll head out and meet her."

Sally started to say something, but Jesse May was already out the door. Sally shrugged and headed back to the kitchen. Jesse May met Jane about halfway home, and Jane immediately knew something was wrong.

"Jane. Thank heavens. I need to talk."

"I can see that. What happened?"

Jesse May relayed her conversation with Mr. Raymond, and Jane cracked up laughing. "I can't believe you're laughing at me."

"Not really. More at you leaving Mr. Raymond standing there as you walked out the door. I don't think he will ever get over the shock of a young woman defying him."

"Well, he made me mad."

"Remind me not to make you mad at me."

Jesse May smacked Jane on the arm. "I'm serious."

"I know you are. But you were right, too. He can't dictate your life. I mean, if you were hanging out in the saloon and entertaining men, yes. But seeing William and going to cafés or whatever, there's nothing improper about that. And you're always welcome to come back to my place. You know that."

"Hmmph. Well, I don't think I'll be teaching anymore, at least after I finish this year. And I might not be able to even close out the school year if Mr. Raymond has his way." They had arrived back at Jane's, but Jesse May didn't go in. "I'll head back home. I may need to start packing."

Jane patted her arm and chuckled. "I don't think even Mr. Raymond would be stupid enough to fire you on the spot. But just in case, I'll keep a room for you."

Jesse May shook her head. "Thank you, Jane, for lending me a shoulder to cry on."

"You just needed to blow off a little steam. Better me than Mr. Raymond. Now get home, and don't worry about things too much. There are more important people in your life than Mr. Raymond."

Jesse May rushed back home, but by then, she had spent her anger and just needed to make sure her belongings weren't outside in the dirt. She relaxed once she arrived home, and everything was where it was supposed to be. But everyday for almost a week, she worried Mr. Raymond would return for another round. Looking back, Jesse May had no idea what had possessed her to stand up for herself. In a way, she was glad she did. But again, she was also scared she had done the wrong thing.

William came over to see her, and they went for a long walk. It was a nice spring evening, and they strolled along until they came to a small café. Deciding to eat a quick bite, they sat and talked for along time. She told him all about her encounter with Mr. Raymond. It was dark by the time William had escorted Jesse May back home. He said goodnight and was just starting to leave when Mr. Raymond came out of the shadows.

"I warned you, Miss Brown."

He shook a finger at her. Jesse May stepped back. Mr. Raymond coming out of the shadows like that had frightened her. William stopped halfway mounting his horse, not sure what was happening. He got his feet back on the ground and started toward Jesse May.

Jesse May finally recovered from the initial shock. "Mr. Raymond. What are you doing here?"

"I'm keeping an eye on you, that's what. Good thing, too. I knew you were a hussy."

William stepped between the two. "Mr. Raymond, is it? What seems to be the problem here?"

"You stay out of this. This is between Miss Brown and me."

"I believe you just made this between you and me, Mr. Raymond. You are threatening my fiancée, and I don't like it. Therefore, I suggest you leave at once before I make sure you can't walk from here."

"Are you threatening me? You can't do that. Do you know who I am?"

"I don't care if you're the president. You can't jump out of the shadows and threaten this girl. Now leave before I make sure you are permanently gone." William walked over to his horse and grabbed his rifle but left it pointed toward the ground.

"Now, you wait a minute here."

"Go," William said.

Mr. Raymond left, but not before telling them he would be back with the law. William took Jesse May and helped her sit on the front step. He put his rifle back and then sat down beside her.

"That man is a menace. Lurking in the shadows just to jump out and scare you."

"I told him I wouldn't stop seeing you. I don't know why he thinks he can tell me what I can do on my own time. I can't believe he's been spying on me all this time. And he called me a hussy!" Jesse May suddenly came to attention and looked at William in the fading light. "Wait a second. You told Mr. Raymond I was your fiancée."

"Oh. That. Well, I thought it sounded more important than a girlfriend. After all, he called you a name, and sticking up for my fiancée would mean more than a girlfriend."

"Oh, I see." Jesse May wasn't sure if she was disappointed or relieved at the explanation.

The two sat there in silence, the crickets singing and keeping them company. Finally, William heard someone coming and stood up. He waited as Mr. Raymond and a deputy arrived.

Mr. Raymond shook his finger at William. "I want him arrested and her gone."

"Mr. Raymond, could you wait out of the way while I talk to them, please?"

"I told you what happened and what I want to be done."

"Sir, please stand out of the way so I can talk to this couple." Mr. Raymond refused to move, but he quit talking. He crossed his arms and glared. "Okay, kid, did you threaten Mr. Raymond?"

"I did."

"Why?"

"He jumped out of the shadows and verbally attacked my fiancée. He called her a hussy."

The deputy turned and looked at Mr. Raymond. "You didn't tell me that part. Why were you hiding in the shadows?"

"I wanted to catch her, and I did."

"You've been spying on this young woman?"

Mr. Raymond cleared his throat. "I wouldn't call it that, exactly."

The deputy scratched his chin. "None of this makes any sense. Someone needs to start from the beginning."

Jesse May spoke up and told the deputy everything from the beginning. When she finished, she ended the story by saying, "And William hasn't even kissed me yet, so I don't think I deserve to be called a hussy. I think Mr. Raymond is jealous I'm seeing someone else instead of him."

"Now, wait a minute. That's not true, Miss Brown."

"It's not? Then why does it matter to you who I see?"

"I told you. No teacher can date."

"That's a lie."

The deputy held up his hands. "Now, wait a minute, you two. Mr. Raymond, go home. I'll take this upon myself to get things cleared up once and for all. I'll see you tomorrow." Mr. Raymond straightened his jacket and headed back into the shadows. "Ma'am, go on inside. I'll talk to other school patrons to find the answer to this. William, go home, and don't pull that rifle on anyone again."

"Just for the record," William said as he got on his horse, "I never pointed it at him. I just pulled it out of my sheath. I only threatened him verbally."

The deputy shook his head. "Go home."

"Goodnight, Jesse May. I'll see you soon."

Jesse May went inside, but she was shaken up over

everything. There were only a few weeks left before school got out, and she didn't know if she could take being followed around by Mr. Raymond or not. And then to have William use the word fiancée; let's just say she had a long sleepless night over that one.

The classes drug on, and Jesse May yawned several times. The children seemed to know something was wrong and were well-behaved. As soon as class was out, Jesse May returned home and took a nap. She had a few things she needed to do but was too tired to accomplish anything. Even after a nap and supper, Jesse May couldn't concentrate. She sat on her front step, munching on an apple, just waiting for Mr. Raymond to step out of the shadows and scare her again.

Back inside, she curled up under her covers and had another restless night. By morning, the bed was a total disaster from all the tossing and turning. She didn't feel like she had gotten any rest at all. Nevertheless, she managed to get through one more day of school. When she closed up the school, she only made it as far as her front porch. That's where she was when she saw a group of people coming to her home. *"Now what?"* she thought as she stood up and waited for their arrival. She recognized some of the parents in the group. Others had interviewed her for the job.

"Miss Brown, I'm Gerald Post. I've been designated to talk to you about Mr. Raymond's complaints." Jesse May began to say something, but Mr. Post held up his hand. "This group does not agree with Mr. Raymond's tactics nor his complaints against you. However, we are here to support you."

Jesse May let out a breath she didn't know she was holding. "You looked like a lynch mob." A woman in the crowd said, "Oh, dear." That broke the tension, and there were a few chuckles. Jesse May gave them a tired smile.

"Thank you."

Mr. Post looked at the crowd and then back to Jesse May. "We also understand Mr. Raymond is paying you a very small amount for your duties. That was not the amount the community had agreed upon. We apologize for everything over the last several months." Mr. Post handed her an envelope with several dollars. "That should cover you until the end of the school year."

"Thank you. I don't know what to say. I appreciate your support."

"Just tell us you will return in the fall."

"Oh. Well. I'm afraid I probably won't. This has been a pretty traumatic experience for me, and I'm in a serious relationship with someone."

"We heard you have a fiancée."

Jesse May smiled. "I have enjoyed teaching this year. Your children have been wonderful. I will let someone know at the end of the year. Of course, I will need to discuss all this with my boyfriend."

"We understand. Again, on behalf of all of us, we are very sorry about Mr. Raymond."

Jesse May sat back down on her front step. She waited several minutes before looking into the envelope and couldn't believe how much money she was holding. From what she gathered, Mr. Raymond took it upon himself to handle things. Jesse May decided that Mr. Self-Importance may have met his match with her. Now she didn't feel so bad about sticking up for herself. She went inside and hid the money. She knew that she would sleep much better tonight.

MAUDE

The winter dress orders were overwhelming. So many Christmas dinners and parties, so many different dresses needed. And heaven forbid if any two were similar. Maude drew on her past experiences to sketch out new patterns. She would sketch, Crystal would cut out the pattern, and they both stitched like mad women. Maude always added some finishing touches to the final product. The shop had never been so busy. Word was out about the fabulous gowns and quality sewing. Crystal began to turn away orders from new customers, saying she could never accommodate them in time for their parties. It was a good problem to have. Unless Crystal stumbled across a new seamstress, they had all the work they could handle for the next few months.

Maude's fingers were sore from all the pin and needle pricks. As long as she didn't get blood on the cloth, she didn't mind. The barn dance was so far behind her that she hadn't given it much thought since she was so busy sewing. When Christmas arrived, Crystal gave her a few days off to spend with Jane and Jesse May. There would be plenty of time to finish the New Years' gowns lying around in several stages of completion.

Maude had a lovely time with her friends and got to know Sally a bit better. She seemed to be a troubled soul but left it to Jane to work her magic. Then, just as she and Jesse May were packing to return home, they were called to the front door to receive visitors. Two dashing young men were standing there. They looked a little familiar, but Maude couldn't put a name to their faces.

The Turner brothers had fancied the girls at the barn dance, but they had left before the men could find out where they lived. Before Maude knew it, Jane had talked the men into taking the girls home. Leave it to Jane to move things along.

Jackson was quieter than William, and Maude enjoyed his company. Three months later, they were still seeing each other on occasion, and Maude was quite taken with Jack. She knew Jesse May and William were still seeing each other, too. On occasion, the four of them would get together. The men came to church, too, when they could get to town. The four of them, plus Jane and Sally, would sit together. Sally always sat at the end of the aisle, so she wasn't near the men.

Maude pricked another finger. Putting her finger in her mouth, she laid the cloth aside and walked to a window to peer into the darkness. There was very little foot traffic this time of night. Maude yawned. She had worked too long today. The coming spring weather had her anxious to get outside in the sunshine again. She had missed seeing Jack lately. He had gone on a trip and wouldn't return for a few more days. She had no idea where he'd gone, but it wasn't her place to ask.

Maude looked at the wedding dress she had been working on. Almost complete, she was anxious to see the bride wear it for her last fitting. The young lady was excited to wed her beau. She had a sudden pang of jealousy for the girl, then anger at her parents for trying to force her into marrying Alan. Maude burst out in tears. She cried buckets of them for the next twenty minutes. She felt much better when she was done, and washed her face. Jane had always told her a good cry was beneficial. It was a good thing she cried easily, she thought.

Once Maude had cried over her parents' letter so many months ago, she had allowed herself to have a good cry once in a while. The thought of her parents' betrayal always upset her. She felt spent. Maude prepared for bed and curled up. Her last thought was how wrong her parents had been about her all these years. Despite tonight's tears, she had been so happy since she and Ada had landed at Jane's place. Jane had been more than a good friend. More like a great Aunt instead. And now that she had met Jack, she knew for sure marrying Alan would have been a terrible mistake. She always knew it was a mistake, but Jack made her realize how much of a mistake it would have been.

Jack returned a few days later and stopped to see Maude before going back to the ranch. He promised to return on the weekend to see her. Crystal always gave Maude a hard time whenever Jack would stop by. Maude would blush and keep right on sewing.

A new restaurant opened just down the street from Crystal's shop. On Saturday evening, William and Jack took Maude and Jesse May out for supper. Jesse May caught everyone up on the fight with Mr. Reynolds and how the parents had gotten together to support her. They all laughed with her, explaining how it had looked like a lynch mob had arrived at her home. After supper, the couples went for a walk, eventually separating. Jack reassured Maude that William and Jesse May would meet them back at Crystal's.

"Did you have a good trip?"

"I did. Everything went as I hoped."

"Anything you can talk about?"

"Oh, I'll tell you all about it in a week or so."

"Kind of sneaky, aren't you?"

"Yes, I guess I am. But I think you'll like it."

"Hmmm. Are you going to make me wait a week or two to find out? It doesn't seem fair."

"You're probably right. I guess I shouldn't have said anything in the first place."

Maude linked her arm through Jack's, and they walked back to Crystal's. It wasn't long before the other couple arrived. A quick goodbye, and the men were taking Jesse May home.

Maude went to her small apartment and thought about Jack's promise to tell her about his trip. She had all the patience in the world, but Jack's secret just might be testing her in ways she hadn't felt before. It was ten days later when Jack stopped by. He took Maude for a walk in the park and eventually found a park bench.

"William and I have always wanted our own place to run a few cattle. Our good friend contacted us about some land for sale, so I went to look at it and talked to the owner. Maude, I don't want to leave you behind when I move to Hastings. Would you marry me and join me in my new venture?"

"Marry you? Move to Hastings? Who is your friend?"

"Greg Walker. You might remember him."

"Greg and Ada Walker?"

"Yes. One and the same."

"Oh, Jack. Of course, I'll marry you. I can't let you leave me behind. And I would love to be close to Ada again. She's my best friend in the whole world."

Jack looked pleased. "Maude, are you marrying me for the right reasons or so that you can live close to Ada again?"

"Oh, Jack. I do love you so."

"I love you too, Maude."

With that declaration, Jack pulled out a ring and presented it to his best girl. It was a perfect fit, just like they were. Then he leaned over and kissed his future bride.

Maude and Jack talked at length about the large house on the property and that William and hopefully Jesse May would be joining them. A second home could be built later on, and they would only be a few miles from the Walkers. In fact, their cattle would be running together on the range.

"William is asking Jesse May to marry him?"

"As we speak. Do you think she will go?"

"Of course. She adores your brother."

"That's a relief. When shall we get married?"

"I'm sure Jesse May will need to wait until school gets out."

"We figured as much. William and I will go ahead and get our cattle on the property and have someone clean the house. Then we will come back for the wedding."

"Oh, Jack. I can't wait."

"Me either, my dear."

"I can't wait to sew our wedding dresses, either. And new bonnets. Oh, Jack. I'm so happy." Maude shed a few tears.

"I'm happy you're happy. Come on. Let's go break the news to Crystal."

"Oh! I need to go to Jane's, too."

Crystal lent the happy couple her carriage, and they rushed over to Jane's. They arrived at the same time as William and Jesse May. The girls hugged each other and showed off their rings. They were still chatting as they burst through Jane's door. Jane heard the commotion and headed toward the noise.

"What is going on out here?" Jane looked at the two couples and grinned. "I assume you have good news to tell me?"

Jesse May and Maude both rushed toward Jane to show off their rings and tell their story about moving to live by Ada. Jane was deliriously happy for 'her girls' and told them all so. After several minutes of bubbling excitement, the men mentioned they needed to get back to work. To save time, Jack dropped William and Jesse May off, and then William would ride over to Crystals so they could get back to the ranch at the same time. They had to tell their boss the good news.

That night, Jane was lying in bed and stared at her ceiling in the dark of night. Her girls were all grown up now. A double wedding in the next few weeks, and then she and Sally would be all alone. Well, not exactly. Chet Arnold was still coming around to see Jane. She smiled. Maybe she would be the next one to get married. One never knew these days. Miracles do happen.

THE DOUBLE WEDDING

For Jesse May, the end of the school year could not arrive quickly enough. Her students were sad that their teacher was moving, but were excited about the wedding. They were all invited, too. Andrew was chosen to walk his teacher down the aisle. They had formed a special bond early on, which had grown over time. Anytime he attempted to pick on other students, Jesse May would point a finger or clear her throat, and Andrew would settle down. Even his parents had noticed a change in his behavior.

After a lot of going back and forth, Maude decided she would notify her parents of her upcoming marriage and the move to Hastings. She didn't ask them to come or accept her decision but sent the information as a courtesy. Satisfied she had done the right thing, Maude sent the letter with the next day's post before changing her mind.

Maude had finished Jesse May's dress and was finishing up her own. Crystal whined about losing such a great seamstress but couldn't find fault for the reasons. She liked Jack and felt he would treat Maude just fine. For selfish reasons, Crystal tried to talk Jack into staying close by. Crystal's business had thrived with Maude helping her.

The girls would have much the same type of ceremony as Ada did, and the reception for friends would also be held at Jane's. Sally promised to cook all the food and make sure everyone was served. Crystal's generosity extended to pay for all the reception expenses. When Maude expressed concern, she waved it off and said it was like a bonus for all the hard work Maude had provided her over the past several months.

The men had gone ahead and done as much as possible to prepare the ranch for their new brides. Ada and her mother cleaned the house and aired out the mattresses. Ada's baby, strapped to her back, rode right along with her, napping or cooing as they worked.

Ada's husband, Greg, would leave the day before the Turners would arrive on the train, so he would be there in time to pick them up. It was a long bumpy road to the railroad station. He would have to stay the night to be there when the train pulled in the following day. He hoped the train would be on time since it would take all day to get back home. Ada stayed home, as it would have been too hard of a trip for her and the little one.

Ada missed Maude so much when she first moved to the farm outside of Hastings. But when her parents arrived, it helped tremendously. And it was nice to have her mother's help when the baby was born. She couldn't wait to see her best friends again. When Greg began to correspond with the Turner boys, she hadn't given it much thought. It was sometime later before her husband mentioned the Turners getting married before moving out to the farm. He mentioned Maude's name in passing, and Ada about fainted on the spot. Who would have ever thought that she and her best friends would be so close to each other once again?

The day of the wedding arrived. It was overcast and threatened to rain, but it couldn't dampen the spirits of everyone involved. Due to the unstable weather, the girls decided to dress and fix their hair after they got to the church. The drizzle that occurred off and on threatened to change to a downpour at any moment.

When the double wedding ceremony was ready to begin, the clouds moved off and left sunshine spilling through the stained-glass windows and a rainbow on the horizon.

Andrew proudly walked Jesse May down the aisle. Another student by the name of Caleb walked Maude down the aisle, right behind Jesse May. The biggest surprise of the week was the arrival of Jesse May's grandparents. They had come for her big day. She had no idea they would, but she couldn't be prouder to have them in the front pew. The trip had been hard on them, but at least they could take the train instead of a stagecoach these days. The early arrival gave her several days of visiting before her big day.

Jesse May was married first. Maude told her that she would be too impatient to wait once they were at the altar. After much laughter and teasing, Jesse May had to agree. Once the two had completed their ceremonies, Jesse May stopped in front of her grandparents and had them walk out with her and William. Maude felt a twinge of jealousy, but just briefly. Her parents did not, and would not, be supportive. It would have been a disaster if her parents had arrived. The feeling only lasted for a moment, and it disappeared completely when she glanced shyly at her new husband, Jackson.

The reception went long into the day. Andrew and Caleb were honored to be invited as their special guests. The train would leave in a few hours, and the new brides and grooms headed to a hotel close to the station. The trunks were packed, and everyone said their goodbyes. The hardest goodbye was Jesse May and her grandparents. She wondered if she would ever see them again.

The couples were brought to the hotel by a friend, and the luggage was taken on ahead to the station. The hotel was a short walk, but everyone needed the rest before leaving town. The train would arrive around midnight. The couples had a quiet supper and then rested in the parlor. The peace and quiet after the busyness of the day were exactly what they needed. They all closed their eyes for an hour or two, trying to get a little rest before their journey started.

THE MOVE

The trip to their new home was exciting for all of them. Once on the train, the movement rocked them all to sleep for a couple of hours. As dawn broke, the men talked about what they wanted to do as the women watched the changing landscape. When they got off the train, the girls waited on the platform while the men retrieved their luggage. Greg was there, waiting, and he helped the men get everything loaded. They were soon on the way toward their new home. The buckboard certainly jarred their passengers as they covered the long, dusty, rutted road. Greg assured them they would have an easier trail into Hastings from their home.

It was nightfall before they arrived at their new home. Ada had stopped by at dusk and lit the lamps to welcome them. Once everyone and their luggage were unloaded, Greg headed for his home. He still had a few miles to go, and he was tired from two days of bouncing around.

All the couples wanted to do was wash up and go to bed. They were exhausted from the last few days. The girls said they would explore the house the following day. Within the hour, the place was quiet except for an occasional snore.

The men had left some money behind so Ada and her mother could fill the larder with food. So, the following morning, the girls soon had coffee warming and biscuits cooking. The men had already been out to check on the cattle. Their property had a river running through it, and the land butted up next to the Walker's place. The cattle were branded with a Lazy T for the Turners and a W for the Walkers.

With the spring rains, there was plenty of grass. William and Jack learned how to take care of a hay field and planned to use some of the land to ensure they had their own hay. They would need extra feed for their cattle with the hot summer sun and the winter months. Their old boss had taught them well.

Ada and her baby, Joseph, arrived after lunch, and the women sat all afternoon catching up. Maude was anxious to see the Parings again and was glad Ada had them close by. But, before Ada went home, she asked the dreaded question.

"What about your parents, Maude?"

"I never heard from them after I wrote my last letter telling them I was getting married. The last time I heard from them was after I sent that letter home with your mother. That was when they sent me a nasty letter demanding I return home to marry Alan."

"You're kidding?"

"I wish I was. Basically, I replied with an emphatic no; that was the last time I heard from them. I technically didn't invite them to my wedding, but I felt it only appropriate I notify them of the event. If they don't care, that's on them. I did my part."

"Good for you. My mother thinks your father has been keeping your mother away from you, but who knows?"

"Mother was always critical of me. No matter what I did. She could always have written me a supportive note but chose not to." Maude sighed. "But I'm very happy. The happiest I've ever been in my whole life."

Jesse May had been listening to their exchange. Maude seldom mentioned her parents, and now she knew why. "Me, too."

The girls hugged and promised to go to Ada's in a few days to see their place. In the meantime, the girls were still making this huge empty home theirs. The previous owner had several children, and the house had several additions to the original space. A terrible fever had gone through the county, and the family had decreased from a dozen to four. Only three of the older children and their mother survived. She pulled up stakes and moved to town. They say she never recovered physically or mentally from the loss.

It was still early enough to start a garden, so the women went to work. The men began dividing the house into two separate living quarters. With all the additions, they found it relatively simple to break up the house instead of building another one. And it was cheaper, too. They would keep the big kitchen and dining area but make two separate parlors. There were two fireplaces already. They divided the house by putting up a wall, but placed a doorway for easy access to either side.

Before long, the garden was growing, and the house now had two front doors. The root cellar needed a little work, and William made it bigger while Jack repaired the barn.

Greg had sent over a few chickens, and he had an extra milk cow. The girls were grateful to have learned some basic cooking skills from Jane, but Jesse May had learned most of her recipes from her grandmother while growing up in Missouri. By the end of the summer, the women worked together to can and store the garden produce. Mrs. Paring had fruit trees, and the women all learned how to keep apples in the root cellar and make pies. It was all hard work, but no one complained. And William and Jack enjoyed the meals even as their wives learned to cook better, too.

Before the winter weather set in, Jesse May and Maude insisted their husbands enclose the back porch. It was used to do the laundry, and they wanted a space they could use year-round. It ended up being more than the women expected, but it was perfect. The men even hung a clothesline inside and put hooks up to hold the wash tubs when not in use.

They planned to run water to the kitchen in the spring and install a pump handle. Then, if Jesse May had her way, William would put in a water closet on their side. Maude laughed and demanded to have one, too. The men shook their heads, but both thought that particular invention was a great idea.

NEW ADDITIONS and SURPRISES

That fall, Maude was under the weather a bit and stayed in bed. Jack was concerned and thought about the previous owners. He asked Jesse May to check on her. Maude wasn't sick, but expecting. Jack was over the moon. Maude remained ill off and on over the winter, and even Jesse May was concerned. Maude sat in her rocker, sewing baby clothes and making sure she had a gown or two she could wear as she grew larger each month. Mrs. Paring visited at least monthly and assured Maude she was doing well. There was a new doctor in town, and as the time got closer, Mrs. Paring sent him out to see Maude. Jack paced the hall as the doctor checked his wife. As soon as the door opened, Jack was there.

"Dr. Johnson. How is she?"

"No need to be concerned. Some women have a more challenging time than others. I've explained to her how things go, and as soon as she tells you, have someone come and get me. You have a big baby in there, so she might have some difficulties delivering, but your wife is healthy."

Jack worried himself into the ground for the next several weeks. Finally, when Maude told him to get the doctor, he about fainted. William rode into town, and, thankfully, the doctor was available. Then, he rode over to the Parings to let them know. Mrs. Paring had promised to come and be with Maude.

Maude spent several hours in labor, but eventually Paul was born. He was a big baby but healthy. Everyone celebrated. Maude took a little time to recover, but she was soon on her feet, trying to build up her strength again.

In the middle of all the excitement over Maude, Jesse May found out she was also expecting. Her first bundle of joy, Effie May, would be born six months later. Ada's second child arrived between the two. The neighborhood was growing, and Mrs. Paring designated herself as grandmother to all the children.

Late in the fall of the second year, everyone had a visitor. Jane had arrived to see her friends. But what surprised everyone more than the visit, was that she was married to Chet Arnold now. Since the Turner house was so large, there was plenty of room for them to stay over as long as they wanted.

As they caught up on the gossip back in Omaha, Jane looked around at her friends. They were so happy, and with children, at that. Jane looked at her new husband with pride. They had sold the boarding house, and she was now the mistress of a new home in a nicer neighborhood. She had dug out the dresses from her chest and altered them to fit the times. They came in handy, between Jesse May needing a pretty dress and now for her new life. Chet would give her the moon if she asked, but all Jane wanted was to visit her friends.

Sally had taken over Jesse May's teaching job. She had absolutely no interest in ever marrying. She had been hurt terribly by someone in her past and vowed to stay away from all men in the future.

Just before Christmas, Mrs. Paring had a letter from Maude's mother. She debated about waiting until after Christmas to give it to Maude but decided it was way overdue. Maude had dutifully sent her parents a notice of their first grandchild, but, naturally, she hadn't heard back.

"Mrs. Paring." They hugged. "Come in out of the cold. Are we going to get snow for Christmas?"

"I hope so. It would help me feel better about these freezing temperatures."

Maude helped with Mrs. Paring's wraps before sitting

by the fire. "What brings you out here on this cold day?"

"Well, I received a letter from your mother."

"I didn't know you still corresponded." Maude clasped her hands together.

"On occasion, your mother would write. I don't think she wanted to be completely out of your life. I always mentioned you when I wrote back. I'm not sure your father knew she wrote to me. He was never my biggest fan."

"Hmmm."

"Anyway, she wrote to say your father died suddenly. She assumes it was his heart."

Maude gasped. "Why didn't she write to me directly?"

"Here. You read this, and you'll know why." Mrs. Paring handed over the envelope. Maude carefully removed the expensive vellum and unfolded the letter.

Cecily, with a heavy heart, I must tell you that Herbert has died suddenly and left me alone. The doctor said there was nothing anyone could have done. He believes his heart gave out on him. I find that looking at his office is quite distressing for me, and I have difficulty functioning day to day. I have kept Maude's letters and reread them every day. They are becoming quite tattered.

Maude has dutifully notified us about the changes in her life, and I was ecstatic over my first grandchild. After she refused to return home and marry Alan Beemer, Herbert washed his hands of the situation. Alan eventually married someone else but has treated her poorly. I'm sure Maude managed to escape from this situation just in time. I am forever grateful that Ada took my daughter away.

Of course, it took several months for me to see what was right in front of my face. Herbert and I were no longer speaking at the time of his death. I feel terrible about the whole situation. I hope you will pass this information on to Maude, as she deserves to know about her father.

I am at odds with what my next step is. Our solicitor is helping me take care of things here. I will sell all our holdings as I want nothing to do with Herbert's business dealings. I apologize to you and Maude for my prudish behavior. I let Herbert skew my thinking and not allow me to support my daughter.

Always, Harriett.

Maude had tears rolling down her face as she read the letter. Her emotions were very mixed as she tried to sort it all out.

"Why didn't she write me once she realized it was father keeping her from me?"

"I don't know. Embarrassment, pride, maybe a refusal to believe she was wrong. Most people don't figure it out until it's too late."

"Father never did."

"No, he didn't. I told you long ago it was probably him. He was a very hard man. But it doesn't matter now. Your mother was trying to be a dutiful wife. She had a part to play in society, too. And she played it well."

"Mother hated that I didn't play along as well. That I wanted other things in my life."

"Yes, but she had to deal with her husband. And she only had you. No male heir to pass things along to. Your father never forgave her for that."

"Yet, I just gave him an heir a few months ago."

"Ironic, isn't it?"

"Now what?"

"It's up to you. Write her back, either way, I think. Acknowledge the information. Whatever else you say is totally up to you to decide. I know there is a lot of pain from the past."

"I'll talk it over with Jack first."

"As you should. I'll leave you the letter. I need to get home before it gets any colder."

Maude helped Mrs. Paring wrap up and watched her leave. Deep in thought, she didn't hear Jesse May come into the room.

"What's going on? I saw Mrs. Paring leave."

"Oh." Maude turned. "You scared me. Here." She handed Jesse May the letter. "I hear Paul. I need to go feed him and change his diaper."

Jesse May sat down and read the letter twice. It was no wonder Maude looked a little distressed when she walked into the room. Jesse May started supper and was hard at it when Maude returned to the kitchen. Then, it was Jesse May's turn to feed Effie May while Maude finished the meal. Maude tucked the letter in her apron pocket and soon had supper on the table. She was quiet during the meal, and Jack knew something was on her mind. Paul and Effie May lay together on the floor during the meal, and the couples went to their separate parlors after the kitchen was cleaned up. Before Jack could ask a question, Maude handed him the letter.

Jack read it and then asked, "Now what?"

"I don't know. Mrs. Paring thought I should answer it no matter what. Acknowledge that my father is gone."

"Probably should, I suppose. This brings a lot of things to light, though. Doesn't it answer a few questions you've had?"

"Yes. Several. But I always thought my mother acted that way on her own, not because of my father. Although, I still believe she had a choice in how she treated me, even if it was all him."

"A little late to figure that out on her part. But it sounds like she and your father were feuding at the end. Maybe she had finally stood up to him."

Maude shrugged. "I suppose I'll write her a note. The

rest is up to her."

"You've always done your part. Which is commendable, I think."

Maude picked up Paul. "I need to get this guy fed and put down. You coming?"

"I'll be up shortly. I need to do the books tonight. The bank payment is due in a few weeks."

"Oh, that's right. Will we have enough?"

"I think so. We might have to sell a few more cattle than we planned, but I'll know more in a couple of days when William and I go over everything."

As Paul napped the following morning, Maude wrote a note to her mother. She was polite about her father's death and made sure her mother knew how well little Paul was doing. She signed off and got it ready to post. No one would be going to town until after Christmas, but it was ready all the same. She set it on the mantle out of the way.

The holiday brought a little snow, making the season seem special. The Turners went over to the Walkers after Christmas and exchanged a few small gifts. It was a joyous time and a blessing to all of them.

THE BANK LOAN IS DUE

Jesse May and Maude dropped their children off with Ada one day as the first of the year rolled around. The two went to town for supplies and stopped by the Parings to say hello. Maude posted her letter, too. They rushed back to Ada's and collected their children before it got too late. The temperature had already dropped quite a bit and only dropped further by the time they pulled into their yard. Their husbands unloaded the wagon while the women hustled their children into the house. The fire was stoked, and supper started before Maude warmed up again. She had a lot on her mind, but the activities around her helped.

By the time Maude and Jack settled into bed, she was worn out. "Jack, I mailed my letter."

"I thought you probably would."

"One more thing. I believe I'm with child again."

Jack turned to his wife. "Really?"

"Really."

Pulling Maude into his arms, he hugged her tight. "Are you okay with that?"

"Of course. I know it's so soon after Paul, but he will surely have a playmate."

"If it's another boy."

Maude chuckled. "Of course. I hope I'm not as sick with this one."

"Me, too, dear. But you managed the last one just fine. I, on the other hand, was a mess. You are good at whatever you do."

"Thanks, Jack. I don't want to say anything until after the New Year to make sure."

"That's fine. This secret will be easier for me to keep now that we have Paul." It wasn't long until they both fell asleep in each other's arms.

Almost a month later, Jack was fretting over the books. William was with him, and they were discussing money problems. Maude tried not to listen in, but she couldn't help but overhear that they didn't have enough money to pay the bank. Moreover, the cold winter storms had taken a toll on the number of cattle, which meant they wouldn't be able to pay the bank unless they sold whatever they had left at a discounted price.

Maude picked up Paul and took him next door to see Jesse May. She shut the connecting door behind her quietly to avoid disturbing the men.

"Jesse May?"

"Back here."

Maude moved to the adjoining laundry room. She set Paul down beside Effie May. "Did you know the men don't have money to pay the banknote?" Jesse May stopped what she was doing, her mouth gaping open. "I'll take that as a no. I just overheard them going over the books. We've lost too many head of cattle this winter. So, they have to sell them all in order to pay the bank."

"No. Oh, Maude, no. What are we going to do?"

"I don't know. The men will have to figure it out. Jesse May, I'm with child again, too."

"I wondered. You have that special glow. But I didn't want to say anything."

"That's okay. I've been meaning to bring it up. This weather has me blue. Cold and snowy, with no sunshine. You know how much I love the sun."

"Yeah. I know. It won't be long before it starts warming up again." Jesse May finished hanging up the clothes, and then they took the children into the parlor. "I'd hate to lose our land, Maude." She nodded. "And the men just want to build a nice ranch for our children and their children. I hope they can figure it all out." They silently watched the children play and worried about the future.

"Here you are," William said. "We were looking for you. It's strangely quiet in the house. Is everything alright?"

"Fine. We're fine. Just resting a bit."

"Good. Jack and I are going to ride out and check the cattle. We'll be back in an hour or so."

"We'll get some hot coffee going for your return."

Maude nodded. "I need to take Paul back to change his diaper. Then, I'll start the coffee."

"Okay. I'll be home soon." William strode out, and the girls looked at each other and sighed.

A week later, Mrs. Paring stopped by. "Maude, I stopped by the post office before coming out to see Ada. They asked me to drop these off for you. I came here first, so I need to get going. I'm already late for our luncheon date."

"Thank you, Mrs. Paring. I appreciate it."

It wasn't until Mrs. Paring left that she looked through the mail. There were three letters. One from Jane, one from the bank, and the other from her mother. Sitting down at the kitchen table, she read the letter from Jane first, then set it aside for Jesse May. She left the bank letter unopened and placed it between the men's places at the table. Then, fingering her mother's envelope, she dropped it like a hot potato when she heard Paul scream. She ran to find him pinned behind the settee. How he got there, she had no idea. He was scared or mad. Maybe a bit of both. Paul was inquisitive, and it would probably get him into many scrapes in the future.

She forgot all about her mother's letter as she soothed Paul. Handing him a cookie, Maude began making biscuits. Jesse May would arrive soon enough. She added more wood to the stove and got the biscuits rising. Paul was busy playing with a toy his father had carved for him. Soon, Jesse May plopped Effie May and her doll down beside Paul and began fixing some lunch.

"There's a letter from Jane on the table."

"Oh, good. Is she alright?"

"Wonderful. Happy."

"Good."

"There was also a letter from the bank."

Jesse May turned. "Oh, Maude. That probably isn't good news."

Maude shrugged. "Did William say anything to you?"

"No. Jack?" Maude shook her head. Jesse May pointed to the other letter. "Who's that from?"

Maude sighed. "My mother."

"Imagine that. What did she say?"

"I don't know. I forgot about it after Paul got stuck behind the settee. Then I got started on lunch."

"Otherwise, you don't want to know."

Maude chuckled. "I suppose I better read it."

She checked on the children, then sat in her rocking chair. The men walked in and washed up for lunch. Jack picked up the bank letter, and William and Jack went to the parlor to read it. Jesse May could hear them talking, their voices rising and falling. If they didn't tell their wives now, Jesse May would ring both of their necks.

Maude was still in her rocking chair when they returned to the table. Jack cleared his throat as Jesse May put food on the table. Maude looked up as the men explained about not having enough money to pay the bank, and without enough cattle left to sell, they could lose everything. The winter had been too hard on their stock, and even with a little hay, it had been much too cold for them to survive.

It suddenly occurred to Jack that Maude was still in her rocking chair instead of joining them at the table. She hadn't said a word. Jesse May, of course, had plenty to say and admonished the men for keeping important information like that from them.

"Maude, are you alright?" Jack saw her holding a letter. "Did something happen?"

Maude stood up, shaking like a leaf. She walked out of the room and up the stairs. Jack watched, then followed behind her.

William turned to Jesse May and whispered. "What happened?"

"I don't know. She got a letter from her mother. That's all I know. I don't know if it's that or possibly losing the ranch. Let's eat and wait until one or both return."

Jesse May got the little ones to the table. William helped Effie May, and Jesse May gave Paul a biscuit. Occasionally they could hear voices from upstairs, but mostly it was quiet. It was twenty minutes before they both came downstairs. Jack looked shocked, and they could tell Maude had dried her tears. They both sat down to eat lunch without saying a thing.

Jesse May was just about to come unglued, unaware of what was happening. But she held herself together when William gave her a look. Jesse May cleaned up the kitchen after telling Maude to take Paul up for his nap. Then she grabbed Effie May from William and stalked to her side of the house. She pointed at William as if to say, "FIND OUT." Then, shutting the door behind her, she managed to click it shut instead of slamming it. *That was the weirdest lunch ever,* she thought to herself.

Jack put on his coat, and William followed. They headed to the barn and began putting out some fresh hay for the horses before Jack said a word.

"Maude's mother is coming for a visit."

William nodded. "Okay. Is she staying at our house?"

"No. I believe at Mrs. Paring's place in town. It's

probably beneath her to stay on a farm." Jack cringed. He hadn't meant to sound mean. He was actually glad, though, as bad as Maude had been treated by her parents in the past.

"So, what's the big deal?"

Jack cleared his throat, leaned on the pitchfork handle, and stared out the door. "She's bringing us money."

"Money. Us?"

"Well, Maude, anyway."

"Okay. I imagine it's just a token to try and make up for the past, isn't it?"

"I'm not sure. It appears that Mrs. Ray sold off all their holdings, and she is giving Maude some money. But you are right. It's probably a small amount to say I'm sorry for things, so here, go buy a nice trinket or two."

"Her mother said that?"

"No." Jack shook his head. "Maude doesn't want the money because that's how she took it to mean, too. All I know is that her parents were pretty much snobs. They even looked down on Mr. and Mrs. Paring, and you know how nice they are."

"So Maude doesn't want to take a bribe."

Jack nodded. "But after the initial shock wears off, I hope she changes her mind."

"So we can pay off the bank, you mean."

"Yes. Now I'm being selfish."

"I'm not sure I feel right about that, either."

"Yeah. Now you know why neither one of us knows what to do."

"Did her mother ask permission or is she coming either way?"

"I gathered she would be here in a week or so. Mr. and Mrs. Paring will go get her and bring her to Hastings. I'm not sure how Maude feels about it, but it's been almost three years since she's seen her mother. I hope they can get along. After all, with another child on the way, it's important Maude doesn't get upset."

"Let's get back inside. I'm freezing. Besides, Jesse May will have my hide if I don't tell her what's going on."

Jack chuckled and slapped William on the shoulder. "Glad you're married to her, not me."

"Thanks, little brother."

Maude was in a slightly better mood at supper time but was still fairly quiet. Jesse May bit her tongue and didn't question her about the letter. William had done his best to tell her what Jack had told him, but she knew that wasn't the whole story. The men played with their children as the two women cleaned up the kitchen.

"Jesse May, I have a question for you."

Jesse May hung up her dishtowel and turned to Maude. "How about some tea, and we sit at the table?"

Maude nodded. "That would be great." They settled down, and Maude started over. "My mother is coming to stay at the Paring's, so I feel like I've been set up. I'm sure Mrs. Paring is behind much of this."

"So? At least she won't be under your feet here."

"I know. But maybe I want her to be?"

Jesse May looked dismayed. "Do you want your mother to visit or not?"

Maude chuckled. "Yes and no. I dread her visit, expect her to criticize everything and tell me I was crazy to do all of this. But then, maybe she's changed, and she will be happy to see me."

Jesse May thought for a minute. "Your parents had all the time in the world to come see you and drag you back home. They didn't,and your mother apologized for her behavior. I'd say she's here to make amends and just as scared as you are. That's why Mrs. Paring got involved. Or your mother involved her. If you two can mend a few fences, invite her to stay here for a few days."

Maude shrugged. "Maybe. Jack and I have discussed just about every scenario, but I don't have an answer."

"I don't think you will until she gets here and you two talk."

"You're probably right." Maude took another drink of her tea. "She's bringing me money."

"William told me something about money, but he didn't know the whole story. So, what's the problem?"

"I feel like she's trying to buy me back."

"Or, she's making up to you for the wrongs that have occurred over the years. Does it matter?"

"I don't know if it does or not. I think it would help us not lose the ranch, maybe. So, selfishly, I couldn't turn it down."

Jesse May nodded. "And, selfishly, I'd agree. If you can help pay this year's note, I would be very grateful."

Maude smiled. "I guess I need to have a face-to-face conversation with my mother. Otherwise, I'll never have an answer."

Jesse May patted Maude's hand. "Listen, my dear sister. I'll do anything I can to help. I think you have the answer. Visit, then decide."

"Thank you, Jesse May. And thank you for considering me your sister."

"Well, we are related as sisters-in-law, so technically, that's a correct term, right?"

"Right." The two hugged and then cleaned up the teacups.

Jack and Maude talked again that night, and Maude explained she would speak to her mother and agree to take the money, especially if it would be enough to pay this year's note. What she didn't say was that the money would probably be enough to take care of the whole note. Her father was very wealthy, and her mother mentioned giving her the money that would have gone for her dowry. She knew it would have been a significant amount that her father had promised Alan. He would have received it as soon as Alan married Maude and got her out of her father's house. But she didn't want to get everyone's hopes up. Not even hers.

Jack knew that her parents were wealthy, but even she wasn't sure how much money her father had. He never spent a dime unless there was something in it for him personally. Unfortunately, Jack and William were due to go to the bank before her mother arrived, and she wondered if there was something he could say to them to stall the payment.

"I could give you my letter to show the banker, but maybe Mr. Paring could help."

"How could Ada's father help?"

"He could tell the banker how much my father was worth. I don't have that knowledge, and mother didn't mention how much she was bringing me."

Jack thought for a moment. "I rather like that idea. Do you think he would do that for us?"

"Sure. I'm like family. I can ask him if you want."

"Well, maybe you can go with me," Jack agreed. "I've talked to Mrs. Paring several times, but not her husband."

"He's not much for socialization these days. He doesn't get around very well. One of his horses spooked and knocked him around. He's lucky to be alive, actually."

"Oh. I didn't know that."

"Let's go see him. I don't know how he will travel to pick up my mother. That road is still awful, and I'm sure it didn't improve with all this snow."

"I'm thinking I better do it, then."

"Hmmm. That might not be good to meet my mother like that. Maybe we should send Greg."

Jack laughed. "Good choice. We'll have a group discussion tomorrow before heading over to the Walkers. Then it's on to Hastings."

"Good plan. Now let's get some sleep."

"Yes, boss."

Jack kissed his wife goodnight. He smiled, hoping that the ranch could be saved from foreclosure. It would give him and William time to rebuild the herd over the following year.

HARRIETT RAY ARRIVES

At the breakfast table, it was decided that Jesse May and William would stay behind to take care of the children while Jack and Maude bundled up to head straight over to the Walkers and then on to Hastings.

Once they sat down and explained about Mrs. Ray coming, Greg agreed that Mr. Paring had no business taking any long trips, especially on that rough road. Ada was pleased to hear that Mrs. Ray was coming. Finally. Leave it to Ada's mother to get that stubborn woman out West. Maude made sure Greg knew what he was getting himself into, as her mother wasn't the easiest person to get along with, but he still agreed to bring her from the train.

Jack and Maude headed into town and straight over to the Paring residence. Thankfully they were home. After pleasantries, Maude explained to Mr. Paring that she wanted Jack to talk to him about something very sensitive. Then she and Mrs. Paring got up to leave the room.

"So, what seems to be the problem here?"

Jack took a deep breath. "We lost half of our herd this winter due to the storms and freezing temperatures. William and I can't pay the banknote due by the week's end without selling everything we own. If we do that, then we won't have any cattle to build our herd to make money for next year."

"You want to borrow money from me?"

"Oh, no, sir. Absolutely not. You see, Mrs. Ray sent Maude a letter saying she has sold Mr. Ray's holdings and is bringing her some money. She didn't say how much or anything, but we hope it's enough to pay this year's mortgage. I'd like you to help me talk to the banker to hold my note until we get the money from Mrs.

Ray. With us selling a few head of cattle and that money, we can probably pay what is due. I'm afraid neither Maude nor I know how much the check will be, but she assures me we can take care of the note and buy some replacements for the ranch. Also, the letter from her mother said something about her dowry money, whatever that means."

"Did she now? I see. So, you believe the banker would believe me over her."

"Don't you, sir?"

Mr. Paring laughed. "So he would, young man. So he would. What would you kids have done if your mother-in-law hadn't sent that letter in time to notify you of her arrival along with some funds?"

Jack gulped. "Sold the ranch, sir. We had big dreams and not enough money to sustain such losses."

"I see. Let me see that letter." Mr. Paring read the letter and handed it back. "I assure you, Jack, your mother-in-law has gone through a lot in her lifetime, but she's not a liar. I believe she is bringing Maude a bank draft made out in a significant amount. I'll go see the banker after lunch."

"Thank you, sir. Do I need to go, too?"

"No, son. I believe my visit with George can be handled without much commotion. There will be enough of that when you take Mrs. Ray's check to the bank."

Jack nodded, even though he didn't really understand. "Before I forget, Greg will get Mrs. Ray and bring her here. He just needs a date and time."

"Wonderful." Mr. Paring rubbed his legs. "This cold weather is killing me."

Jack smiled and went in search of Maude. They made their way to the mercantile for a few items and headed for home. They stopped briefly to tell Greg the travel information to get Mrs. Ray and then went straight home.

They made it just in time for supper.

The train arrived and a gentleman sitting close by helped Harriett from the train. She was dirty, her clothes were wrinkled, and her hat was askew. How her daughter could live under these conditions, she had no idea. She thanked the gentleman for his assistance and stood on the platform. The Parings were nowhere to be seen. Harriett was mumbling about being in primitive surroundings when someone cleared his throat behind her.

"Mrs. Ray?"

She turned to find a young man with her luggage. "Yes. That's me. Have you seen the Parings?"

"I'm their son-in-law, Greg Walker. I'm Ada's husband. Mr. Paring has been recently injured, so I offered to provide your transportation."

"Oh, well. Thank you, young man."

"I'll load your luggage. Is it just this one piece?"

"Oh. Yes. And my valise." She placed it on top.

"I'll be right back." Greg disappeared around a corner and soon returned to retrieve Mrs. Ray. "Come this way, Ma'am."

Greg helped Mrs. Ray into the buckboard. Ada had provided a pillow to sit on and plenty of blankets. Unfortunately, it would be dark before they reached their destination. After much jarring, Harriett couldn't help but complain.

"Young man, do you have to hit every hole in the road?"

"I'm sorry, Ma'am. This is a terrible stretch of road, and there isn't a good place to be. The horses will follow the established path. I really don't do anything except hang on to the leads."

Harriett grumbled and resituated herself. "Thank you for the pillow and blankets."

"You can thank Ada when you see her. She thought

only of your comfort on this long, bumpy trip. Even she doesn't like this road. We never take it unless we have to."

They slammed into another hole. "I can believe it." It was several minutes before she asked about Maude. "Tell me about my daughter and her husband."

"They are lovely people. I can see where she gets her looks." Mrs. Ray blushed. "The Turners are good people. Jack, Maude's husband, is the younger of the two. William married Jesse May. The Turners bought a ranch that connects to mine. It actually has more acreage. We run our cattle together in the open range. Unfortunately, it's been a hard winter, and we've both lost several head."

Harriett looked around. "It's pretty barren. I'm used to more trees."

Greg nodded. "There are more by the river. Unfortunately, the prairie is too dry most of the time to sustain much more than a gopher."

"This Jesse May that's married to the other brother."

"William."

"Yes, William. What type of girl is she?"

Greg scratched his head. He wasn't sure what Mrs. Ray was asking. "Well, she was a teacher when William met her. I believe her grandparents raised her on a large farm in Missouri. She's very nice and perfect for William. They have a little girl named Effie May."

"And my grandson?"

"Cute little guy. Maude is a very good mother, and Paul keeps her running. He adores his parents and is very inquisitive."

"You use big words for a farmer."

Greg about choked, trying to keep from laughing. "Thank you, Ma'am. I'm well-bred. I just choose to raise animals instead of following in my father's footsteps."

"And what footsteps would that be?"

"He is a lawyer, back East."

"Really?"

"Yes, Ma'am. You will find that many of us that choose to move out here do so because we hated the city. Of course, there are many farmers and ranchers that have moved out here, too, but you will find a variety of people who have chosen this new life."

"I see."

"I'm not sure you do. Just like you questioned my breeding, you might question others. That is quite inappropriate, and others will not take kindly to your snobbishness. It's a warning I suggest you take before you get around others."

Greg flipped the reins to hurry along the horses. He was getting tired of Mrs. Ray already. It was no wonder Maude was worried about the visit. Greg kept the horses at a brisk pace and ignored the cries when the wagon hit bumps and holes. It was some time before Harriett said another word. Her pride had been hurt, and she realized that no one in this area of the country would care one way or the other about her. She had tried to change after Herbert died, but her pride often got in the way. She knew people talked about her behind her back. What hurt worse was when the gossip was about Maude. Her husband hadn't helped in that department. In fact, he made it well known that Maude was a thankless daughter and had run away. Harriett, when asked, would say she left to get away from Alan Beemer since her husband wouldn't listen, and she was happy living away from home. And it was the truth. She had stopped supporting Herbert, and every one of her friends knew the type of person Alan was.

Her pouting done, Harriett noticed the sun beginning to set. "How close are we?"

"We have several miles to go yet. If you're tired, we

can stop at my house, Maude's house, or continue on into Hastings. It's only five miles further to town."

Harriett sighed. "I suppose we best go to the Parings tonight. Cecily will be expecting me."

"Good decision. There's another blanket or two in the back. I'd appreciate you handing me one."

"Certainly."

Mrs. Ray threw a blanket over Greg's legs and put another one over her own. As they passed by the Turner land, Greg mentioned where they were. Then he told Mrs. Ray when they were going by his land. Finally, just as Harriett thought she was frozen stiff and would never be warm again, they arrived at the Parings. Greg helped unbundle Harriett and assisted her down. Mrs. Paring heard them arrive and rushed to the door.

"Harriett. Come in here. You must be cold clear through."

"Cecily. I'm so glad I'm here. What an awful ride."

The two women went inside, and Greg soon followed with the baggage. Mr. Paring offered Greg some brandy to warm him up. He took it gladly and stood by the fireplace for a few minutes.

"I better head for home. Ada will be expecting me."

"The trip go alright?"

Greg understood the question Mr. Paring really meant to ask. "Yes. It was a little bumpy sometimes, but we got through it."

Mr. Paring smiled. "I'm sure you did."

Ada questioned Greg the minute he walked in the door. He admitted to scolding Mrs. Ray, but Ada laughed. "That probably threw her for a loop."

"Between those roads and her long trip on the train, she was probably exhausted."

"I'm sure."

"I left the pillow and blankets in the barn. We can get

them tomorrow. Right now, I could use some food."

Ada got a plate off the warm stove and put it on the table. "I'm glad you're home."

"Me, too."

Mrs. Ray was still cranky the following day. She bathed and tried to stay warm. The temperature had dropped outside again, and Harriett stayed wrapped in a quilt all day. Mrs. Paring hoped she didn't get pneumonia. She fixed her some hot tea and honey, and all her meals were served by the fireplace. By the following morning, Harriett was feeling better and apologized for her behavior.

"It was such a difficult trip. I'm not used to such hardship. How did you two manage?"

"Oh. It was difficult, of course. We had to rest up just as you did, but it wasn't freezing cold when we arrived. I don't know what possessed you to come out in the winter."

"Oh, Cecily. I'm such a fool. First Herbert, then Maude, and now this trip."

"Harriett, I'm just glad you're safe. I'll have Maude come to town. We will wait for a good day to go to her house. I have someone I can use to send a message out to her."

"Okay. I should talk to her soon."

"I'll plan a noon meal for tomorrow. I'm sure it will be fine. You will like her husband. Jack is a very nice man."

"Sounds lovely. That will give me one more day to recover."

Mrs. Paring sent a message to Maude, and a message was returned that they would both arrive mid-morning. Both Maude and her mother were nervous wrecks.

Maude walked up to the Paring doorway with great trepidation. Taking a deep breath, she knocked lightly. Jack was right behind her, holding Paul. Mrs. Paring opened the door and invited the family inside. After removing all their coats, gloves, and hats, Mrs. Paring brought them into the parlor. Mrs. Ray was standing by the fireplace with a worried look. Maude stood looking at her mother for a few seconds.

"Mother."

"Maude." The Parings left the room and shut the door behind them. "Come in, dear, and introduce me to your family."

"Mother, this is my husband, Jack Turner. And this is our son, Paul."

Jack went forward and extended his hand. Mrs. Ray reached out and gripped it warmly. "It's good to meet you both."

Paul turned and hugged his father's neck. "He's still a little shy with strangers."

"That's alright. I don't blame him."

"I'll leave you two to visit. I believe you have some catching up to do, and you don't need us hanging around distracting you." Jack gave Maude a quick kiss and let himself out.

"You have a fine-looking family." She peered at her daughter. "And another one the way, I assume?"

Maude blushed. "Yes. And one on the way."

"Very nice."

"Is it?"

Her mother was taken aback. "Why, yes, it is. Very much so."

Maude walked to a chair and sat down before she collapsed. Seeing her mother brought back so many memories — none of them good, at the moment. Harriett sat across from her daughter and rushed to explain things before losing her nerve.

"I'm sorry for everything. I had no decisions to make, no life to choose. Your father told me what to do and when to do it. I had lived like that for so many years I lost sight of what was important. I refused to listen to you. It was easier not to deal with Herbert. Even though doing something like making you marry Alan would have been a horrible thing to make you do. I can't blame it all on your father, though. I allowed myself to be submissive, which worsened over the years. I lost my way. After he died, I felt lost. No one was there to boss me around and tell me what to do. Your father's solicitor helped me through it all. From what I gathered, he really wasn't too fond of your father." Mrs. Ray offered a sad smile. "In the end, I wasn't either. I had moved to your old room a few months after you left. I missed you so much. I would smell your clothes or play with your ribbons. I didn't want to lose you or forget you. I hadn't talked to your father for a long time. He made me write those awful letters. I almost didn't send them. I knew he was watching me or had me watched. So, I knew I could never correspond with you behind his back." Mrs. Ray shivered.

"He turned out to be an awful, manipulative man. By the time I realized it, it was too late. You came along, and you were all I lived for. Even that he took away from me. I tried to make you into the person he wanted, but, bless your heart, you didn't bend. I should have helped you run away. But I would have been punished terribly. So, instead, I turned a blind eye when you left. I knew you wouldn't be back. Mother's instinct, I guess. I played along. I'm glad you didn't tell me ahead of time. Your father would have beat it out of me." Maude looked surprised.

"Yes, dear. I did what I was told to do or paid the consequences. Believe me. I did what I was told. I would guess that is why he wanted Alan Beemer as your husband. Like minds and all." Mrs. Ray took a breath.

"Anyway, another poor decision was to come out here in the freezing cold. I don't know how you stand this weather."

"You get used to it."

Mrs. Ray shrugged and poked at the fire to make it flame up again. "Back to the solicitor. His name is Bertram Benjamin. He is the one that suggested I liquidate your father's holdings. I think he enjoyed selling it all. As I said, he wasn't too fond of your father. He said I'd be set for life, and I agreed. I didn't want any of those slimy creatures around me. They were at my doorway immediately after Herbert died, offering to take care of everything. A couple of them offered to marry me immediately. You know, to help take care of the business. Bertram handled all of it and got a fair price for me. Those men thought I would also let them have it all cheap, so they were quite surprised by how Bertram handled the sales. Even though I'm not that big of a pushover, I'm sure they believed I was, the way your father talked about me." Harriett dug around in her purse. "Ah. Here it is." She held some papers. "This is the information I thought you might want to have." She handed it to Maude.

After a glance, she looked at her mother. "This is my dowry information. You mentioned in your letter about this."

"Yes, of course. I guess I did write about that. This account was set aside for you and was still intact. I was surprised your father didn't spend it or close the account. I think you might have Bertram to thank for that. He didn't always do what Herbert told him if Bertram thought it was a bad idea. Herbert just expected things to be done and never went back to check." Harriett handed over a bank draft. "This is in your name to do with whatever you wish, but I'd like you to use it as your dowry, as intended. If I could have had anything to do with your wedding, that would have been available to you both then. It would have made a nice start to your married life."

"Thank you, Mother." Maude looked at the amount on the bank draft. She gasped. Of course, she knew it would be a lot, but it still took her by surprise.

"You're welcome. After everything was said and done with your father's assets, you and I are now rich."

"Mother, you've always been rich."

"No, dear. Your father was rich, and my father was rich. Women are never rich in our circumstances. But now, we are rich. The money is mine to do with as I choose. I had Bertram get a bank draft for your half of the proceeds. You suffered as much as I did over the years. And if you and I were still under the same roof, I wouldn't do anything different. You are my daughter, and I am supposed to care for you. The last three years have been devastating for me. I'm sure they have been for you, too. Not Jack, of course, but our relationship. Please tell me you'll forgive me."

The tears had welled up for several minutes in both of their eyes. Finally, the dam broke,and they held each other tight. Mother and daughter embraced for several minutes as a healing emotion washed over them. They were both spent by the time they were done. As they dried their tears, Harriett remembered she hadn't given Maude the other check yet. She opened her purse and pulled out the other bank draft.

"Before I give this to you, I have one more request."

"What's that?"

"I want you to put this in an account with your name on it. Then, if, God forbid, your husband ever acts as mine did, you will have the funds to leave."

"But Jack..."

Her mother held up her hand. "Jack appears to be a nice man. Greg Walker told me so. And if all of these people are good enough for Cecily Paring, they're good enough for me. But promise me you'll put this in your own account. If something happens to Jack, you need to be able to take care of your family."

"Yes, Mother. I promise."

Harriett smiled. "I love you, Maude. I always have."

"I love you, too, Mother."

They hugged and cried a few more tears. Then, Harriett handed the bank draft over to Maude. Maude looked at it several times and then had to count the zeros.

"Are you serious?"

Harriett smiled. "I told you we were rich."

"My heavens. And you have one just like it?"

Harriett nodded. "Plus, the house, the stables, the vacation house, and a few other things. I haven't decided whether I'll keep any of the property."

"That's unbelievable."

"My father gave your father a huge dowry. I never knew where it went, but it doesn't matter now. I believe your father made good use of the money. He was good at making money."

"Thank you so much, Mother."

"Again, you are very welcome." Her stomach growled. They both laughed. "Do you think dinner is ready?"

"I hope so." Maude's stomach chimed in. "Let's go eat."

Maude put the drafts in her small purse, and they

walked arm in arm out to the dining room. Everyone was pleased to see mother and daughter smiling.

Later that day, Maude and Jack walked into the bank. She had given Jack the dowry bank draft. He reacted about as she did, and it took a few moments for him to breathe again. Maude told him to pay the whole bank loan to start with. All he could think about was that William and Jesse May wouldn't believe their luck.

After putting the money in the ranch account, Jack took his receipt over to the banker, George, to conduct some business. While Jack was busy completing the paperwork, Maude opened an account in her name, just as her mother requested. The teller about fell over when he saw the amount. Maude took out a few dollars to have at home in case of an emergency. Otherwise, it would be sitting in the bank as her nest egg. Like her mother said, you never knew if she would need the money in the future. If she didn't, it would be there for her children.

When they left the bank, they paid their bill at the mercantile. Then, Maude and Jack filled the wagon with goods for everyone. She picked out yards of material to make baby clothes and dresses with, for her and Jesse May to wear when they were with child. They had left Paul napping at the Parings and stopped to get him on their way out of town. The sun had come out that afternoon, and Maude smiled. It was just dropping down to the horizon as they began the last mile to the house.

"Jack, I may have failed to mention something. I opened an account in the bank, too." She pulled out the receipt and showed it to her husband. Jack about fell out of the wagon as he looked at the paper, so Maude took the reins until he could control his emotions. "You can't tell anyone about this money. It's just between you and me."

"How could you forget to tell me about such a thing?

That is huge!"

Maude laughed. "I know. I'm still in awe. Mother sold my father's business holdings and split it with me."

"Good grief. I don't even know what to say." The wagon was almost at the house.

"We can talk about it another time, but as far as Jesse May and William, all they need to know about is my dowry, alright?"

"That's enough in itself. They will be thrilled that we saved the ranch."

"Mother saved the ranch."

"I'm glad you two have made up."

"We're working on it, but I am, too."

THE RANCH

They pulled up to the house, and William came out to help unload the wagon. And unload they did. Maude took Paul inside and cleaned him up before joining Jesse May in the kitchen. Before Jesse May started on how the visit went, Maude assured her that it went fine and that they would talk about it at the supper table. Jack and William ran out of places to put the stuff they brought home and stacked things on top of each other until the girls could decide where it all went. Then, they washed up for supper and sat down just as dinner was set on the table.

Maude smiled at everyone, and Jack was just about bursting at the seams. "My visit with my mother went well. Better than I expected. We have a long way to go, but most of the misunderstandings of the last three years have been solved. My mother handed me a large bank draft that was meant for my dowry. Since I'm married now, it would have gone to Jack had my mother been allowed to do so."

Jack couldn't stand it any longer. He took the bank papers out of his pocket and held them up high. "The loan is paid off. We own the ranch free and clear."

Jesse May and William shouted with happiness, and they all talked over each other. Even Paul and Effie May decided to join in on the fun and screeched out. Everyone laughed.

Once things settled down again, Maude continued. "Now that we can get back on our feet and replenish the stock, I expect you boys to do what we need to do to stay profitable. Figure out how to stop losing cattle in the winter. Learn what it takes. Find the answers. That money won't last forever, but it should keep us going until your herd is built up and we have a good hay crop every year."

Jack smiled. "Listen to you. All bossy all of a sudden."

"You boys kept this loan problem a secret. You can't do that. So, from now on, we work as a family, we worry as a family, we problem solve as a family."

"Yes, Ma'am. Whatever you say," Jack and William said at the same time. Maude reached over and slapped Jack on the arm, and Jesse May did the same to William.

Jesse May said, "We had to grow up quickly. We came together as friends, and when we had problems, we got together and solved whatever it was."

William hugged Jesse May. "Well, you women are much more sensible than us men."

"True."

Jesse May and Maude went through the stacks of supplies brought into the house, trying to find a place for it all. Jesse May admired the cloth and couldn't wait to see what Maude made from each piece.

Soon, the children were put down, and Maude was exhausted from the stress of everything that had happened that day. However, Jesse May was still full of questions, so Maude sat in her rocker while Jesse May questioned her.

"It was just so emotional, and it's hard to explain. But we've made our peace. For now, anyway. She will be out for a visit in a couple of days."

"I just can't believe that she gave you all that money."

"Technically, it would have gone directly to Jack. And in this case, since he and his brother own the ranch together, everyone benefits."

"Just how big was that check?"

Maude laughed. "Big. Our bank account is pretty flush right now, and as long as the boys remain responsible, it should stay that way. I know they want to raise their boys to take over someday, but they won't be able to if we have more winters like this last one. Unfortunately, we were ill-prepared."

"I know they have some ideas, but we've never been involved much. I suppose we better be from now on and not let them get too carried away. My grandparents were successful because they took great care in their decisions. I remember them talking late into the night sometimes when they had to make a big decision. I'd like us to do that."

"Me, too. Right now, I need to go to bed. My feet are killing me, and I must have done too much today."

"I'll finish up here. You head on up to bed."

Maude did, and Jesse May finished putting things away. The larder was full, and there was a big box of food to take to the root cellar tomorrow. The cloth was settled over on a table where Maude did all the mending and sewing. Jesse May never did get the hang of a needle and thread. She would have to have Effie May learn from the best.

Jack and William were working on the books. Jack entered the new balances in the books, and they both sat back and stared at the total.

William scratched his stubble and looked at his brother. "You know I'll never be able to repay you for this."

"You know you don't have to. It was a gift."

"I feel bad we ended up in such bad shape. And we didn't let the girls know until we had almost lost the ranch."

"A little prideful, are we?"

"I suppose, a little. What did you think of Maude's speech at supper?"

"She's right. We were ill-prepared to deal with the problems that arose. We need to think ahead. Drought, too much rain, tornadoes, hail, heat, you name it. We just sailed in here like we had the world by the tail and never thought that we would be in the mess we got ourselves in."

"I bet the banker was hoping we failed."

Jack laughed. "Yeah. He had no use for us, did he? Then Mr. Paring asked him to put off the collection for a bit, and all was good. Money does talk, doesn't it?"

"I bet old George was surprised when you took that check in there."

"I'll say. I mean, he knew there would be money, but not that much. He was about as surprised as I was."

"At least we can replace the herd, get a good bull, and start with a few repairs around here. It looks like your wife bought enough material to sew for weeks."

"She said it's for Jesse May and her, so when they get big, they have something comfortable. It wouldn't surprise me if she made something for Ada, too."

"Wouldn't surprise me a bit." William fingered his shirt. "She is a great seamstress. I've never had such well-made shirts before. Jesse May is lucky to be able to darn my socks."

"Let's head to bed. We can start discussing repairs tomorrow, but the first thing is to make sure the girls are involved."

"Right. Right." William shook his head. "I'll try to remember that."

"You won't have to. Jesse May will remind you."

The men laughed and began putting out the lights and going their separate ways. William thought, as he climbed the stairs, that he would let Jesse May think she was involved in the decision-making. But he underestimated the woman if he thought he could get away with that.

Jack headed up to the bedroom, peeking in on Paul first. His firstborn was growing so fast, and here he had another on the way. He curled up next to his wife and soon dropped off to sleep.

Maude awakened to the sun streaming in the window. Sunshine. It made her so happy. Jack was long gone. His side of the bed was cold already. Surprisingly, Paul hadn't awakened her. Then she realized there was a lot of noise from the main floor. By the time she got to breakfast, Paul and Effie May were playing, and Jesse May was still trying to find spots for all the goods.

"Well, good morning, sleepyhead."

"Good morning."

"You get a little carried away with all of your buying yesterday? Unfortunately, we don't have room for all of this food. I've tried since last night to find spots for everything."

Maude shrugged. "We can put it in the laundry room or somewhere for now."

"So much cloth. Are you planning on a new wardrobe? I thought I had found it all last night but ran across more this morning."

"It's for you and me and the babies. I might even make Ada a new dress. Aren't the colors beautiful?"

"I bet you've missed all that sewing."

"I have, in a way. I didn't like the pressure I was under to get things done so quickly, but you know I love it. I'm getting as big as a barn again, and I need something to do since I can't even see my feet. And none of my clothes are comfortable."

Jesse May frowned. "You do seem to have bloomed overnight. When are you due again?"

"I thought June, but maybe I'm off a few weeks."

"Hmmm. I'll have the doctor come out to see you."

"Yes, I need to see him anyway. I promised him I wouldn't wait until the last minute."

"You are doing much better this time, though."

"Thankfully."

After Paul laid down for his nap, Maude cut out a dress for herself and Jesse May. She worked on Jesse May's first, which was done a couple of days later. It felt good to get back into sewing. The dress she made for herself was patterned, so no matter how big she got, it would fit. It was a shapeless dress, and she would look like she was wearing a tent, but Maude didn't care. She was uncomfortable. Her feet were swollen, and she couldn't put on any shoes. A couple of days later, Dr. Johnson stopped by. He was driving past and remembered that she hadn't made an appointment with him yet. They went to her room, and he checked her out thoroughly. Maude was much healthier this time, and he congratulated her.

"Where's Jack?"

"I'm not sure. Why?"

"Oh, I need to tell him something. Come on down when you're dressed. I'll see if I can find him."

When the doctor reached the bottom of the stairs, Jack burst into the house. "What's wrong?"

Dr. Johnson laughed. "I just stopped to check on your wife and congratulate you."

"Oh. Thank you."

Maude got downstairs without difficulty and walked over to Jack. "The doctor was going to go look for you."

"I saw the buggy and came running. I thought something was wrong."

The doctor smiled. "Nothing is wrong. But I know why Maude got so big so fast and couldn't see her feet. She's carrying twins."

"Twins?" the couple gasped. Maude sat down in a chair, and Jack plopped down beside her. "Good grief."

Jesse May walked into the room carrying a load of laundry. "Good grief, what?"

Maude smiled. "We're having twins."

"Good grief!" Jesse May exclaimed as she dropped the laundry basket. Once she recovered, she said, "So, Dr. Johnson, since you're here, you want to check on me, too? I believe I'm carrying. But it better not be twins."

William walked in the door. "Twins? We're having twins?" Everyone laughed.

Dr. Johnson shook his head. "Jack is having twins, but I was just informed you might be having another one soon. Come on, Jesse May. Let's have a quick check."

William sat down. "Good grief." That made everyone laugh once again.

As the doctor followed behind Jesse May, he looked over his shoulder and said, "You Turner boys are doing your best to fill this house back up."

Maude looked over at Jack. "Twins?"

Jack nodded weakly. "Twins."

"Well, Mr. Turner, I do believe the doctor is right. We're going to fill this house up in no time."

Jack replied, "Good grief."

Mrs. Ray visited that sunshiny day and found Maude sitting in her rocking chair, with a shocked look on her face. Dr. Johnson had left only a few minutes ago, and they were still trying to digest the news. When Maude told her mother, Harriett just about fainted on the spot. The doctor had left from Jesse May's side of the house and managed to miss Mrs. Ray, who would have peppered him with questions. As it was, Jack and Maude were under fire instead. Finally, Jesse May walked in and stopped the drama.

"Mrs. Ray. We all share your concern, but the doctor said she is doing just fine. The babies will probably come a little early, but we will make sure she is taken care of."

Harriett was wringing her hands. "Oh my. Oh my."

Maude got herself together once her mother stopped throwing questions at her. "Mother. I have felt very well this whole time. It wasn't until a couple of days ago that I began to get so big. I'm making good use of my time by sewing baby clothes and gowns."

"I'm sorry. It's just such a shock."

"For all of us."

"You mentioned you were working for a seamstress in Omaha," her mother tried to ask without causing problems. "I thought that to be a..."

"Menial job?"

Harriett had the sense to blush. "Uh, yes. We've always hired someone else to do that for us."

"Well, I was the one you would have hired in Omaha."

"I see."

"Mother, stop. Jesse May, go get your new dress. I finished it, and it's hanging in the laundry room."

Jesse May brought it out for Harriett to examine. "Take a close look at it, Mrs. Ray."

Harriett checked all the seams, the hem, and then looked at the trim. "This is perfect. Where did you learn to sew like this?" She handed the dress back to Jesse May.

"You taught me the basics if you remember. Then, I continued to sketch and plan my own patterns. The finest women in Omaha wear my ball gowns."

"Really?"

"Really."

Maude got up and walked to her sewing basket. "Right now, I'm making clothes for the baby, but it looks like I'll have to double the amount. Diapers, too. Paul is still in them."

Harriett looked at the little clothes Maude pulled out of her basket. "These are cute and practical. Babies grow so fast."

"I know. I made a few things for Paul to grow into. But, it will be a full-time job keeping my children in clothes. Especially if we have twins every time."

Harriett burst out laughing. It was a sound Maude hadn't heard for years. She couldn't remember the last time her mother had a true laughing spell. It was contagious, and soon everyone joined in.

Her mother looked at Jesse May. "Would you show me around? I don't want Maude up and down those stairs right now." Jesse May looked at Maude, and she nodded.

A half-hour later, the inspection was complete. Jesse May had even walked her to their side of the house, but didn't take her upstairs. Jack had gone outside to finish his latest project, and William was just riding in from checking the cattle. Jack informed his brother that Mrs. Ray was inside, so William joined Jack.

Jesse May went back to her side of the house and left Maude with her mother. Harriett had come up with some solutions that her daughter struggled with. It was all

Harriett could do not to walk in and take over, but she reminded herself that Maude was married now.

As she got ready to go back to town, she told Maude, "I'd like to move to Hastings permanently. Somewhere close to the Parings. If it's all the same to you, I'll sell the house and all of the other properties. I'd like to live by my grandchildren and watch them grow up."

"Are you sure, Mother? I mean, you hated your trip out here."

"And I'll hate it again, but look what will be waiting for me. Grandchildren that I thought I would never get to meet. And if I don't move here, they will never get to know me."

"You're right. If Father were still alive, they would never get to know you. But I don't want you to move and be sorry about it."

"Pshaw. If I can't stand it, I'll move back. Simple as that. Those old biddies can just gossip about me easier if I'm not there."

Maude laughed. "I'm glad you're not leaving yet. I think these babies will be a hand full."

Harriett smiled. "I'll contact my solicitor. Bertram will have to take care of my staff, too. I will return home and pack up what I want to keep." Harriett looked around. "It doesn't look like you will need any of the fancy ball gowns now."

Maude chuckled. "After all of these babies, nothing will fit anyway. I have an idea. You can ship them off to my old boss, Crystal, in Omaha. She can remake them for her snooty clients there."

"Give them away?"

"What else would you do with them? No one back home will wear them."

"True." Harriett sighed. "We'll talk about it later. My driver is back."

"Who brought you?"

"Mr. Walker. He is showing me how to handle a small carriage so I can get back and forth on my own."

"How nice of him. Tell him hello. And make sure you have him tell Ada about the twins."

"Is that appropriate conversation?" Harriett raised an eyebrow.

"We don't stand on ceremony out here, Mother."

Sighing, Harriett promised she would.

The weeks flew by, and Maude had more and more difficulty getting around. She and Jack had multiple decisions to make, and some included Mrs. Ray's suggestions. The house was large, even after the Turners split it into two sections. Jack discussed some of the options with William, and the two made a few changes. The parlor was changed into a bedroom, so Maude didn't have to take the stairs any longer. One of the upstairs bedrooms became a nursery for the twins. A door was placed between two rooms for a nursemaid to stay on one side and babies in the other room. Maude had agreed to have live-in help for the twins, especially since Jesse May would have her hands full with her own children. Harriett tried to talk them into a cook, too, but Maude put her foot down. Harriett had sent for the nursemaid, and the woman arrived as frazzled as everyone else had in the past. But once she saw her accommodations and got a little rest, Bea settled right in. Maude would be paying her double the amount since she was having twins, and that meant Bea could send more money home to her family.

Maude filled the dresser drawers with new diapers and gowns for the twins. Paul was growing fast, so Maude cut long pants and stitched in long hems so she could let them out as he grew. By May, Maude knew it was almost time. Bea was established, and Paul had taken to her easily. While waiting for the twins to be born, Bea helped clean the house and cook. She was surprised to learn she would sit with the family to eat. Bea sat by Paul and assisted him with his meal, which made her feel better about sitting there. Maude deferred some decisions to Bea about Paul's care; she was soon just another family member.

Dr. Johnson stopped by whenever he was in the neighborhood and checked on Maude and Jesse May. Then he would go see Ada, who was now with her third child. The doctor mentioned they would have to build a school just for the Turner and Walker children.

Harriett had traveled home for a couple of weeks to take care of selling her property but was soon back in Hastings. Her trip, although just as frustrating, was at least warm so she didn't get frozen stiff. She had several chests of goods this time, and, as promised, she had sent Maude's gowns off to Crystal. Harriett even packed a few of her own fancier gowns, too, though there was nowhere to wear them here. She took lessons from Cecily Paring on how to dress appropriately for her new surroundings.

Harriett found a house close by the Parings and attempted to settle into a new regimen. She finally found someone to cook and clean for her. Cecily did all of that by herself, but Harriett drew the line there. She was still astounded how Maude enjoyed all that domestic work. Then, of course, she had to have someone for the stables. Cecily offered to have their man work between the two places. She was grateful for Cecily's help. After all, Harriett had barely been civil to her in the past.

Greg stopped by one day, alerted Harriett to Maude's time of labor, and hitched up the carriage for her. He had already notified Dr. Johnson. Harriett took the reins and followed Greg. She had been doing very well with the carriage but was nervous for Maude, and the horses knew it. Once on the road out of town, Greg reminded Harriett to let up on the reins and let the horse have their head.

"Remember, Mrs. Ray; the horses know their way now that you've been out here a few times. You're making them a tad nervous with all of that twitching."

Harriett smiled at Greg. "You're right." She loosened her grip a bit. "Thank you for riding with me." Greg nodded and soon turned his horse to his own home.

Harriett let the horses take her on to Maude's, and they came to a stop where they always did. *Amazing animals,* she thought. William came over and helped her down.

"I'll take care of the horses, Ma'am. You'll be here for a while, I assume?"

"Probably so. Thank you, William. It won't be long before you have another, right?"

"Yes, Ma'am. We're going to fill this house to the rafters soon."

Harriett blushed and rushed inside. Jack was pacing, and she shooed him outside, then she went to the bedroom. The doctor was diligently checking over her daughter. Finally, she took Maude's hand and nodded at the nursemaid, who was helping the doctor and preparing the bassinet.

The doctor smiled. "It won't be long now. These babies are anxious to get out of there and have a little more room to move around."

Maude had another contraction and smashed her mother's hand. Harriett grimaced. After the contraction, she peeled her hand free and rubbed it.

"That must have been a hard one."

"I'm sorry, Mother." Maude was already sweating and disheveled.

"That's okay, dear. It just took me by surprise, and I wasn't prepared."

An hour later, the first child arrived, followed quickly by the second. It was a good thing the nursemaid was helping, as the second baby didn't give the doctor much time with the first. Dr. Johnson announced a boy followed by a girl. The babies both cried lustily as they were rubbed clean and dry. Jack heard the cries and came barreling into the room. He didn't pay any attention to the doctor but went straight to his new babies. Bea wasn't sure what to do. She had never had a father burst into a room like that before. He took the first baby from her and checked him out. Jack gave him back and checked out his daughter. Then, smiling, he rushed over to Maude.

"They're beautiful. Just like you."

Harriett wasn't sure what to say or do at this point. She finally went over to help Bea while the couple visited quietly. Soon, the babies were placed in Maude's arms. The doctor finally finished up and congratulated them all.

"Go on ahead and feed them. They sound hungry."

Bea helped Maude situate the baby boy to feed. A few minutes later, the girl was latched on. Dr. Johnson approved.

"Everything is going well. If you don't have enough milk for two, you'll have to supplement them a bit." Bea said she knew how to make a formula if needed. "It looks like you're in good hands. Bea, very nice help. You'll come in handy for when Jesse May delivers. And maybe you'll be available for Ada, too."

"Thank you, Doctor."

Jack walked Dr. Johnson out. William had heard the babies cry, so he took the liberty of having the doctor's buggy ready to go. William slapped his little brother on the back. "Sounds like you'll have your hands full in there."

Jack rubbed the back of his neck. "I guess so. Wow. You should see them! I have one of each."

Maude saw the sunshine through her window. *What a beautiful day to have babies,* she thought. Then she dozed off. Harriett and Bea took the babies to the nursery, bathed, dressed, and swaddled them. There was a bassinet in the bedroom, and they would sleep together until they were too big to share. Bea would stay on a small cot in the bedroom to assist Maude until she was strong enough to get around. Then Bea would take the babies up to the nursery so Maude could get more rest between feedings. But there wouldn't be much rest with two bellies to feed.

A few months later, Jesse May had her second child, and Ada shortly after that. Bea did help with all the deliveries, and the doctor told her that if she ever wanted to give up being a nursemaid, she could be his full-time nurse. Thanking him for the compliment, Bea knew her heart was in caring for the little ones. And she had her hands full at the Turner home.

NEW PROJECTS

With all the babies being born, there was no one left to put a garden in except the men. They prepared the soil like usual but had to get some help to do the planting. The women gave them a hard time. Bea had never planted a garden, nor had Harriett. Jesse May was too big now to help plant, but her mouth worked well. Ada was also early in her pregnancy, and needed to have help with her own garden. Now that the twins were born, Maude was finally getting around good enough to water and weed. Bea would help occasionally, but she was busy with the twin's care.

William and Jack drew up some plans to build a large lean-to for the cattle to protect them from storms. After talking to other ranchers in the area, they decided to use a side hill and build some type of protection. The cattle would gravitate to the lean-to on instinct. The men had no idea if it would work or not, but there was no way to build a barn big enough for their herd. Their land didn't have box canyons to protect them from the wind, but they did have some gentle hills.

William and Jack walked their horses through their land until they had found the right place. The cattle were grazing, and the new additions had fit right in. Greg Walker was able to increase his herd, too. But, without more grazing land, they couldn't add many more. And they needed some good rains to keep the grass green and growing.

Using the hill as the back of the lean-to, William and Jack, along with Greg, built a long and wide structure. Digging post holes took a lot out of them in the heat, so they dug early in the mornings and late in the evenings. The Turners worked their hay fields in between that work, and Greg Walker raised wheat.

One day, Jack was checking the cattle. He noticed they had migrated toward the lean-to. It was providing shade in the heat of the day. He was happy to report to his brother that the lean-to was a success.

The river was running low these days. The heat wouldn't let up, and the rains didn't come. Greg got his wheat in and was grateful for the harvest. Everyone was crabby from the heat, and the babies lay around with nothing on except a diaper. The house was stifling, and there wasn't even a decent breeze. They ate a lot of cold meals and sat on the porch. Harriett hadn't been out to see Maude for several days; the heat was too much for her. Her house in town was surrounded by trees, which kept her house much cooler.

Maude looked at the cloudless sky. "You know, I love the sunshine, but even I could take a break from it all."

Jack laughed. "We better get some trees planted."

"Not in this heat."

"No, not in this heat."

After a hot and dry three weeks, the storms finally rolled in, and the skies opened-up. The river swelled, and the grass greened. Life had gotten much easier with showers off and on for a couple of days. The hay crop wouldn't be lost after all.

By the end of August, Maude walked down to the river. She looked at all the cottonwoods growing along the banks. Some were huge and had been there for years. She found a few smaller ones to use as starters and spent the next several minutes digging them up. By the time Maude got them back to the house, she was exhausted.

Jesse May came out of the house to see what she was doing, then offered to dig the holes to plant them. They would need to plant them several feet apart. The two decided to place one on the northwest corner, then one on the southwest corner of the house. They eventually hoped to have shade for the house and provide some protection from the winds. By looking at the huge trees by the river, Maude said they needed to be far enough away from the house to allow them to grow tall and wide.

Jesse May decided they needed to have a whole row of trees, so every day Maude would dig up two more trees, and Jesse May would plant them. They were so proud of themselves; they planted trees all over the farmstead. If they all made the transition, the place would finally have shade.

Jesse May took Effie May and Paul and walked around and watered the trees daily, a little bit for each one. It gave them all a little exercise. Bea would keep Jesse May's baby while she worked outside. The door between the two sides of the house stayed open most of the time these days. With all the little ones in the house, Bea stayed busy helping both families.

The two couples were sitting on the porch one late day in October. The cattle were lowing, and the sun was beginning to set. Jesse May listened to the children through the open windows. Effie May was trying to talk to her new little brother. The twins were cooing. Paul, being the oldest, thought he should be the boss of them all. What a good life she had. She looked around at her family. Blessed. Truly blessed. And with friends like the Walkers just down the road, and the Parings and Mrs. Ray in town, what more could they ask for?

Maude daydreamed of their future. A house full of children, a school just down the road, and their families surrounding them. She was glad that her mother had moved close by and that they had made amends. Jane and her husband came for another visit to see the new additions. Good friends and family. That's all she needed.

The sun dropped down below the horizon, and the crickets became the loudest they had heard in a long while. The birds were settling in for the night, and the frogs could be heard croaking in the background. Most of the trees had made it through the transplanting. Come spring, they would see how many they needed to replace.

Cattle were sold to pay for next year's expenses. They hoped their herd would handle the winter storms and give them calves in the spring. The men had saved back a couple of hardy bulls for their breeding program. The hay was in the loft to supplement the feeding.

Bea sat by the children, knitting winter caps and sweaters. She loved her job and had encouraged her family to move out West. The air was crisp and clear, and she was sure they would enjoy it. Once they got there, of course. The road was still a bumpy mess. She had just gotten a letter from her mother. They would come in the spring to see if they wanted to stay. Smiling at the children, she felt blessed, too.

It was time to go inside and prepare for bed. Before they did, Jesse May asked Maude to go for a short walk. Arm in arm, they strolled down the lane as the full moon began to rise. Jesse May stopped and looked at Maude.

"You have no idea how grateful William and I are that you saved the ranch. The men felt foolish for not being more prepared."

"Oh, Jesse May. Thank my mother."

"I have, but if you hadn't agreed to see her and take the money, we'd all be back in Omaha again. When we got married, I gave my savings to William to help buy this place. It was all the money I had left from my grandparents after they sold the farm."

"I hadn't realized that."

Maude began to walk again. They eventually turned and headed back to the house. They could hear the children start their fussiness, and it was time to put them to bed.

"My father was a tyrant. My mother realized it too late, but somehow, with Ada's help, I managed to escape. I always thought my mother agreed with him. Jane helped me stay strong, and of course, you and Ada." Maude stopped before reaching the house. "Jesse May, the family solicitor hated my father's actions, but he was paid to do a job. Mr. Bertram has helped my mother care for everything now that Father is gone. To say I am grateful for my mother's generosity is true. Still, more than anything, I'm grateful she is back in my life. We've had our difficulties, of course, and sometimes she forgets no one cares about high society out here, but with a little guidance from Mrs. Paring, she has changed. And she didn't just help us save the ranch. She made the future possible for our children and her grandchildren. We have a good future here. I can feel it."

One of the children began screaming. The women laughed, and, arm in arm, they went inside. The men soon followed. They went their separate ways, and soon the house was settled for the night.

City life to the prairie life was hard–but worth every minute with family and friends around you.

PART TWO

THE NEXT
GENERATION

LIST OF CHARACTERS
PART TWO

Bertram Benjamin – Herbert Ray's solicitor – lives on the East Coast.

Chet Arnold – married to Jane Peterson.

Greg and Ada Walker – children: Joseph, Gary, Penelope, Sarah.

Jackson and Maude Turner – children: Paul, Carla and Jackson II (twins), Donna, James, Georgia, Thomas.

William and Jesse May Turner – children: Effie May, Charlie, Mary Ann, Carrie, Henry, Mark.

TWELVE YEARS LATER

The William Turner side of the family had grown to six children. Effie May, Charlie, Mary Ann, Carrie, Henry, and Mark.

The Jackson Turner side bested that by one. But, as Jesse May always said, Maude cheated by having twins. Paul, Carla and Jackson II, Donna, James, Georgia, and Thomas.

Early on, the doctor had teased the Turners about filling the large house with children. It took a few years, but they managed to do just that. It was filled to the rafters. And in the middle of all this was the nursemaid, Bea.

Once the last child was out of diapers, Bea moved to town to help Dr. Johnson deliver other babies in the area. Her mother and sister had moved West a couple of years after Bea. Her sister, Noreen, helped with the William Turner household, because Bea had too many little ones to care for. Even with the parent's help. Their mother stayed in town and assisted Maude's mother, Harriet Ray.

The Turner's best friends, Greg and Ada Walker, were their closest neighbors. Their cattle shared the open range. The families celebrated together on important occasions. The Turners frequently teased the Walkers about only having four children. Greg quickly pointed out they had a much smaller house, which was full. Their children's names were Joseph, Gary, Penelope, and Sarah.

Summer arrived early that year. Unfortunately, the spring rains never arrived, and it went from cold and blustery to hot and downright windy. As the weeks went by, the river became a small stream and then all but dried up.

Jack and William had to dig the well deeper to reach the water. Maude and Jesse May seldom did laundry. If they did, they poured the dirty water on the garden. No one had water to waste.

Greg and Ada Walker's wheat crop was shriveled up and almost worthless. The return was virtually nothing for their effort to harvest it. Ada saved enough to make her flour, even as poor a quality as it was. The Turners would get their share in exchange for garden produce. Ada had no idea if there would be anything from anyone's garden this year. She hoped the apples would also produce since they were by the river. The roots would have to be deep to get moisture these days.

The skies occasionally clouded up, but they floated on by and left everyone's hopes shattered. The cattle couldn't survive in this heat, and the Turners took many to market early in the summer. The ones they kept were woefully thin. The men fed them hay sparingly, trying to make it last. There would be no more hay harvest this year. With insufficient water to go around, Jack had an idea to bring in someone that did water witching. William laughed at Jack and told him he was crazy.

Jack went over to Greg's and asked him about it. Greg had heard of it before but didn't know anyone who knew how to perform that job. Jack thought he had nothing to lose, so he made a forked stick from a willow branch. He practiced different methods of holding the stick and began wandering around the pasture. Unfortunately, he wasn't finding water, or he just didn't know how. He did manage to get a terrible sunburn.

It was another scorcher of a day in August. Jack wandered around the pasture again, holding his forked stick in front of him. He stopped to wipe his brow for a moment. Then, looking at the horizon, he noticed something that didn't look quite right. The strange cloud didn't look like a storm building, but it was moving fast and right for him.

"No! No! No!" he screamed as he ran. Jack dropped his stick and screamed at the top of his lungs as he headed for the barn. He was a long way from home, and he had never run so fast in his life. The family came out to see what Jack was yelling about, thinking he might have found water.

"Fire! Prairie fire! Everybody get out of here!" Jack kept running to the barn. It took Jesse May and William a moment to realize what Jack was saying, and then they began running themselves. Jesse May yelled at all her children and then went to the house and screamed for Maude.

By the time the wagons were hooked up, the cloud was getting closer, and they could smell the smoke. Two wagons were loaded with children. Jesse May and Maude counted to make sure the children were all accounted for. Jack and William sent them on their way. The men put halters on their horses, skipped the saddles, and followed their families as fast as they could go. They were heading to Walker's place first to make sure they were getting out of the way. The men told their families to keep going while they checked. When they arrived, the Walkers were in the wagon, ready to leave.

The prairie was so dry; it only took a moment to burn a path. Then, the wind picked up behind the fire and pushed it harder. No one stopped to watch the fire. All they wanted was to get away as fast as possible.

Jack and William took turns warning neighbors as they passed by. Their goal was to get to town and let them know, too. The Turners didn't look back. The smoke was thick, and, more than once, Jack thought the fire might catch up and consume them all. He had no idea if the farmers they had warned along the way had gotten away.

William yelled that they needed to change directions.

The Walkers had managed to stay right behind them, but the fire was covering more ground and catching up to everybody. They turned the wagons and continued their pace, angling off from the fire the best they could. The horses had no intention of slowing down. They didn't like the smell and heat from the fire, either.

The group slowed the horses to a walk when they were safely away, but continued toward town. They were almost to the edge of town when they noticed multiple other farmers and ranchers had arrived before them. Many others were joining them, coming from different directions. All were glad to find a safe haven for the moment.

The little children were glad to get out of the wagon and play with their friends while the parents visited. The older children stood by their parents, still scared from the close call. No one could keep their eyes off the fire as it continued to consume the land in front of it. The wind had changed direction enough that it missed Hastings by just a short distance. Men were standing by to douse embers as they floated through the air. No one wanted any structures that survived the firestorm to be lit on fire by the flying embers.

The horses were watered, the children rounded up, and families began their treks home. Of course, some knew they wouldn't have a home to go to, but there wasn't a person there that wouldn't go see for themselves.

The Turners and Walkers plodded home together, and all hoped for the best. No one knew if their cattle had survived, either. As they drew closer, the Walkers could see their house was still standing. The fire had burnt off the fields very close to the home, and a couple of trees were still smoking. Greg said he would stop by the Turners later to see how they fared.

The Turners continued home and were happy to see

their house still standing. The barn had scorch marks, but somehow it was still there. The women rushed their children into the house and left the men to care for the horses.

William and Jack took care of the animals and began walking the pasture. Burnt to a crisp, they saw their dead cattle scattered and burnt. The smell was atrocious. They changed direction and walked toward the Walkers. They could hear cattle long before they saw them. Some were hurt, but most of the others were fine. Their cattle were mixed with several others from other ranches. As they walked toward home, Greg rode up. The men explained to Greg about the dead cattle and how they found several head gathered together. It would all be worked out later in the days to come.

The next few days were spent dragging the carcasses by the feet into a depression. The men would wrap a rope around the hind feet, and then the horse would pull it down until it was close to the others. This was repeated over and over until there was a large pile. The men poured a little kerosene on it all and then lit it on fire. With nothing left to burn in the area, the men left the stinky mess to burn. They didn't need coyotes to start coming by, and when the fire burned out, they would cover the bones and hides with as much dirt as they could.

Greg helped sort the wandering cattle, then drove the strays back to their homes. In a couple of cases, there wasn't a home to go to anymore, and they wouldn't be back by the looks of it. So, Greg brought the cattle home instead of leaving them to the elements. If the owners returned, they would return them then.

It was another week before the clouds built up, and the hopes for rain finally came true. It started with just a few splatters, but soon the sky opened and poured buckets of water. The rain washed the smell of smoke away. It must have rained upstream, too, because the river began running. It wasn't much, but the cattle started to gather around the water and drink their fill.

It rained off and on for the next week. Too late for crops, gardens, hay, or grass this year, but it was still a welcome sight. The river wasn't back to normal yet, but at least there was enough for the animals again. The women were happy to do the laundry and clean the house. The smell of dirt and sweat was finally gone.

The drought cycle was broken, and the moisture continued into the winter months. The area struggled with piles of snow. It seemed as if spring would never arrive. However, the snow melted gradually as the warmer weather began, and the river filled its banks. The Turners and Walkers bought more cattle to replace their losses. Thankfully, the lean-to the Turners had built ten years earlier had held up for the cattle through the heavy winter storms. The snowpack was heavy, but the roof remained intact.

The grass came back greener and healthier than it had been in years. William had heard from other farmers and ranchers that their land also looked better. However, it would be years before it was established how burning off pastures resulted in positive regrowth.

For the neighbors that had been burnt out, some stayed and rebuilt. Others sold out and left. The Turners took some savings and bought a quarter of land that was located close by. The Walkers purchased another quarter of land on the other side of their property. It was good wheat ground, and Greg looked forward to expanding his fields.

Surviving a prairie fire reminded the Turners of the stories from the ranchers that had come before him. About thirty years before they arrived, the grasshoppers had come through as a hoard and eaten everything in sight before moving on. It had been like a plague, moving from state to state. It was one the Turners hoped would never happen again.

DISASTER STRIKES

The flu was running rampant throughout the countryside. Jack and William remembered back to when they bought the original homestead. The family that had built the home had an illness spread through the large family, and only a few survived. The Turners hoped that this would not be the case for their families.

It started with little Georgia, and then it spread quickly to all the other young ones. The men and oldest boys stayed in the barn, hoping they wouldn't get sick so they could take care of the ranch. It wasn't long before the whole house was ill. The men and their boys moved back inside, dropping like flies one by one.

The fevers weakened them all, but Jesse May somehow managed to care for everyone. Maude was very ill, and Jack tried to care for her, but he was soon delirious with fever. By the time Maude knew she would be alright, Jesse May had collapsed with a high fever. Even in her weakened state, Maude managed to start caring for not only the children but Jesse May, too. The little ones were beginning to feel better and were hungry. However, Maude wasn't sure she had it in her to fix a meal.

A knock on the door interrupted the whining of the children. She slowly walked to the door to find Ada Walker.

"What are you doing here? We're all sick. You need to leave."

"You must be really sick if you didn't notice how bad I look."

"What do you need?"

"I came to help. Greg and I have recovered, and he is keeping the children. I thought you could use a hand if your household were sick, too."

"Come on in. I have to sit down."

The children ran to Ada and asked for food. Maude sat in her rocker and laid her head back. Ada had brought a few things with her and soon had the youngest children seated at the table. Ada found that all of them had been stretched out on the main floor, wherever there was room. Jesse May had collapsed on the settee, and her fever was raging. Ada brought some willow bark to boil down for tea to help with the fevers. While that boiled, she made Maude drink water and had her eat a little something. Surprisingly, Maude felt a little better but was still too weak to care for the children properly.

Ada stayed for two days. By then, Maude was well enough to care for everyone by herself. Jack and William were finally on their feet once Ada got their fevers under control. It took Jesse May another week to recover because she had worn herself out taking care of everyone in the house. Ada checked back in a couple of days and brought more willow bark. Greg made her rest between visits so she didn't relapse. If it hadn't been for Ada, Jesse May probably wouldn't have made it through.

The horses were pretty hungry by the time the men got out to the barn. They made sure all the animals were cared for, brought in the eggs, and milked a very uncomfortable and cranky cow. Then, dragging themselves back to the house, the men decided that they would split the chores. One would take the morning, the other the evening. Until their strength was back, they would have to limit their activities.

Two weeks later, things were pretty much back to normal, except for Jesse May. She was still weak, and Maude made her rest off and on throughout the day. She would have her sit at the table and work on making biscuits or anything else Jesse May could sit and do. It was another week before Jesse May could take over the care of her children without wearing herself out.

Dr. Johnson made his rounds once he had recovered from his own bout of the flu. By the time he stopped by the Turners and Walkers, everybody was on the mend. He encouraged Jesse May to drink plenty of water and rest. The doctor reported that both the Parings were fine. Bea was caring for her mother at Mrs. Ray's when she came down with the flu. Then, the whole house became sick. Mrs. Ray, the staff, and Bea's entire family. Dr. Johnson reported they all came through, having milder symptoms than some. Mrs. Ray still coughed, but he was certain she would be fine over time. Maude promised to go see her in a few days after Jesse May was stronger.

Jesse May was sitting on the front porch enjoying the sunshine but was wrapped in a heavy quilt. The house had been cleaned from top to bottom, and the bedding freshened. Maude sat beside her, and the two listened to the cattle lowing in the snow-covered fields. They felt blessed that everyone in their families had survived. A few minutes of crisp fresh air felt wonderful.

The winter was less severe than the two years previous. The snow was welcomed because the moisture was always needed for the land and to replenish the water. Once the flu had gone through, the everyday routines returned.

School was always a priority for the children —as long as the weather held to get them there and back, that is. Effie May and Paul, the eldest children of William and Jack, were both avid readers. They took turns reading stories to their youngest brothers and sisters in the evening. If the weather didn't allow travel to school, the two would also play school at home and spend a little time teaching numbers and listening to the children read. Effie May always brought home a book or two just in case the weather kept her home.

Once the family was able to return to church again, they found out the devastation the flu had caused. Families from all over the county had either been completely wiped out or lost a member of two. The Turners and Walkers realized once again how lucky they were. And if Ada hadn't shown up when she did, Jesse May, for sure, would be gone. So, from then on, the Turner family made sure they kept the willow bark on hand.

LIFE SETTLES DOWN

The years had been good to the Turner families. Yes, the weather didn't always cooperate, and sometimes the garden was ruined by grasshoppers, hail, or heat. Sometimes all three. But they were generally all happy and healthy.

The cattle they raised had kept them afloat, and after their first disastrous year, the Turner men had been better at managing the ranch. They added a little land when they could to have more grass for the cattle. They never had time to build that second home, but after all these years, their big farmhouse divided down the middle worked out just fine.

The children were sometimes a handful. If they got to bickering with each other they would be sent outside to play, and sometimes Jesse May and Maude joined in and chased the children around the yard.

After all these years, the cottonwood trees that had been so carefully transplanted and tended to were now providing shade all around the house and down the lane. They had somehow survived the fire two years previous and would continue to grow for years to come.

Once more families began to move into the area and brought more children, a schoolhouse was built, and a teacher was employed. The children spent most of their free time learning from October through April. September was harvest time, and May was planting season. Since most of the children helped around the farms, especially the boys, the school year was a little shorter than the school in town.

The families in the area had been lucky to find someone able to teach for years. A house was built close to the school for Miss Anderson to live in. The Turners built her a chicken coop and gave her a couple of hens.

During the months without school, Miss Anderson could be seen tending her chickens, garden, and flowers. Since the school was centrally located in the area for the farmers and ranchers, a church was eventually built next to the school. The area was an excellent place for the neighbors to get together.

THE ACCIDENT

A new neighbor had moved in next door to the Turner property. He didn't want the cattle wandering around his land, as he planned on putting in crops; the cattle would destroy his fields. The Turners reluctantly agreed to run a fence along that edge of the grazing land as soon as possible. It would take most of the summer to enclose their land. It was becoming harder to allow the cattle free range these days.

Jack and William grumbled every night about the time it was taking away from other jobs that needed to be done. The older Turner boys would be helping their parents soon, with school almost completed for the year. Paul, Jackson, and Charlie were old enough to help these days. Paul's education would be completed this year, and Jackson and Charlie would finish the following year. All three lads had grown into the spitting images of their fathers. In fact, when all the children were together, it was difficult to tell them apart, and to tell which family they belonged to if it weren't for the occasional flaming red hair that proved they were Maude's.

Jack was in the field working on a corner post when a storm started building. He was rushing to get the post set and wasn't paying much attention to anything else except the darkening sky. Then, he felt something come up behind him, and before he could react, their prize bull butted him so hard that Jack went flying. Dazed, his reaction time was off. The bull lowered his head, hooked Jack with a horn, and threw Jack several feet in the air. Everything went black when he landed.

When Jack woke up, he was in terrible pain. It was raining, and he lay there trying to figure out why he was on the ground. A clap of thunder scared him, and his body jerked. Pain shot through him, and he screamed. He tried to sit up but dropped back down because the pain was too much to move. Jack didn't know how long he had been lying there, but he was soaked clear through and getting chilled.

Jack heard someone hollering, and eventually William rode up. Jack's horse had returned to the barn without him after the storm began, so everyone knew something had happened to Jack. They'd figured he'd been thrown from his horse, so William was surprised he didn't find him walking back to the house. He got off his horse and checked his brother. He noticed Jack was losing a lot of blood, so William pulled his handkerchief out and stuffed it in the wound.

"What happened?"

"I'm not sure." Jack could barely get his answer out. "I hurt everywhere and can't get up."

"Hang on. I'll get help."

William rode back home as fast as possible and rounded up the boys. They got the wagon ready, and Maude came running out of the house. She demanded that she go with them. She also sent Effie May to the Walkers to ask if Greg would ride out to get the doctor.

Maude and the oldest boys rode the wagon and pushed the horses to go as fast as possible across the range. Carefully, they picked Jack up and placed him in the wagon. Jack screamed in pain and passed out. Maude was in shock over her husband's appearance. She rode with Jack in the back, holding his head in her lap as the boys sent the wagon flying back home. It was a rough ride, and she was glad Jack was still unconscious.

Everyone pitched in to get Jack into bed. Thankfully, they had never moved their bedroom from the main floor. Maude sent everyone out of the room except William. They peeled all the wet and bloody clothes off him. When Jack woke up, all the commotion made him scream, and he passed out again. Maude stuffed the wound with clean dressings, and then they bundled Jack up in blankets to get him warmed up again. The spring rain was cool, and Jack's skin was so cold he was blue. But the poor coloring wasn't all from being cold, but from blood loss.

It seemed like hours, but Effie May returned and said Greg was on his way to find the doctor. She rushed to her room and changed out of her wet clothes. Jesse May had lit the fireplace, and Effie May stood in front of it to warm up.

The house was quiet, the mood somber. Greg and Dr. Johnson arrived two hours later. Dr. Johnson went straight to the bedroom. He brought Bea with him in case he needed the extra help. Maude had managed to all but stop the bleeding in Jack's side; as long as she had a wad of cloth in the ragged hole, it applied enough pressure to keep it from bleeding.

Maude stepped aside as the doctor checked Jack out from head to toe. Bea helped him clean and stitch up the terrible wound in Jack's side. Jack occasionally mumbled something, but with the doctor's prodding, it was a good thing he had passed out again. Dr. Johnson had given him a little laudanum to settle Jack down and help him rest.

"Maude, I can't be sure, but he probably has several broken bones. I'll wait until tomorrow to check on him again. My concerns are the things I can't see. Whatever happened to him, it was pretty traumatic."

"We don't know what happened for sure. At first, we thought he was thrown from his horse. But that doesn't explain the wound in his side."

"I see. Well, I'll be back tomorrow sometime. Give him the laudanum when he needs it. With those broken ribs, he is going to hurt pretty bad."

Maude pulled her rocker next to the bed. Bea

promised to send her sister out the following day to help around the house and help tend to Jack. So, Maude settled in for a long night. She alternated a nap with tending to Jack.

Just as the sun began peeking in the window, Jack awakened. He blinked several times, trying to clear his fuzzy mind about where he was. He tried to take a deep breath, but instead, it was a sharp intake from the pain. He heard movement and saw Maude sitting in her rocker, but the noise had not awakened her.

Jack's mind began to clear, but his mouth was like he'd eaten cotton. He didn't have enough spit to swallow. Then, finally, Jack noticed the laudanum bottle on a small table by his bedside and knew why everything was so fuzzy and his mouth was so dry. He took smaller breaths through his nose, and things began to clear.

Any slight movement caused pain, even when he tried to move his arms. He must have made too much noise as Maude suddenly awakened.

"Jack. Oh. You're awake. Do you need something for the pain?" She reached for the medicine.

"Water," he croaked. Maude helped him get a glass to his mouth and offered small sips. "Thank you."

"What happened to you? We've been so worried. Your horse came back without you, and we found you in the pouring rain on the ground."

"How did you find me?"

"William rode out when the boys said your horse came back alone. He knew you had been working on the fence. Can you remember what happened to you?"

Jack asked for more water. His thirst finally quenched for the moment, he answered Maude's question. "I saw the storm coming and wanted to get that corner post set in before I came home. I wasn't paying any attention to anything else. By the time I noticed, it was too late. King evidently didn't like me being so close to his harem, and I was rushing around. Normally, he paws the ground and snorts if he's upset, but my back was to him, and there was a lot of thunder. I was also busy pounding that post into the ground, so I probably didn't hear his warning." Jack stopped for more water.

"I started to turn, and there he was. He slammed his head into me, and I went flying. When that wasn't good enough, he charged at me again and tossed me up into the air. I think he hooked me with his horn. I blacked out when I hit the ground. I don't know if he touched me after that or not. If he thought he'd killed me, he probably wandered off."

"You have a terrible wound in your side. The doctor doesn't think the horn got any organs, but he will be back this morning. You were in awful shape when we got you back home and in bed. Dr. Johnson wanted you to rest before he checked everything over again."

"Can you prop me up? I can't breathe very well."

Maude paused. "You better wait until the doctor gets here. He will be bringing Bea to help. And Bea said she would bring Noreen to live here while you are laid up, and I'm preoccupied taking care of you."

Jack sighed and then grimaced from the pain. "No more laudanum for now. I want to keep my head clear."

"Okay, but when we move you, I have a feeling you'll beg for it."

"Probably, but I'll wait as long as I can."

Maude heard the household waking up. She left the bedroom to help with the children. They came flocking into the room to see their father, promising not to touch him or bump his bed. It was rather difficult for the little ones, but Maude caught them in time. Soon, Jesse May called them all for breakfast, and off they went. Food always rated higher than anything else.

Jack grimaced, the pain becoming almost too much. Maude reached over and poured a very small dose of laudanum into his water. It wasn't very pleasant, but soon, Jack felt a little better.

"I didn't want to sleep. I need to think."

"That's fine. I didn't give you very much this time."

"Good."

Dr. Johnson arrived shortly after breakfast was over. Noreen went right to work helping Jesse May with the children. Bea followed Dr. Johnson into the bedroom. It took all three of them to turn Jack and then position him more upright in bed. The bruises were much more apparent this morning. Since Maude had given him a little laudanum earlier, he tolerated the doctors poking and prodding. The worst was turning and getting him settled again.

After Jack said he was comfortable, Maude gave him a touch more pain medicine. Finally, Jack was ready for a nap after the doctor's exam. The three left the bedroom as Jack began to doze.

Jesse May and William were waiting in the kitchen. Noreen had taken all the children outside to do the chores. Jesse May poured everyone coffee and then sat down at the table with everybody. William was on pins and needles.

"Okay, Doc. What's the verdict? How bad is he?"

Dr. Johnson sighed. "He's bad, William. Real bad. I know he has to have several broken ribs. I'm not sure how many. Last night I put a dislocated shoulder back in. That was part of his severe pain. I'm pretty sure he has a concussion. Lots of bruising, a deep wound in his side, and maybe a few other things. The biggest thing is, he isn't moving his legs."

Maude gasped. "I hadn't noticed."

"I didn't want to say anything last night. I'm not sure if

it's permanent or not. Did he say what happened?"

Maude told everyone about the bull. "King is pretty temperamental and protects his territory."

William shook his head. "We all know not to turn our back on that bull. Darn it."

"So, what's next?" Maude worried her hands around the coffee mug.

"You take care of him. Don't let him up yet. Keep him clean, feed him, but don't, and I mean don't, let him try and get up. I'll let you know in a few days when he's ready. Keep that wound clean and dry. He should live unless he gets a terrible infection. But he may never walk again. So, you all need to be prepared for that."

William hit the table with his fist, and everyone jumped. "Sorry. Jack won't like being an invalid. Not one bit."

The doctor shrugged. "Then don't make him one." Everyone looked puzzled. "Once he gets healed up, make him do everything he can do. If he can't walk, I'll bring him a wheelchair. He can gather eggs or feed the chickens. Supervise the children's chores. Dress, shave, whatever. But if you wait on him hand and foot, then he becomes an invalid and probably a very angry man. He's going to be angry enough without your pity."

William nodded. "That makes sense. I can make a way for him to get him in and out of the house."

Jesse May had been quiet during the whole conversation, making sure everyone had coffee and even got out a plate of cookies. "Maude, I want you to do what you need to do to take care of Jack. Noreen can help when needed. William and I will take care of the chores and ranch. I think we'll pull the older boys from school to help William."

Maude sighed, and then the tears flowed. She hadn't had time to think about the next few days. She was barely getting through the moment. "I'll need to get more sleep. Can we put another bed in the bedroom for me until I can sleep with Jack again? He hurts too much for me to toss and turn."

William agreed. "I'll bring down Noreen's old bed, and Noreen can use Bea's old room. I want her close by in case you need her."

"Thank you, William. I appreciate it."

Dr. Johnson stood up. "Bea and I need to leave. I'll be back in a couple of days, but send for me if you need me sooner."

Maude checked on Jack and then went outside to talk to her children. She gathered them around and tried to explain their father's condition and how the accident happened.

"Now, you can see why I don't want any of you near the cattle, except for you older boys, of course. But none of you will ever get near King unless you are with William. So, you must do everything he tells you to do. Is that understood?" The children were all wide-eyed as their mother told them about King attacking their father. "Noreen will be here for a few days to help me, so you do what she tells you. I'll be helping your father a lot, so if you need me, check the bedroom. If I'm sleeping, let me sleep. Understood?"

Everyone nodded, even though the little ones didn't understand everything that was going on. All they knew was Momma was sad, and Poppa was sick.

THE RECOVERY

It was five days before Jack realized his legs didn't work. "Maude. When is the doctor coming back?"

Maude yawned. It was late afternoon, and they had both taken a nap. Noreen had taken the children to school, and the older boys went with William to take care of the hayfields. It was mid-April, and it was time to make sure the hay survived the winter. If there were bare patches, new seed would be sewn in the soil once it was roughened up, and then a little water added. Each boy had a job to do as they walked the field.

"I think in the morning. How was your nap?"

"Very good. I think I'm finally on the mend. How was your nap?"

"I can't believe I slept so hard. I may have to keep Noreen around so I can nap every day."

Jack smiled. "Getting spoiled, are we?"

Maude smiled back. "Maybe a little bit. I better get you some more water. Do you need a cookie or something?"

"No. I'm fine. Help me sit up first."

"Sure."

Jack was able to help more, and he was soon propped up in bed. He looked out the window and saw the cattle scattered across the pasture. When Maude returned, Jack sent her out to find William. As Jack waited, he thought about all the work that needed to be done, and he wasn't sure how William could do it all by himself. Their boys weren't quite old enough to pull the weight of a full-grown man. William arrived several minutes later, carrying a large glass of lemonade for himself and a smaller one for Jack. He took it and sipped on the tart drink. William practically inhaled his.

"You've got the boys working?"

"I do. They're finishing up seeding some spots in the hayfield. They always did get along well, and they work well together, too. So, what's on your mind?"

"That stupid fence. William, I can't help put it up."

William shrugged. "I'll teach the boys. It will put some muscle on them. One post at a time, and we'll get it done."

Jack growled. "Listen, big brother. My legs don't work. I will never be able to help you again."

"Well, little brother, you'll have to do what you can. I expect you to do something besides laying around."

Jack looked shocked. "How am I supposed to do things if I can't walk?"

"Your arms and brain work. And I see your mouth is still functioning."

Jack leaned back on his pillows. "You don't understand."

William got to his feet and took the empty glasses with him. "Listen. We will get you out of this bed when the doc says and not a minute before. What you do after that is up to you. I will not put up with you sitting around feeling sorry for yourself. Now, I need to see if the boys are done seeding. We need to take care of a few other things today. Then, we will begin work on that blasted fence tomorrow."

With that, William walked out of the bedroom and left Jack glaring at his brother. What Jack didn't see were the tears on William's face. He went to the kitchen, held his wife for a moment, and told her that was one of the hardest things he had done in a long time. He nodded at Maude on his way out the door. The bedroom door had remained open, and the women had heard the whole conversation. Maude thought William very brave and promised herself to try to do likewise.

Jack fussed and fumed and then tried to get out of bed.

151

He failed miserably. He hollered for Maude, and when she came into the room, he yelled at her, too. She shook her head and walked out during his rant. Jack couldn't believe his own wife had walked out on him. It was several more minutes before his tantrum subsided. By then, he was exhausted. He managed to get himself repositioned, then dozed for a few minutes.

When the children came home from school, they streamed into the bedroom to see their father. He welcomed them and was glad someone was happy to see him. It was suppertime before Maude returned. She had brought both of their meals into the bedroom and assisted Jack as needed while eating her meal. Tonight was a sad affair, as Jack refused to apologize for his outburst. Maude didn't bring the episode up, either. By bedtime, he was still sulking. Maude went to bed and let him wallow in self-pity.

When the doctor arrived the following day, Maude left the men to visit. Bea hadn't come today. She had stayed in town with her mother, who wasn't doing well. Maude began working on the laundry with Jesse May, and the women caught up with their visiting. Dr. Johnson came to find her before he left. He promised to send a wheelchair out later in the day. He had met the Walkers on the road as they headed into town, and Greg would load it up before coming home. Jack's wound was healing well. He congratulated Maude on keeping it clean and dry.

"Oh. One more thing. I told him he wasn't allowed to feel sorry for himself and make everyone else's lives miserable." He tipped his hat and left.

Jesse May laughed. "Well. I bet that conversation went over well."

Maude looked at Jesse May and cracked up laughing. She laughed so hard that she had to sit down. When Maude finally calmed down, she wiped the tears from her face with her apron. "I needed that, Jesse May."

"I did, too, but I'm glad to see you are doing better."

"I'll be fine. But I think Jack's struggles are just beginning." About then, they heard Jack calling out for Maude. She glanced at the pile of laundry left to do. "I better go."

"Don't worry about the mess. This pile is almost washed."

Maude walked into the bedroom and found Jack tangled in the bed sheets. "What in the world?" She rushed over to untangle his legs from the bedding.

"Doc says I can get up today."

"Okay. Where do you plan to go from here?"

Jack looked around the room. "I hadn't thought that far ahead, I guess."

Maude shook her head. "I'll move my rocker over here. You can start with that."

"Okay."

Maude moved the chair close to the bed and watched as her husband tried to figure out how to move from the bed to the chair.

"I'm not sure I can move over there. My ribs are still in bad shape."

"So, what do you want to do?"

"I don't know. Maybe I'll just sit on the side of the bed for a time. It feels good."

"Fine. I'll go help Jesse May finish the laundry. Holler if you fall on the floor."

Maude rushed out of the room before she could change her mind. She wanted so badly to help Jack, but she knew it would hurt him if she tugged and pulled to get him moved into the chair.

Once the laundry was done, Maude checked on Jack and found him lying sideways in bed. Unable to get his legs back into bed, he did the best he could. Maude helped Jack get situated and then left to gather fresh bedding and bathing supplies. When the Walkers arrived later, she wanted Jack to be clean and sitting in the rocker. After talking it over with Jesse May, they decided to have William help get Jack moved. It would be much easier for William to assist him than Maude.

Right before lunch, William transferred the newly bathed Jack into the rocker. Jack could put on a clean shirt once he was sitting up. Maude was able to slide some underclothes on him while Jack was still lying down, but it was difficult with Jack being unable to help.

Eating while sitting in a chair was a much more pleasant experience. The bath and clean clothes had lifted his spirits, too. After lunch, Maude set his mirror and shaving supplies by his chair and told him to get to work on getting that scraggly beard cut off. Then, she left him to it and went to check on the garden.

Maude, Jesse May, and their girls had taken a whole Saturday getting the garden in early. They would plant more things next month, but they got a head start on the peas and lettuce. A couple of years after the Turners were established, they realized apple trees were on the back of their land. The men hadn't noticed them until they happened to be riding the range and saw the bright red apples from afar. Since then, taking the wagons and picking fruit had been an annual treat. Some years were better than others, of course. It depended on if they got a late frost, hail, or bugs. The weather had been perfect this spring, so the families were counting on a big crop this fall. It was a long time between the apple blossoms and ripe apples, though. Anything could happen.

Once lunch was over, William got the boys together and built a ramp on one end of the porch. The porch was only off the ground a few inches, but there was no way Jack would be able to maneuver off and on the porch.

Just as they finished, Greg and Ada arrived with the wheelchair in the back of the wagon. The men tried out the chair on the ramp, then modified it to make it easier for Jack to use.

The men found getting the chair through the house's doorways challenging. So, the men began tearing into every door between the outside and the bedroom. Jack heard all the commotions and yelled for Maude.

"What is going on? It sounds like the place is being torn down."

"Well, it kind of is. Your wheelchair doesn't fit our doorways very well, so the men are fixing them. It won't be long before they get to our bedroom."

"Good grief."

Maude interrupted and pointed the finger at him. "Don't start. It's all to make it easier for you, so you should be grateful that they care enough to do this. Now. Sit tight. The men will be in here soon enough. I'm going to join Ada and Jesse May on the front porch."

Jesse May and Ada were chatting in the kitchen, but Maude drug them out the door and out of the middle of the mess. No one could talk with all that racket. Eventually, the noise and hammering were done, and the women didn't hear anything for a few minutes. The next thing they knew, Jack, sitting in his wheelchair with a blanket over his legs, wheeled himself out the door. He took a deep breath of fresh air and then complained about hurting his ribs when he breathed too deep. The men encouraged Jack to try the ramp. He rolled down easy enough but found it was too hard to get back up to the porch. His ribs were still too delicate to put so much strain on them.

Jack rolled toward the barn and found he could maneuver over to his horse's stall. He rubbed the horse's nose and talked to him. Then he came back to the house.

William rolled him back up the ramp.

Jack stayed outside long past when the Walkers left. He waited for his children to come home from school. The boys had helped around the house but were now playing in the back. They had helped put in two fence posts today and then helped widen the doorways. They were learning a lot about keeping the family ranch running.

THE CATTLE DRIVE

School was now out, and the thirteen children were underfoot all day. Jack hadn't realized how noisy the place was all day long. The doctor stopped by several days after the wheelchair was delivered. Dr. Johnson had been reading about cases like Jack's, trying to give him some hope. He offered Jack and Maude suggestions but basically said it would be up to Jack's body whether he walked again or not. Nevertheless, the doctor encouraged Jack to do as much as possible, no matter what the outcome.

Since his ribs had finally healed, Jack was able to do more. He could even get up the ramp by himself. However, he missed riding the range and was often found out as far as he could go so he could look at the cattle.

The neighbor heard about Jack's accident. Since Jack had been putting up the fence that the neighbor had practically demanded to be strung between the properties, he and his boys helped string the wire along the boundary between the two parcels. Then they went back to working their land and putting in their crops. It took weeks for the Turners to complete the whole pasture, but King was now contained with his harem. Greg Walker and his boys helped after their crops were harvested. The countryside was beginning to have more and more settlers, and many were trying to raise crops of corn and wheat. The cattle would be a nuisance to them all. Once the fencing started, the Turners kept going around their property. Finally, they were fenced up to the Walker fields. Thanks to Greg and his boys, the work went much faster.

There had been little rain since early spring, and the grass was beginning to brown. Having learned the hard way about too many cattle and not enough grass, the Turners and Walkers decided to cull the herd and send several to market. With the new fence line in place, they didn't have to chase the cattle as far; they decided that was one benefit for all that work. Jack was involved in the decision-making, but he wished he could be out there with the men and boys as they worked the cattle.

William separated King and a few cows to a corral while everyone branded and moved steers to be taken to market. King was so big and strong that his pen had to be exceptionally sturdy. The Turners had had a couple of other bulls over the years, but nothing like King. He produced great heirs, many of which were sold to other ranchers trying to build a good, strong herd.

Jack watched all the activities from the sidelines. The Turner boys were growing into tall and strong young men. They worked hard and kept up with William and Greg.

Then, one evening, the boys had been in the barn for a long time. Jack could hear banging and sawing. He had no idea what was happening, and when he asked William, his brother told him to mind his own business. Jack wasn't sure if he should be offended or not. But the smile William was trying to hide let him know something was up.

The following morning, everyone who could help was going to move the cattle to town. After an early breakfast, the boys grabbed Jack's wheelchair and pushed him outside and into the barn. Maude and Jesse May stood on the porch and waited. It wasn't long before a smiling Jack was up and inside of the wagon. A portion of the seat was missing so he could sit up front and grab the reins. He pulled the horses to a stop outside of the house, where everyone was waiting.

"Look what those boys did! They made a ramp to get me up here so I can go on the cattle drive."

Everyone clapped and cheered, slapping the boys on

the back and congratulating them on creating a way for Jack to stay more involved. The men were anxious to get on the trail. William, Greg, and the boys opened the gate and got the cattle moving. Jesse May, Maude, and the girls all stayed behind, but they had prepared a couple of picnic baskets full of lunches for the men to take with them. Maude lifted all the young boys up inside the wagon to go along. Jesse May packed the baskets and threatened them within an inch of their life if they got into the food before lunchtime. Jack yelled for the horses to get going, and soon, they followed the cattle. Jack had a huge smile on his face.

The house was so much quieter with all the boys gone. Jesse May gave Noreen the day off, so she went to town, passing the herd as she hurried on to spend the day with her family. Maude and Jesse May sat on the front porch and relaxed. The girls were doing their chores, and then they could play. Maude, as usual, had sewing in her hands. It was relaxing for her. Today she was making new dresses for the oldest girls. Effie May and Carla were growing up fast. Mary Ann and Donna weren't far behind them, but they could wear some hand-me-downs. It wouldn't be long before the neighbor boys would begin to notice their girls. They may already have noticed Effie May. Turning fifteen, she had blossomed, and even William was starting to worry about boys taking his little girl away from him. It seemed like it was just yesterday when she was born.

THE CHILDREN

Paul, Charlie, and Jackson worked hard all summer. Finally, with school inching closer, they decided to talk to their fathers about not going back. Paul had already completed his studies, but Jackson felt like he should stay home and help his Uncle William now that his father couldn't. Charlie flat-out hated school. Their oldest sisters had agreed with them. Effie May was also done with her classes, but she felt she hadn't learned anything new in the last year. Carla nodded her head in agreement. She didn't want to go back either. Mary Ann and Donna still had a couple of years to go, and they both said they would miss their friends if they didn't return.

Once the younger children were down for the night, the oldest five came together and asked to talk to their parents. They sat at the kitchen table. Paul, being the oldest, was designated to be the one to tell their parents.

"We've been talking. No one wants to go back to school. Effie May and I, of course, are done, but the other three don't want to return. However, Mary Ann and Donna do want to go back."

William glanced at the other parents, then back to the children. "Do you have a good reason? Charlie?"

Charlie cleared his throat. "Pa, you know I hate school, and I didn't learn anything new last year. So, I might as well quit rather than go over the same stuff Paul and I learned last year."

William nodded. "Jackson?"

"Same here."

"What about you, Carla?

Carla nodded. "I agree with everyone else."

William took Jesse May's hand. "Okay. We will go home and talk about this. Your Aunt and Uncle can decide on their own about the others. Let's go."

The four left the room and went to their own side to discuss the issue. William closed the door between the sides and led the children to the parlor.

"What's the real reason?"

Charlie shuffled his feet. "I really don't want to go back. I'd rather be here working with you."

"Effie May, is he telling the truth?"

"Yes, Pa. He's actually the one that brought it up first."

"I see. Your mother and I will discuss it and let you know. Now head up to bed."

William walked over to his chair and sat down. Jesse May picked up some darning and promptly stuck a finger with her needle. Then, mumbling, she put the cloth down on her lap.

"I hope Effie May can learn how to sew. I certainly haven't managed over the years."

William chuckled. "Good thing Maude is around, or we'd all be naked." He picked up the latest newspaper.

The house eventually quieted down. Jesse May put the darning away and stood up to go to bed. "I'm okay with Charlie staying home. We need the extra help."

William nodded. "I'll see what Jack has decided about the others."

Jack watched William take his family to their own side of the house. The first thing he asked Paul was, "Did you put them up to this?"

"No, Pa. Charlie brought it up, and then Jackson agreed with him."

"Carla?"

"It's true about not learning anything new. Miss Anderson said we could go to the mercantile and order more reading material. We've all read every book at school. Except maybe Charlie. He doesn't enjoy reading very much."

Jackson grinned at his sister. "Yeah. He hates school."

"So you two want to stay home with your cousins and brothers and sisters?" Jackson and Carla nodded their heads. "You'll have to work hard."

"We know, Pa."

Maude reached over to Carla's shoulder and lightly squeezed it. "You will learn to cook and can and sew."

"I know, Ma. I like to sew and want to be as good as you someday."

Maude turned to Jack. "What do you think?"

"As long as they keep their nose to the grindstone around here, I'm okay with it."

Jackson let out a big breath. "Thanks, Pa. You won't regret it."

Maude shooed them up to bed. Jack frowned. "I hope they aren't doing all of this because of me."

"What if they are? They need to learn someday, anyway. A year sooner shouldn't matter."

"I hope you're right. Those boys have come up with some great ideas on their own. Like how to get me into the wagon. We need to encourage them more."

Maude smiled. "Paul always was inquisitive. He wants to know how things work and why things are the way they are. We probably should send him off to college somewhere."

"Do you think he'd go?"

"I don't know. Maybe not yet. He's still a little young. But someday. You're right, though. We need to encourage all our children more so they can find their path in life."

Jack and William assigned specific chores for the boys to do every day. Earlier in the spring, they were given their own horse to take care of and use for riding the range. Jackson wanted his father's old horse, but Jack told him the horse was getting too old for hard work. So,

Jackson asked if he could use the horse for a stud and begin raising horses. It was something Jack had wanted to do someday, and he was proud that Jackson had possibly found his calling.

Paul was still working on making his father's life easier. He had rigged up a pulley in the barn where his father could strengthen his arms by pulling the ropes with small bags of grain tied to the ends. Paul discussed options with Dr. Johnson, and the doctor lent him a book with pictures of medical devices. One day, he took his father to the corral fence. There were a couple of scraps of leather tied around the rough wood on two of the railings. Paul demonstrated what he wanted his father to do.

"Now. You roll over here and grab this first railing to help get you out of the chair. Then you reach up here to the top rail and hold yourself up. That way, you can stand on your feet. You can do that as long as you can hang on. That will stretch the muscles in your legs and make them feel better. What do you think?"

"I think you're trying to kill me. The bull couldn't do it, so you have devised ways to do it for him."

"I know Ma rubs your legs every day, but you need to do something while the weather is good. If this works, I'll have to figure out something in the house."

Jack shook his head. "Okay, son. I'll try."

It took several attempts before Jack managed to hang onto the top rail. Sweat poured down his back as he toiled to do what his son wanted. He couldn't hold on for long, so he was soon back in his chair.

Paul grinned. "I knew you could do it."

Jack, breathing hard, said, "I have to admit, that felt good for a moment. After I rest for a minute, I'll try again."

"That's great, Pa."

"Son, don't tell your Ma. Not just yet."

"Okay, but why?"

"I don't want her to watch me struggle." Jack wiped the sweat off his face. "It's a pride thing, son."

Paul smiled. "Yes, Pa. I understand. Pride can be an awful thing."

Jack chuckled. "Yes, it does get in the way sometimes."

Maude and Jesse May began assigning the girls more tasks. Although they had helped in the past, Effie May and Carla were now ordered to take care of the garden. Maude would set them down in the evening to learn basic sewing skills. She even made Jesse May do it, too. But even Jesse May's youngest could sew better than her. It was great fun to tease Jesse May, and she took it well.

Noreen returned to her family once a routine had been established in the Turner household. Unfortunately, Noreen's mother had never recovered from her illness and could no longer work for Mrs. Ray. So, Noreen decided to care for her mother, and help Mrs. Ray, too. Once school was out and the older girls were home, they took turns helping with the younger children. Again, everything worked out for the best.

With canning season arriving, Ada and her girls would be coming to help. The three families took a day trip to the apple orchid. First, they would picnic and pick apples. The following day would be spent canning and making pies. Since the trees were close to the river, the orchard did well on its own most years. It was a sight to see seventeen children and six adults picking apples and picnicking. Paul's invention to help Jack get into the wagon had made it so even he could enjoy the day with his family and friends.

After several days at the Turners, the women went to the Walkers and did the same thing for a few days. It wasn't until the last day at Ada's that Jesse May noticed Ada's oldest son, Joseph, and her daughter, Effie May, had been spending time together. And it didn't look like just visiting, either. Those two went out of their way to be off by themselves. Effie May twirled her hair and giggled. Jesse May elbowed Ada.

"See that?"

Ada smiled. "I wondered when you'd notice."

"How long has that been going on?"

"I'm not sure. But I think it suddenly occurred to them that they liked each other. Before, it was like cousins or brothers."

"Well, you are like a sister to us, but I'm not sure William will like this."

Ada laughed. "No one will ever be good enough for your Effie May when it comes to boys. William is pretty protective."

Jesse May sighed. "I guess I should be happy it's Joseph and not one of those Harder boys."

"Oh. Those troublemakers? Yes. Yes. Maybe you could point that out to William."

"Good point."

With harvest completed and the cattle sold, Maude and Jesse May took Effie May and Carla into town after they dropped everyone else off at school. Effie May got a list of books from Miss Anderson that she thought would interest the oldest Turner children. The stop at the mercantile was always a treat. Now that the train had a line through town, more and more people were moving to the area, and more stores were opening their doors. Maude didn't want to change where she shopped but promised the girls they could look around in a few more stores.

The mercantile had a few books to select from but promised to order whatever the Turners wanted. Effie

May gave the owner the list, and he promised to do what he could. Maude's list of goods was also handed over, and they said they would be back after lunch to load the wagon.

Everyone walked down the street, and the girls enjoyed their morning looking in different shops. Jesse May picked the place to have lunch. The four of them enjoyed themselves immensely. As they readied to head back to the mercantile, Maude was stopped by George Carsten, the banker.

"Mrs. Turner. May I have a word?"

Both Jesse May and Maude turned and answered, "Yes?" at the same time.

Mr. Carsten smiled. "I apologize. Of course, you are both Mrs. Turner. I meant this one." He pointed to Maude. The girls tittered at his mistake.

Maude smiled. "Of course, but we were on our way to the mercantile and then home."

"It will only take a moment."

Maude nodded. "Jesse May, go on ahead. I'll be right there." Then, turning to Mr. Carsten, she said, "Alright now. What is it?"

Mr. Carsten looked around. "I'd rather we discussed this in my office."

"Is there a problem with my account?"

"Oh, no." He rushed to offer an apology. "I'm sorry. Could you and Jack come and see me at your earliest convenience? I have a proposition for you."

"I suppose. Can you tell me what this is about?"

"Not on the street, no. But I would very much appreciate it if you would come to see me in the next few days."

"I'll do my best, Mr. Carsten."

"Thank you. I'll let you get back to your family. Good day." He tipped his hat and headed for the bank.

Maude was puzzled but soon put it out of her mind as they finished loading supplies. The girls were excited about the new fabric for the dresses. A fall dance was coming up soon, and they both talked about the boys who would be there. Their mothers couldn't help but laugh, remembering when they attended dances as young women. Jesse May had attended actual barn dances. Maude's were more cotillions. But still, the young girls' hearts and minds were on handsome boys asking them to dance.

The wagon pulled up in front of the school and only had to wait a few minutes before the children were released for the day. As they waited, Jesse May asked Maude about the banker, but she couldn't tell her much. Before Jesse May could question her any further, the school door burst open, and the flood of children came rushing through. Other parents were arriving for their young ones, and the Turners greeted them as they headed home.

THE PROPOSITION

It wasn't until bedtime that night before Maude remembered to tell Jack about the encounter with the banker. He agreed to go see him but thought they should have either Paul or Jackson go, too. Jack still needed help getting in and out of the wagon, which was too hard on Maude. It was no easy feat, even though Jack was getting stronger all the time; Paul's exercise program was definitely helping. Even Maude commented that his leg muscles seemed to be in better shape. The first time she saw him hanging on the corral fence, Maude thought Jack was actually standing. She had gotten her hopes up briefly until he landed back in his chair with a thump.

Jack visited with William the following day to find out what the boys would be doing that week. It was decided Paul would go to town to assist. With his analytical mind, they thought Paul could fix the problem if something went wrong. While in town, they would stop by Dr. Johnson's for a check-up and show off his increased strength.

It was a few days before they left for town. The weather had turned cold and rainy, so the couple had to wait until the skies cleared. Maude promised to check at the mercantile to see if they got the books the children had ordered. It certainly hadn't been long enough, but she promised to check, anyway.

With all the errands they had to do, Effie May promised to get the young ones from school, and Carla promised to help Jesse May start supper. Jack, Maude, and Paul dropped the children off at school on their way into town. Maude stopped at the mercantile first, and the owner thought it would be next week before the books would arrive. Then they stopped to see Dr. Johnson. He was out on a call, so they headed to Mrs. Ray's place.

Paul helped his father out of the wagon. They enjoyed tea and visiting for an hour or so. Mrs. Ray offered them lunch, but Jack said he'd promised Paul a meal at the diner. Mrs. Ray declined the invitation to join them and sent them on their way.

A stop at the doctor's office found Dr. Johnson returning from his call. They spent several minutes in the office. The doctor was pleased with Jack's progress and encouraged him to keep up the excellent work. It was on to the diner from there, where Paul dove into his food like he hadn't eaten for a week. He was still a growing boy and would soon be taller than his father.

By the time the Turners arrived at the bank, Maude had become nervous. She had no idea what the banker had in mind at all. Jack held her hand as Paul rolled him inside and to Mr. Carsten's office. Paul shut the door and sat down in a corner chair. The banker looked at Paul and hesitated. Jack noticed the banker look at his son.

"Mr. Carsten. Whatever you tell my wife and me, let me assure you Paul is old enough to know."

"I see." He cleared his throat and looked at Maude. "Since you have the largest amount of money in this bank, I'd like you to become the new owner." Everyone gasped. "You see, I'm not well, and the doctor assures me I will not be around another year from now."

Maude exclaimed. "Oh, no!"

"Yes, well." Then he looked at Jack. "I thought that with your current condition, you could take over my position. Unfortunately, I don't believe people are quite ready for a female banker." Jack and Maude looked at each other in shock, and were speechless.

Paul finally spoke up. "Mother, what does he mean you have the most money?"

Maude turned to her eldest son. "I'll explain it to you on the way home. I promise." Turning back, Maude reached out and took Jack's hand. "So, you want to sell the bank to me and have Jack run it? Is that what you're telling us?"

"Exactly. I have the paperwork drawn up right here. I believe you will find it is a fair price. Jack has been meticulous with the ranch's money since that first disastrous year. I'm sure he could also help other farmers manage their money. At least he would understand what it takes to manage those farms." Mr. Carsten handed over the paperwork, but Maude didn't read it yet.

"Mr. Carsten, since we are in a state of shock, we will have to get back to you. When do you need an answer?"

"Soon. I can still work, and if I don't get too sick over the winter, I'd like to turn everything over in the spring. Sooner if needed. We can make the contract to read whatever date you choose. But if you decline, I'll need to find someone else."

Maude nodded. Jack was still speechless. Paul had many questions but tried to hold them all for the drive home. Anytime a word started to come out of his mouth, his mother looked at him. Finally, he wheeled his father out of the bank and loaded him into the wagon. Maude held the papers tightly in her fist as Paul guided the wagon away from the bank. Finally, Paul couldn't hold in the questions any longer, and they spilled out one after the other.

Maude put her hand on Paul's shoulder. "Paul." He stopped talking and took a deep breath. "Let me start from the beginning."

She told him about how they just about lost the ranch. Then she explained about her father passing away and how her mother became a wealthy woman. She left out all the details of the hurt and anger from the past. It wasn't necessary.

"And no one other than you and your father knows

about that money."

"So, we're rich?"

Jack piped up. "No, son. We are not rich. Your mother is rich."

"Isn't that the same thing?"

Maude shook her head. "My mother stipulated that no one touch that money. It was there just in case something happened to your father, and I was on my own with you children and no income."

Paul thought a moment. "So, if father had died in his accident, then you would be able to take care of us."

"Correct."

"What now?"

"We go home. Your father and I will discuss this offer between us. You, young man, will not mention a thing about my money to anyone. Ever. Is that understood?"

"Yes, Mother. But how will you explain the banker asking you to buy it?

Maude shrugged. "I don't know the answer to that. I guess we could take out a loan."

Paul cracked up laughing when Jack gasped and looked appalled. "What do you mean a loan?" Jack exclaimed.

Even Maude chuckled. "Well, how else do we buy a bank and not use my money? How do you explain that to your brother? And Jesse May will question us till we keel over." Maude shook her head. "No one has agreed to buy the bank. Let's read the paperwork first."

Jack agreed. "Jesse May will hound us with questions as soon as we're home."

Maude laughed. "Paul, you better make yourself scarce and play dumb about everything."

"Not a problem. I'm used to Carrie acting the same way. She follows us around and questions everything."

"She is her mother's daughter. And she can't sew a

lick." They all laughed and were soon home.

Paul helped his father out of the wagon, then left for the barn. He didn't plan to come to the house until necessary. Jesse May started in as soon as Jack and Maude were through the front door. Maude removed her wrap and said that Jack was tired and needed to rest before supper. She pushed him back to the bedroom and closed the door. That left Jesse May standing there with her mouth open.

Carla joined Jesse May in the kitchen to help prepare supper and knew better than to question her aunt, considering her mood. When her parents came home, Carla was out back getting some things from the root cellar for supper. Then she talked to Paul before going back into the house. He warned her that Jesse May might be upset.

Effie May had gotten the younger children from school, and she had them playing outside. It was a good thing. Her mother was in a mood. She washed everyone up and helped Carla get supper on the table. Carla walked back to her parents' room and knocked on the door. She yelled that supper was ready. She heard her mother answer and went back to the kitchen.

William came into the house, along with Paul, Charlie, and Jackson. They had washed up outside and were ready to eat. William took one look at Jesse May and kept his mouth shut. Paul had already warned him that his parents wouldn't answer her questions when they came home.

Suppertime was always chaotic, with everyone around the table talking over each other. The little ones were especially noisy that night. It was almost too much for Jesse May. After an argument over the last biscuit between Henry and Mark, she jumped up, took the two youngest by the collars, and headed them to their side of the house. She slammed the door. William looked at Jack, who shrugged. He took his last bite of supper and excused himself. Every child at the table was silent for the rest of the meal. Finally, Maude told them to stay put and that she would give them a cookie.

After supper, Paul, Charlie, and Jackson went outside to make sure the chickens were in for the night and the horses were settled. They took James and Thomas with them and left all the girls to help clean the dishes. Finally, the kitchen was clean, and the girls sat on the floor around Maude as she gave them a sewing lesson. Jesse May came into the room, looking ashamed.

"I'm sorry. I was completely out of line. I don't know what's the matter with me."

"Not a problem. We're doing fine here. Even Carrie is making a fine stitch. Of course, we all have our bad days."

Jesse May looked around. "Okay, girls. Let's get ready for bed." Her girls put their sewing away and headed to their side of the house.

Maude stopped Jesse May when she turned to leave. "We'll talk tomorrow instead of tonight like Jack and I had originally planned."

Jesse May nodded, then shut the door quietly behind her. William hadn't returned, either. Maude had the girls put their sewing away and sent Carla outside to tell the boys it was safe to come inside.

Jack had gone to his office to do the books, but his mind wasn't on the pages in front of him. The banker's paperwork was lying on the desk, and he'd read it multiple times by now. Maude said she would join him after the children had gone up to bed. It was a little earlier than usual, but that was because Maude had Carla take care of the youngest this evening. Nobody wanted to rock the boat after the episode at supper. The children seldom saw one of the adults get that mad and knew not to press their luck with anyone in the house.

Jack patted the chair next to him, and Maude sat down. He said, "Maybe we should have answered a few of her questions first."

Maude shook her head. "It wouldn't have been enough. Jesse May isn't one to stop asking questions, even if we answered some of them. But I could have been a little more diplomatic about things when I got home. I'm sure she's actually madder at me than the fact that we didn't answer her questions. We'll be fine by tomorrow."

"You sure?"

"Positive. Now. Let's discuss this whole thing. What did you think of the contract?"

"Mr. Carsten was right. It's probably a fair price. He gave us all the details, which included information about how much the bank has out in loans and how much money the bank has. Thanks to you and now your mother, the bank is flush with money. So, I'd say the bank is in excellent shape."

"Okay. So, it's a good investment. Second question. Do you want to be a banker?"

"I'd never thought about it before now."

"Well, you are good with numbers. I think Paul takes a little after you in that department. I don't know why Mr. Carsten thought I could be a banker. Heavens. I would hate to sit at a desk with numbers in front of me all day. Give me a needle and thread any day of the week."

Jack scratched the stubble on his chin. "First of all, Paul is smart. But he needs more stimulus than sitting behind the desk. His mind travels paths that even I will never understand. I think you were right about sending him off to college. I have no idea where he should go, though."

"We've gotten far off the subject of whether you could

work at the bank."

Jack smiled. "I don't know. We'd have to move to town and uproot the children. This is the only life they've known."

"I wondered about that. I'm not sure any of us want that."

"Which is why we will sleep on it and then talk it over with William and Jesse May."

"Okay. But how do we explain why Mr. Carsten approached us?"

"My injury. And he mentioned how I had the knowledge of both handling the books and understanding what is needed to run the ranch."

"That sounds good. And it's the truth, too. Let me see the contract." Jack pushed the papers toward her. She looked at the amount he was requesting for the sale. "I know we could pay for this, but I'd really like Mr. Carsten to make us a loan instead. He can use my account as collateral."

"I don't know. Let's talk about it in the morning."

"Agreed."

After a restless night, Jack and Maude didn't have any better answers. They were glad not to have to make any decisions for the time being. Mr. Carsten wanted to line things up and set a date, and the Turners didn't blame him. With the man's health failing, it was only prudent that he took care of his business. After all, he had no one to leave it to, which begged the question, what was he going to do with the money he got from the sale of the bank? The more Maude thought about it, the more questions she had. Finally, just as they were leaving the bedroom, Maude stopped and had Jack go back inside the room. She shut the door and leaned against it.

"I have an idea."

Jack cocked an eyebrow. "What?"

"How about instead of you and I own the bank, the four of us buy it? Then the loan could hold the ranch as collateral, but you and I would know that if we got into trouble, I'd have the money to take care of the loan balance. And nobody's feelings get hurt in the process." The more she talked, the more ideas she had. "Paul promised not to say anything. And between our families, surely some of them will have enough mathematical understanding to take over when they get old enough. From what I've seen out of Henry and James, those two are possibilities. What do you think?"

Jack was amazed. "You might be on to something. But that doesn't solve me having to be there every day."

Maude looked deflated. "I know."

"Let's get out to breakfast. We will get everybody off doing chores so the four of us can discuss this."

"Deal."

Breakfast was back to its usual hubbub, and then Jack asked the oldest children to get everyone outside doing chores. He winked at Paul, who patted him on the shoulder as he walked by. It wasn't long before the house was quiet. Maude poured everyone another cup of coffee and sat down. She nodded to Jack to begin.

"We're sorry about not discussing things yesterday. It's just that we were, and maybe still are, in a bit of a state of shock. Mr. Carsten offered to sell us the bank." Jesse May and William were taken aback. She started to question him, but Jack held up his hand. "I know you have questions, so I'll explain all I know first."

Jack told them about Mr. Carsten's illness, then explained why he chose Jack to run the bank. "Because I'm in a wheelchair, he knows I can't help much around here. But I have learned a thing or two about finances over the years. Honestly, we would have to get a bank loan and use the ranch as collateral. Then there is the issue where I'd have to move to town in order to be there every day. In my current state, I can't jump on a horse and be there in a few minutes. But I don't know if I could uproot the children from here. Or even me. We had no idea what to say or how to explain it yesterday. And we have a lot of questions of our own. But we needed to start by having this conversation first."

Jack pulled out a few pages from the contract. It was only the part about the bank's financial status and how much Mr. Carsten would sell it for. Handing them over to William, he and Jesse May looked at the papers. William looked at Jesse May and then back to Jack and Maude.

"I can see why you needed to talk to each other first. Are you seriously considering this?"

Jack shrugged. "I don't know. Of course, I can't be of much use out there in the hayfield or rounding up cattle without legs. But I could run a bank and increase our fortune that way."

Jesse May had been unusually quiet. "I'm sorry I got so mad. We agreed not to keep secrets between us, and then you wouldn't tell me anything. What sense would that have made if you casually walked in and said – do you want to buy a bank?"

Jack cracked up first, followed by William and Maude. Jesse May eventually couldn't help but laugh with them. Maude poured another round of coffee, and they talked about it until the children came running in with eggs and milk. Paul followed, and Maude nodded that it was okay. She got up and followed him back outside.

"Thank you for giving us some time alone. No decision has been made, but I'll let you know. In the meantime, I appreciate your silence. One more thing. If you would like to attend college somewhere, let us know. You might visit with Miss Anderson to see what college

177

she would suggest according to your interests. Your father and I think you are old enough to go now."

"Thank you, Ma. I'll think about it. I hadn't given it much thought since Pa's accident."

She nodded, and Paul went back to join the older boys. They were going to head out and check the cattle and fence line.

It was chaos when Maude went back inside. The children were trying to get ready for school, and Effie May was about at her wits end getting all of them prepared to go. Maude laughed and gave her a hand. William and Jack disappeared to talk business, and Jesse May sat at the table. She had already poured Maude a cup of coffee.

"I'm sorry, Maude. William scolded me for my behavior. I acted like a spoiled brat and took it out on my babies."

"It's okay. I understand. We just didn't know what to say. And we hadn't even looked at the paperwork Mr. Carsten had given us yet. I knew we would be fine today. It was just such a shock and totally unexpected. I figured it was a problem with our account, or he wanted us to buy someone's land. If that had been the case, we would have said something right away."

"I understand now. I get crazy when I don't know what's going on."

Maude laughed. "We all know that, Jesse May. We all know."

STAKING OUT A FUTURE

It was several days before Jack and Maude went back to town. Effie May wanted her books, and Carla had forgotten to buy ribbons that would match her new dress. After a long conversation with Miss Anderson, Paul wanted to visit Dr. Johnson about college. It appeared that his scientific mind led him to possibly be a doctor. With his inventions that were helping his father, it wasn't that much of a stretch.

Jackson wanted a new bridle for his favorite horse, and Charlie wanted to hang out with everyone else. William and Jesse May decided they better stay home and make sure the younger ones got back and forth to school. Maude promised to pick up something for the younger girls and toys for the boys.

With so many going, the group took two wagons. One that Paul had modified for his father and the other for the rest of the family. It was a rowdy bunch; Jack and Maude were glad they were in their own wagon.

The first stop for the children was the mercantile. Effie May had several things to pick up while there. Maude went in briefly to let the owner know it was alright to charge a few items. Paul had gone directly to Dr. Johnson's office, and Jackson and Charlie went to the tanners. Next, Maude and Jack rode over to the bank. Maude helped Jack roll down his ramp. Stronger now, he could help get up and down the ramp with only a bit of help from Maude.

"Mr. Carsten. We have several questions."

"I'm sure you do."

"First, if we agree to do this, would you sell it to all of us?"

"All of you?"

"My brother and his wife, too."

"Well, I suppose that could be arranged. Are you afraid of hard feelings?"

"You might say that is one reason. This is the thing. They are not aware of Maude's money. I mean, they knew about the money we used to pay off the original loan, but not about her special account. Her mother asked that she not tell anyone about it, you see. And we have abided by that."

"I believe I understand the circumstances now."

"So, if we buy the bank, we'd have to take out a loan using the ranch as collateral. If things got tough, Maude could use her money to bail us out, but we hope that will never be necessary again."

"Interesting." Mr. Carsten steepled his fingers.

"Mr. Carsten," Maude said. "If I may be so bold to ask, what do you plan to do with all of this money from the sale of the bank? I mean, since you are ill and not expected to live another year, that is."

"Fair question, I suppose." He smiled. "Of course, I'll have expenses. I also plan to take the train to California. I'd like to see it while I still can. I'll probably leave some to the town or some such thing. I hadn't given it a lot of thought. Did you have something in mind?"

"No, not really. I just can't imagine what anyone would do with that amount of money in so short a time. You see, my father decided he couldn't get rich enough quickly enough. But he never enjoyed the fruits of his labor. So, in the end, my mother is. As you can see, I've never touched mine. My husband and his brother make enough for even our huge families. But it's good to hear you will try to enjoy yourself."

"Thank you. I'll give it some serious thought. But, to be honest, my lawyer has been after me to make some decisions, too. Now, then, I assume you are interested?"

Jack nodded. "The biggest problem is my drive into

town. It wouldn't be such a problem if I could ride a horse. But we would have to move into town for me to be here every day. We aren't sure we'd like to move from our home, and we're pretty sure our children won't."

"Yes, I can see that. You two take your time discussing this. The good doc says I'm doing fine right now."

Jack handed the contract back to Mr. Carsten. "I'll let you know. If you believe we can buy it as a family and take out a loan, we'll seriously consider how to make this happen."

Mr. Carsten stood and leaned over the desk. Holding out his hand, Jack took it. They gave each other a hardy handshake. "Good doing business with you, my boy. Mrs. Turner, it was nice to see you again. I'll be anxiously awaiting your final decision. In the meantime, I will have a new contract drawn up and loan papers ready. We will leave the date empty until we both decide it's time."

It wasn't long before everyone arrived at the diner. Effie May's books had arrived, and Carla had found the perfect ribbons for her hair. Jackson purchased a halter, and Paul was excited about the possibility of going East, to college. Dr. Johnson said he would enquire for him. Charlie managed to get Effie May to let him buy some candy since she got everybody something that day. Paul asked to ride back with his parents so he could discuss college. They trailed behind the children's wagon. Sensing Paul didn't want the others to hear their conversation, Jack slowed the horses' pace to leave a bigger gap between the wagons.

"What's on your mind, son?"

"How did things go at the bank?"

"We don't know if we'll buy it yet. We'd have to move to town."

"That's what I thought. If I stayed home for another

year or two, Jackson and Charlie would be old enough to manage the ranch."

"Son, do you want to go to college?"

"Yes, but I'm still a little too young. Dr. Johnson says he'll get me some books to start studying, but he thinks they won't take me yet. Effie May and I can keep an eye on everyone, and they don't have to move."

Maude interrupted. "No, Paul. It's the parents' job to raise their children. We could leave you older ones at the house, but never the younger ones. By the time we do this, if we do, Donna may or may not be old enough to stay. But I'd have to take James, Georgia, and Thomas with me. We haven't got it worked out yet."

"Okay. But it's alright if I start studying with Dr. Johnson?"

"Absolutely."

Jack reached out and grabbed Paul's head and knuckle rubbed it. The two wrestled a bit, and the horses picked up speed. "Okay, you two. Settle down before the horses think they need to run full speed ahead."

DECISIONS

Jack and Maude made the tough decision that they would move into town in the spring. The banker wanted to stay until then, so Jack spent a day or two every week learning the banking business. It turns out the bank's price included Mr. Carsten's house, too. It was about a block behind the bank. The home was a large and prominent two-story; Jack would only be able to use the main floor, of course. He stayed in the house when in town.

On a cold day in February, George Carsten announced he needed to go to California soon if he was going to be well enough to enjoy the trip. The papers were drawn up to include both Turner families, as planned. The loan papers were signed, and on March first, George handed over the keys to the bank and house to Jack. Paul had been busy modifying the house as soon as he knew his father would stay there. He built a ramp at the front of the house and made sure the doorways were wide enough to get Jack's chair through them easily.

George left every piece of furniture, saying he did not need anything. Maude kept the housekeeper and cook on staff. She planned to stay in the country for the time being. Jack found he could wheel himself back and forth to work. If the path was muddy, he would have one of the house staff help him get to and from work. Paul placed a ramp on the back door of the bank. His father's office was just inside, and no modifications were needed elsewhere. There was no need for Jack to go to the lobby area.

The bank was a small building, and Jack could see everything from his desk. Once Maude realized she didn't need to stay to help him, she returned home to take care of the younger children. The plan was to keep them in school, then move them all into town before the fall term. Carla, Jackson, Effie May, and Charlie were all finding their way. Paul looked at college in the fall, and Effie May was stuck in her books. She felt like she might want to teach and had been visiting with Miss Anderson about helping out at the school; it had grown, with so many new settlers in the area over the years. Jesse May worried about Charlie. His interests changed with the wind. But he worked hard and stayed by his father's side. William knew his son was restless, but he learned the ranch chores and could take them on without supervision.

Times were changing at the Turner house, and William missed having his little brother around every day. Maude went to town on Fridays and helped Jack get home for the weekend. Then she would help him get back to town either early Monday morning or Sunday evening. A lot of times, it depended on the weather. Paul installed a large cover over the wagon where his parents sat to protect them from the elements. It had been an added blessing. It was hard for the children not to see their father every day, and they spent a lot of time with him on the weekends.

George Carsten sent a letter from California. He was enjoying the warmer weather and was feeling better. He hoped all was going well and thanked the Turner family for taking over the bank. He knew it was in good hands. The letter included a check for half the amount the Turners had borrowed. Mr. Carsten instructed them to put it back on the loan. He said Maude was right; he would never be able to spend it all in what time he had left. Whatever was left over after his death, his lawyer would pass on to the city for improvements. He closed out by saying he was moving on and had no permanent address to contact him, only his lawyer would know where he was. The Turners knew they wouldn't hear from him again.

Jack held on to the check for several days. He wanted his family to see it and the letter before he put the money toward the loan. The family was astonished and promised they would make sure to give others a helping hand when needed. Jack mentioned that if someone came into the bank for a loan but they weren't a good candidate to lend to, he would tell his family to help them somehow.

Jack didn't take any income from the bank. He made the loan payments and took enough for the upkeep of the staff at the house. Otherwise, he lived as he always had; on the ranch profits. The sooner he paid the loan off, the better. One or two bad years at the ranch could make all the difference in the world.

PAUL

Over the winter, Paul studied the books Dr. Johnson had given him. But the more he learned, the more he knew being a physician wasn't his calling. He wanted to make life easier for people like his father, which meant making his inventions instead of healing. Paul felt that expanding on the things he learned from helping his father could only help others. So, Paul rode to town to find Dr. Johnson. He brought the books back, too. Paul waited while the doctor finished examining the patients.

"Paul. Come to my office. I see you're returning my books. All finished?"

"Yes, sir. I realized my main interest remains not in the patient's health but in taking care of them afterward, like my father. I want to continue my education to understand how things work, and how I can make life easier for people. Having come up with several ideas for my father and then improving them has made me see I could do so much more if given a chance to learn."

"I see. Quite commendable. I sent off a request to Johns Hopkins after we visited last fall. I explained your interests and what you had done to help your father. With great results, too. I had honestly hoped you wanted to be a physician and would come back here to help me. Funny how things work out, isn't it?"

"What do you mean?"

"I got a response back in the last week or so. Unfortunately, I haven't been able to stop by your house and discuss it with you. So, I'm glad you stopped by. It's been weighing on my mind."

"And?"

"They encouraged you to apply around your next birthday."

"My birthday is in May. But I don't believe I'll go to

medical school."

Dr. Johnson smiled. "No? How about a brand new program the college is starting in mechanical engineering?"

"What is that?"

"Exactly what you want to do. Exactly what you have been doing, actually. But they will train and educate you to be an engineer, and it's an exciting new field. That's why it took so long to hear from them. The college thought you would be a perfect candidate for their new program. They hadn't announced it until recently." Dr. Johnson opened his desk drawer, pulled out a large envelope, and slid it across his desk. "Take this home and visit with your parents. Fill out the application if you choose to go, and by the end of the summer, you will be headed to Johns Hopkins in Baltimore, Maryland."

Paul was trying to absorb everything but failed. A special school where he would learn to do the things he wanted to do. Impossible. Bea stuck her head in and told Dr. Johnson he had another patient.

"Paul, let me know what you decide. But I believe this is an excellent opportunity for you."

"Thank you, Dr. Johnson. I appreciate all you've done for my family."

"Bah. Get out of here."

Paul left with his envelope, not believing his good luck. He pushed his horse hard to get home to his parents. Paul rushed into the house; he hadn't even cooled down his horse or taken it to the barn. Jackson saw Paul ride in, thought something terrible had happened, and came running.

"Mother! Father!" Paul yelled as he flew through the door.

"Good heavens, son. Quit your yelling. What happened?" Maude put her dishtowel down and stood with her hands on her hips.

Paul saw his father wheeling toward him from his office. "I heard back from the college Dr. Johnson wrote to."

Jackson came barreling in and saw everyone in the kitchen. Jesse May, Effie May, his parents, Paul, and Carla. "What is going on?"

Maude looked at Paul. "That's exactly what we're waiting to find out."

"You left your horse all lathered up. This better be important."

"I'm sorry, Jackson. Would you take care of him?"

Jackson looked around. "As long as no one has died and someone explains all this, I'll go."

Paul smiled. "I'll come out to the barn after I'm done talking to Ma and Pa." Jackson nodded and left to walk the horse, then brush him down.

Maude shook her head. "Okay, son, sit down and tell us what has you all excited."

Paul explained about his conversation with Dr. Johnson and pulled out the envelope. "I haven't even opened this yet. I couldn't wait to get home."

Jack looked at his son. "So, you tried to kill your horse over this?"

"I'm sorry, Father. But I couldn't wait to get home and talk to you."

"You better hope that the horse is okay. Jackson will never forgive you." No one said anything for a short time. Then, finally, Jack said, "Leave your paperwork here and go see about your horse. Once you've settled down and we've all recovered from your outburst, we'll go sit in the office and talk about this."

"Yes, Pa."

Paul took off like a shot. He still hadn't read the envelope's contents but knew better than to leave a horse as he did. He ran to the barn and helped Jackson brush down the horse. Paul explained about college and was excited about the possibility of going. Once his horse was cared for, he thanked Jackson for not yelling at him. When he returned to the house, Carla told him to go on back to the office, that their parents were waiting for him. Paul found the paperwork laid out across the desk, with his parents reading over each page. When Paul entered the office door, they looked up, and Jack waved him to a chair.

"So, this school of engineering is what you are interested in? I've never heard of such a thing. What will you learn there?"

"When Dr. Johnson sent his letter asking about me attending medical school, he let them know about my interests. One of which was inventing ways for you to become stronger, and how you get in and out of the wagon. This new school will teach me how things work. Expand my knowledge so I can make proper equipment to help people like you, Father. After reading the books Dr. Johnson lent me, I realized I didn't want to be a physician, but to help afterward. Build things that would make your life easier and others like you. Someone built that wheelchair. Maybe I could build a better one."

Pride swelled in Maude as she listened to her firstborn. The always inquisitive one. The one that got stuck behind the settee when he was barely old enough to crawl. Now, here he was, ready to go to college. Maude picked up the application and handed it to Paul.

"Fill this out. You proved to us long ago that you are at your best when you are building something. So, if you get accepted, you can go. Right, Jack?"

"Right."

Paul beamed. Picking up the application, he looked it over. "Wow. There's a lot of questions here."

"Take your time. Ask if you don't know the answer."

Jack pushed over another piece of paper. "They included this in the information. It's a scholarship, which means the college will fund your tuition. It's a new program, and they want people like you to go so they can prove its successful. According to the information about the school, they are also offering room and board. Basically, they will pay for you to go. We will need to give you some spending money for your personal expenses, but this is a good offer. After the first year, if you don't like the program, then come home."

"I have to be accepted first."

Maude smiled. "Take your time filling out the paperwork. Have your father help you. I think the college has already accepted you. You just need to send all the information back to them." Maude got up, patted her son on the shoulder, and then left the room.

Paul and Jack worked on filling in all the blanks. There were a lot of questions to fill out, and it took quite a bit of time because Paul had to do it right to ensure he was accepted. With no envelope the right size to send it back to the college, Paul said he would ride to town and take care of it personally. Jack gave him a little money and told him to have lunch while he was there.

"Paul, I'm proud of you. I always have been. This is a great opportunity, and if you're accepted, we'll make sure you get there in the fall."

"Thanks, Pa."

"Before you go up to bed, I have a question for you."

"Sure. What is it?"

"What do you think Charlie wants to do?"

Paul smiled. "Depends on the day."

Jack nodded. "Your Uncle William says the same thing. Between you and me, do you think he'll stay on the ranch?"

"I doubt it. But I don't know. He's not that much younger than me, but I can see him leaving someday if he completely loses interest. He never liked school and isn't seeing any girls. Outside of working hard for his father, I think he just goes through the day."

"Well, if you can think of something he might enjoy, tell your Uncle William, okay? I know they worry about him."

"Okay, Pa. Goodnight. Thanks for helping me with the paperwork."

"Goodnight, son."

EFFIE MAY

Reading everything she could get her hands on, Effie
May found it very frustrating when she didn't have a
book in her hands. Finally, Jesse May visited with Miss
Anderson, and she agreed to let Effie May work with the
smaller children. Her brothers, sisters, and cousins didn't
want her help, though. That eliminated five students from
getting her assistance.

Thankfully, with all the farmers in the area, there were
always new students arriving, and Effie May was happy
to help them. Unfortunately, some hadn't had any type of
formal education, so Miss Anderson ended up having
Effie May tutor any child not up to their perceived
reading level. After Miss Anderson made a few changes
in the room, Effie May had her own corner to help those
in need. With a little trial and error, Miss Anderson found
the perfect use for Effie May, which made her job much
more manageable. With one-on-one tutoring, Effie May's
students could learn much faster. She took great pride in
her results.

By the following school year, Miss Anderson had
purchased more books in all the subjects for every age
group. Effie May poured over each one.

Effie May had grown into a lovely young woman, who
still enjoyed the company of Joseph Walker. They had
been friends all their lives, but in the last year or so, they
had attended every dance together and sat in church side
by side. Joseph was almost two years older and worked
with his father. The families approved of their
relationship and found no fault, except that Effie May
was too young at first. William had the hardest time
accepting the relationship, but as Jesse May pointed out,
at least it wasn't one of the Harder boys.

The Harders were known to cause trouble everywhere

they went. In school, after school, or at dances. Their father was known to cuff the boys at the slightest thing, so it didn't surprise anyone when they did the same thing to other children.

One day, sweet little Carrie and Donna were playing with a doll at recess when one of the boys their age came by and tore the arms off the doll. The girls stood up and then knocked him down. The boy lay on the ground, surprised at the girls retaliating. With a finger pointed right in his face, Carrie looked straight at him and told him that he'd never have a girlfriend, as mean as he was. His brothers came over and picked him up, yelled at the girls, and walked away. But those two were never bothered again. They told their parents about it that evening, and William had to hide his laughter. Jesse May tried to explain about hitting people, but Maude interrupted Jesse. They were just defending themselves, after all.

The youngest boys made sure they didn't back down from the Harders after that, and said they'd have their sisters come over if they didn't leave them alone.

With the summer coming on and school out once again, Joseph rode over to the Turners. He asked to speak with William alone. Jesse May knew what that meant, and she was in tears. Effie May was down by the river supervising the younger children, while she and Maude were preparing supper. Joseph left, stating he would be back after supper. Jesse May grabbed William and went behind closed doors for a little bit. She came out wiping her tears.

Effie May hadn't been asked yet, so no one was to say anything about Joseph having been there earlier. Joseph would have talked to her while he was there, but since she was busy, he promised to return. It wasn't long before all the children came tumbling into the house. Effie May had them clean up outside and made the boys take the frogs out of their pockets.

The oldest boys had come in from the barn, and Carla had been in her room sewing. Supper went as usual, except for Jesse May wiping away a tear or two. By the time Jesse May heard a knock on their door, the supper dishes were cleaned up and put away.

William answered it and yelled for Effie May. She was surprised to see Joseph but agreed to go for a walk with him. It was a lovely spring night. She threw on her wrap and went outside. The two walked for a few minutes, walking hand in hand. When they returned to the porch, Joseph asked if they could sit and visit.

Once they were sitting side by side, Joseph cleared his throat and finally asked Effie May to marry him. She was ecstatic when he produced a ring for her. Then he explained he had already been there once that day to talk to her father, but she wasn't home. Effie May couldn't believe it. She had dreamt of this moment many times but was still surprised that her Pa had given Joseph his blessing, as protective as he was. Moreover, her birthday was coming up, and she would soon be eighteen.

Joseph said he and his Pa would build a home on their property for them to live in but wouldn't start until Effie May said yes. So, she told him to get it started. Then they went inside the house, where Jesse May and William were waiting for them.

There were congratulations all around, and suddenly, the room was filled with the Turner family from both sides. Apparently, Jesse May announced it the minute Effie May walked out the door with Joseph. After Joseph left that evening, Effie May sat visiting with her parents. The only thing she requested was to have the wedding before Paul left for college. She couldn't imagine getting married without him there.

CARLA

Sitting around her mother's feet and learning to sew was a great memory for Carla as a young girl. The two oldest girls would work on scraps of cloth to learn different stitches, how to tie knots, sew on buttons and lace, sew on patches, and darn socks galore. Watching Aunt Jesse May fail one lesson after the other was funny; Effie May would show up her mother every time. When Mary Ann and Donna were old enough, they joined the little group. By then, Jesse May had given up and stuck to darning socks. It was a good thing all her daughters ended up being able to sew.

Carla, Donna, and Georgia worked on Effie May's wedding dress. Maude had supervised cutting out the material, but she left it all to Carla to put the dress together. Donna and Georgia sewed on the beads and lace. Carla had inherited Maude's love of sewing and excelled so much that Maude insisted she was better than her.

Mary Ann and Carrie were sewing new tablecloths, napkins, and piecing a quilt. When all the pieces were ready, Maude, Carla, Donna, Georgia, Mary Ann, and Carrie would take it to the church for a quilting party. Other women from all over the county would come and help finish the quilt. It would be gifted to the young couple after the ceremony. Jesse May would join them, but she wasn't allowed to stitch. Instead, she was in charge of thread, needles, and refreshments. That, she could do. Maude was also making a couple more nice dresses and nightgowns for the bride.

With all the talk of wedding plans, most of the male inhabitants of the house made themselves scarce, but they got new clothes and shoes, too.

The wedding would be a neighborhood affair, held at

the church. The reception was going to be there, too, because they needed the outside space for the dance to be held that evening. Jesse May was going all out for her eldest child.

In the meantime, Joseph and his father started a cabin. They would build on later when the couple began to expand their family. The most important thing was getting a roof over the new couple's heads. Effie May and Joseph picked out the spot. It was near a grove of trees. Joseph had played there as a child, and it held many memories for him. William, Paul, Jackson, and Charlie came over to help as much as possible to build the cabin in time for the wedding. The youngest boys were just old enough now to help hold boards and get supplies. But, mostly, they got in the way or snuck off to the river.

The men stopped building long enough to get the wheat crop in, and then returned to work. Once the main part of the house was enclosed, the Turners went home and caught up with the work on their own place. The hay needed to be swathed, and, with the plentiful spring rains this year, the hay crop was bountiful. Depending on the rain and heat of the summer, sometimes the Turners managed to bring in a fall crop, too.

Mr. and Mrs. Paring promised to outfit the house, so Effie May rode to town and went shopping with her grandmother-to-be. Mrs. Paring had been considered everyone's grandmother for so long that it would be a special moment to be related now.

Everything settled down a couple of months after Effie May's announcement. The wedding was scheduled for late August. Paul would leave shortly afterward for college.

Carla spent a lot of time on a special project for Effie May. First, she made a crocheted veil, adorned with tiny beads. Intertwined was a special gold thread that Carla specially ordered for the occasion. Then, it was crocheted around a comb that would push through her hair and keep the veil in place. Next, Carla planned to fix Effie May's hair so there would be shining beaded ribbons that matched her gown. When she looked at the finished project, Carla sighed. It was at that moment she knew what she wanted to do.

The summer wore on, but all the sewing projects were completed. Carla helped Effie May pack her trunk. It would be taken to her new home by Paul on the morning of the wedding. Mrs. Ray arranged for the cake and other provisions for the reception.

The weather had been hot and dry like an ordinary August day, but that wouldn't dampen anyone's spirits. Jesse May, Maude, Effie May, and Carla went to the church early to prepare Effie May. Ada showed up and joined in, too. Effie May was a vision to behold when it was time to walk down the aisle. Carla's creations were absolutely gorgeous.

The wedding went according to plan, and soon, the couple was married. The reception was a hit, and the dancing ran late into the night. Effie May and Joseph sneaked off for home as the party continued.

Carla danced a few times, but she had a lot of things on her mind. Eventually, she offered to take the little ones home and leave their parents to enjoy the evening. Jackson, Charlie, and Paul were having a great time dancing with all the girls and were flirting shamelessly. However, Mary Ann wanted to stay at the dance, and once she got permission she was thrilled to be included in the older group. Donna couldn't make up her mind but finally decided to go home with Carla.

It was a couple of days later before Carla took her mother aside. Her father had already gone back to town, but she didn't want to wait until he was home again.

"Mother, you know how much I love to sew."

"Yes, dear. I do."

"I'd like to open my own shop in town."

"What?" Maude was taken by surprise. "Isn't there already a seamstress in town?"

"Yes, but I don't like her."

"Carla," Maude admonished her daughter.

"Well, she's mean. I don't know why she gets any business at all."

"How do you know she's mean?"

"I walked in there one day, and she complained about me touching the fabric."

"Were your hands dirty?"

"No. She doesn't want anyone to touch things. And it's awful-looking cloth, too. Drab and colorless."

Maude couldn't help but chuckle. She thought back all those years ago to Crystal's shop in Omaha and the beautiful cloth displayed. "So, tell me what you had in mind."

"Well, I thought I could live with Father and use one of those rooms as my sewing room."

"You want to use the house as a shop?"

"Oh, no." Carla grasped her hands together and took a deep breath. "I just meant to work out of the house. Get orders from people and work from home."

"Take in sewing, you mean. Not have a shop."

"Yes, to begin with. If I make a go of it, then I can open a shop later."

"I see. We better go to town and talk with your father. I was thinking of moving to town this fall, but the young boys are having a fit. I can't leave them here with Jesse May and the older boys. They are too busy themselves. Maybe if you move in with your father, I won't worry so much about him."

"Or you will just worry about the both of us."

Maude laughed. "Yes, probably so."

It was decided they would go to town on Friday and bring Jack home with them. First, they went to the seamstress shop and looked around. The surroundings were drab, the cloth was drab, and the woman was drab – just like Carla said. The owner was crabby and didn't appreciate Maude asking questions. After all, what they were wearing far surpassed the quality of work this woman did. Even the seamstress could know that by looking at their clothing.

Then they visited Mrs. Ray and stayed for lunch. Maude's mother thought it a wonderful idea and would send her new friends Carla's way. Maude, and now Carla, made all of Mrs. Ray and Mrs. Paring's dresses.

As Carla and her mother looked around the house, Carla chose a bedroom to live in. Then they decided on a room off the back with several windows to allow the natural light inside. She could have a customer come in the back door if needed, and it wouldn't disturb anyone else in the house. Even Maude was getting excited and offered to help sew if Carla became too busy.

"The one thing I learned at Crystal's shop was you can't take in more work than you can promise. So, we had to turn work away on occasion. Do not be afraid to say no."

"That would be hard to do."

"No rush jobs, because your end product won't be right."

"Mother, you must move to town and help me."

"Dear daughter, my eyes are fading from sewing all these years in poor light. Plus, we need to discuss this with your father."

"Okay. Let's go get him."

They arrived a little early at the bank, but Jack agreed to leave anyway. Things had been slow, and his teller could handle closing up just fine. So, Maude helped Jack into the wagon, and off they went.

"Father, I want to talk to you about something."

"You do? Are you getting married, too?" Jack's eyes twinkled.

Carla laughed. "Heavens, no. Although I bet one of those Harder boys would marry me."

Jack visibly shivered. The three oldest had been jailed more times than he could count for disorderly conduct. "Uh, that would be no."

Carla and Maude both laughed. Maude nodded in encouragement to Carla. "I want to move into town. I've picked out a bedroom already."

"Really? That would be nice. But I sense there is more to this move."

"Yes, quite a bit."

Carla began telling him about the visit to the seamstress' shop. Carla wanted to take orders and sew using the back room in the house. Jack nodded as he listened.

When Carla was done, he said, "Sounds like you two have it all planned out."

Maude smiled. "Well, we had time while waiting for you to get off work."

Jack pondered the idea of Carla sewing for a living, but that wasn't what was on his mind. Then, finally, they pulled into the yard, and his children came running. "Help me down, Maude. I need to hug my children."

Jackson came out of the barn and took the team away. He and his father nodded to each other, and Jackson knew something was up. Paul had just ridden in from checking the cattle. The two brushed down the horses, gave them grain, and headed for the house. Charlie had gone over to help the Walkers with a cow that was struggling to calve.

"Pa has something on his mind."

"Now what?"

"I don't know. You're leaving next week. Maybe that's it."

"Could be. I guess we'll find out soon enough."

Jack's family got together every Friday night in his office and talked about the previous week. It kept Jack involved in his children's lives and gave him a chance to offer suggestions for running the ranch. After the children said all they wanted, Jack reached out for Maude's hand.

"My turn. I heard from Mr. Carsten's lawyer. George passed away sometime in the last couple of weeks. He stated that his last days in California had been wonderful. I'll let your Uncle William know when we're done here." After the comments died down, Jack continued. "Carla would like to move into town and be a seamstress. She would use one of the rooms at the house for sewing. Now, I'm all for that, but I think she should set up a small shop on main street by the mercantile. That way, the mercantile can order the material for the patron, and Carla would only have to sew, so she isn't spending money upfront. If things work out, she can expand. What does everyone think?"

The whole room erupted in cheers and positive thoughts. Then, when Jack got everyone's attention again, he said, "One more thing. You should probably order one of those…" Jack paused a few seconds and then continued, "I think it's called a Singer."

Carla jumped up. "A Singer? Really? Oh, Pa! I would love to learn to use one of those."

Jack laughed. "The mercantile just got one in, and I'll be happy to donate the money to buy it for you."

"Oh, Pa." Carla smothered her father with hugs and kisses. Maude had tears, of course, because she cried at the drop of a hat.

"Now that we have that settled, I have one more thing to discuss." He looked at his youngest children. "James. Thomas. Georgia." Then he looked at Donna and Jackson. "I want my family in town with me. I've been living alone for too long. I know you don't want to leave this house, but I need my wife and children by my side. I miss you all too much. Paul will be leaving next week. Carla wants to be in town now. Jackson, you have your horses and ranch work to deal with here. The question would be, Donna, if you stay or move to town. The rest of you will have to move."

There was silence as the children stared at their parents. Donna finally stood up and hugged her father. "I've missed you, Papa. I'll move to town."

That's all it took for the rest to agree to move. The family talked until bedtime, then off they went. Jackson and Paul stayed behind for a few moments to discuss the ranch further. The weekend flew by, and the discussion of moving and Carla's shop were the biggest topics. But Paul leaving on Tuesday's train was too difficult for Maude to discuss. It was a good thing she would be too busy packing and helping Carla the next few weeks to keep her mind off Paul being gone.

JACKSON

Jackson's reputation for his horses was known far and wide. So, when the Turners were able to buy extra land, they did. Jackson needed the additional pasture for his growing herd.

The neighbor that had demanded the Turners put up a fence had failed in his attempts at crop farming. The river flooded his fields twice, and the sun baked it the rest of the time. He offered up his place to the Turners, and William snatched it up. They left the fence between the properties and added a new fence line around the rest of the property to keep the horses in. Before Jackson moved his herd onto the quarter of ground, he let it all go back to native grass. The land wasn't very conducive to crops anyway. William and Jack had talked about that when the farmer moved in. The land had been available more than once, but they could never afford it before now.

There was a house and barn, and Jackson made good use of them. He left the barn doors open so the horses had shelter from the storms. Charlie and Jackson repaired the roof on both structures. If a horse had difficulty foaling, sometimes Jackson stayed in the house to be close by. Charlie was spending more and more time at that house and finally asked permission to move in. William agreed, and Jackson certainly didn't mind. They were young men now and didn't need to live under their parent's roof.

The whole family pitched in and moved the Jack Turner family into the house in town. Jackson now had the entire side of the house to himself. It certainly was quiet without everyone there. Jesse May continued to run the household. Charlie always stopped for lunch and occasionally for supper. Never for breakfast. So now, instead of seventeen around the table, it was seven or eight. It took Jesse May a few meals before she cut the size down to fit the number of people at the table.

Jackson rode over to the Walker's place quite frequently. He would check the cattle and end up at the Walkers, give his horse water, and then ride home. It turns out he was seeing Penelope Walker. They had, of course, known each other forever, but when he danced with her at Effie May's wedding, he suddenly became a little tongue-tied. Penelope wasn't that much younger than him, and he remembered her visiting with his sisters frequently over the years.

Penelope seemed to return his feelings. One day, he invited her to go to Hastings with him to pick up some supplies. Ada agreed to let her go, smiling as they moved off down the road. She would have to let Greg know another wedding would be happening soon. Their son, Gary, had been seeing a young woman, and it looked like they would be getting married, too.

Jackson took Penelope to lunch before returning home. They were getting along great, and Jackson was as starry-eyed as Penelope. Several years previously, Jackson had taught all the girls in both his family and the Walkers how to ride a horse. The girls would put on long pants, and Jackson taught them to handle horses as well as anybody in the family. It had come in handy more than once over the years, as they had needed to saddle and ride for one reason or another. Penelope loved to ride, so talking about Jackson's horses greatly interested her.

By spring, Jackson had asked Penelope to marry him. Since he had the house to himself these days, she could move right in. But they left Jack and Maude's bedroom for their visits to the ranch. Jackson fixed up his parents' old bedroom upstairs. Jesse May even repapered the walls for the couple.

Jackson's horses were fine-looking animals, and he earned a nice living selling them.

With Penelope by his side, he was a happy man.

CHARLIE

Restlessness seemed to follow Charlie wherever he went, no matter whatever he did. He couldn't sit still for long and was happiest when he was running around with half a dozen different projects going on. School had bored him, and he didn't have any particular interest like his cousins did. That irked him, too.

Paul was inventive, and Charlie often helped him make things. Jackson loved his horses, but they didn't hold Charlie's interest. He found assisting animals in distress the more exciting part of running the ranch. He willingly helped any of the local farmers when they had trouble with their stock.

When he moved into the house on the newly purchased land, he found the silence wonderful. The noise in the Turner house had bothered him, but he hadn't realized how much until he spent a night alone. He always felt his mother was disappointed in him for not having plans for his life. But other than ranching, there was nothing special he wanted to do.

It wasn't until Charlie had to see Dr. Johnson for an injury to his leg that things began to change. Charlie had been helping pull a calf when the cow kicked him hard enough on his leg, breaking the bone. As Charlie flew backward, the calf came with him. It was a good thing his father had been helping that day. William took care of both the calf and cow while Charlie scooted backward out of the way. His leg had gone numb initially, so he hadn't realized it was broken. It was only when Charlie tried to stand that he knew something was wrong.

William settled both the animals in a clean stall and then yelled out the barn to get some help. Jesse May and Mary Ann came running. They got Charlie into the back of the wagon, trying not to hurt the leg any more than it already was, while William hitched up the team of horses. Charlie reassured his mother it was just a broken leg and not to fret about him. Charlie asked Mary Ann to take him to town and left his parents at home, much to Jesse May's distress. Mary Ann laughed as they got down the road.

"You never let a chance go by to make mother upset."

Even though the wagon was softened by straw, the bumps nearly made Charlie scream from the pain when he was jarred. "Can you imagine me putting up with her all the way in and back? No way would she let me go back to my house."

"Heavens, no. And she will be upset if I leave you there, too. Besides all the questions I'll have to answer when I get home."

Charlie smiled before the wagon banged through another rough patch. "Can you just rush the horses along? I'm dying here. Get this ride over with."

Mary Ann yelled at the horses and flicked the reins. "Hold on!" she shouted.

And Charlie did. He'd broken out in a sweat by the time they arrived, but thankfully the ride was finally over. He lay there waiting for help and tried to keep from screaming in pain. Finally, Dr. Johnson, Bea, and Mary Ann got him inside and on the exam table. Mary Ann waited in the other room. She only heard Charlie yell once on the trip and once inside the room. She had to hand it to him; Charlie was one tough brother.

Dr. Johnson gave Charlie a little laudanum to dull his senses, and then they removed his britches. The leg was swollen, bruised, and out of alignment. Another bit of laudanum, then Dr. Johnson set the leg. He applied splints and wrapped the leg in soft cloth tight enough to keep everything in place.

Bea cut off one pant leg, and then they pulled his pants

back on. Dr. Johnson came out to talk to Mary Ann and explained he would keep Charlie overnight to make sure things looked alright the following day. Somebody could check on him the next day to see if he could go home. Mary Ann gave it a little thought. She decided to have Aunt Maude check on him, and maybe Charlie could stay at her house for a few days. Dr. Johnson thought that might be a good idea. Mary Ann rushed over to the Turners to explain what had happened. Maude agreed to the plan immediately, and Donna said she would prepare a room for him. Knowing Jesse May as well as she did, Maude scribbled a note to her, saying they would keep Charlie in town until he could get around. That way, the doctor would be close by if needed. It was going to be up to Mary Ann to reassure her mother that Charlie would be just fine. But Maude also expected a visit from Jesse May sometime tomorrow, no matter what anyone said.

Charlie's leg was very swollen, but the doctor thought if he could stay with his Aunt Maude, then he could stop to check on him every day. Charlie agreed that it was a better option than going home. Besides, with her experience with his Uncle Jack, Charlie knew he was in good hands.

The rain had started mid-morning and hadn't quit by the time he was well enough to move. Dr. Johnson and Bea got Charlie in a carriage, so they were out of the rain. They managed to get them all into the Turner house before they were thoroughly drenched. Charlie was grateful for the rain. Not because the hay field needed the moisture, but because it would keep his mother home one more day. He wasn't ready to have her hovering over him. His Aunt Maude was thinking the same thing but didn't say it out loud. When Jesse May was stressed, she was a handful.

The following morning, Dr. Johnson came to see

Charlie. He was doing much better with his leg splinted. The swelling had gone down a little, so the doctor tightened the dressings to hold the splints in place. Then, Dr. Johnson sat down beside Charlie to visit about his injuries.

"Mary Ann said something about a cow kicking you. What were you doing?"

"Pulling a calf. The momma wasn't happy, but we didn't want to lose them both."

"Sounds like you've done that before."

Charlie shrugged. "Yeah. I've helped a neighbor or two out with sick animals or trouble calving. Jackson had a horse that had trouble foaling not that long ago. I seem to have a knack."

"Hmmm. Sounds like it. I did a little research before I stopped by. What would you say about going to a veterinarian school in Pennsylvania?"

"A what school? I hate school."

"Veterinarian. It's like a medical school for animals. They could teach you a lot about different animals, and you could get paid to do all the work you're doing now for free."

"Really?"

Dr. Johnson nodded. "Back about twenty years ago, they started this program. I'm sure it's probably only gotten better since its inception. But, as far as I know, it's the only one of its kind right now."

"But, I'd have to go to school."

Dr. Johnson laughed. "Yes, but you'd be learning about the health of animals. How all of their organs work, and what you do to care for their specific diseases. You would probably enjoy it, actually."

Quietly, Charlie remarked, "You really think I could do it, Doc?"

"I don't know why not. Would you like me to contact

them?"

"Yes. I think so. But don't tell anyone."

"No problem. It's going to take a few weeks to get you back up and around, so we've got plenty of time to do a little investigating. And Pennsylvania isn't that far from Baltimore, where Paul is attending college. So maybe you two could see each other over holiday breaks."

Charlie smiled. "That would be nice. I sure miss him."

Dr. Johnson got up to leave. "I'm sure your mother will be here as soon as she can get through the mud. I need to get back to work. I'll see you every day until I think you can go home."

"How long do you think that will be?"

"Not sure. A week, maybe two. It might be longer. It was a bad break."

"Thanks, Doc. I'll think about the school."

"You do that."

Dr. Johnson let himself out of the house and thought about his help in getting another Turner boy off to college. He had delivered everyone one of those children, and it was like they were his own. Whatever he could do to help, he would.

Jesse May made it to town right after lunch and questioned Charlie as if he'd just robbed the bank and was on trial.

"Mother. Stop," Charlie raised his voice. Jesse May shut her mouth and didn't know what to say. Her son had never talked to her like that. "Mother, I'm not a little kid anymore, nor have I done anything wrong. It's a broken leg, and it will heal. It's as simple as that. You don't need to make a big deal over the whole thing."

"So you're saying I'm overly dramatic?"

"Aren't you always?"

Jesse May dropped into a chair. "Yes, I am. Your father warned me before I left home. I didn't listen to him again."

Charlie shook his head. "We all knew it would happen."

Jesse May looked surprised. "What do you mean we?"

"Dr. Johnson, Bea, Aunt Maude, Mary Ann, Pa, and me. I probably missed someone."

Jesse May began laughing and then laughed so hard Charlie started to laugh. Jesse May finally said, "I'm terrible." The two laughed a little longer but ended up having a good conversation.

Dr. Johnson brought crutches over when he came the next time and made sure Charlie could get around. Then the doctor told him he could go home in about a week. Once the swelling was down and with the splints remaining in place, he thought Charlie could manage with a little bit of assistance.

Maude, James, and Thomas eventually took him back to the big house. Charlie agreed to go home only if he got to stay with Jackson instead of on his mother's side. He didn't want to be smothered.

Maude made up the downstairs bedroom for him and told Jesse May not to drive him crazy, or he'd move back to his little house.

Charlie got along well, and the weeks flew by. Dr. Johnson stopped by on occasion to check on him. Jackson was the perfect roommate. He and Penelope left him alone, and if his mother got under his feet, he would hobble out to the barn and just stay there for a couple of hours. He would prop his leg up on a bale and daydream. He knew it was time to go to his own house when he started to put more weight on his leg, and his mother was yelling at him about the whole thing. Jackson took him to town to see Dr. Johnson. The trip alone was worth the peace and quiet.

Jackson left Charlie at the doctor's office and went to

get supplies. His twin, Carla, had opened a shop close by the mercantile, so he stopped to say hello. His mother happened to be there helping Carla by doing some finishing touches to the dresses she had been working on. Mrs. Ray and Mrs. Paring had kept their promise to tell their friends about Carla's shop. As a result, she was inundated with orders immediately.

Maude helped Carla accept or decline orders at first. She knew how much Carla could do at a time. It took Carla a couple of months to figure out her speed. Now, her mother only came in occasionally to do some finish work and left the decision-making to her daughter. Even if Carla didn't necessarily need the help, Maude would sometimes come to the shop just because she loved to sew. It also gave them time to visit.

Jackson breezed in and hugged them both. "I hear the old bat down the street is mad you have a good business already."

Maude shook her finger at Jackson. "That's not nice."

Carla tried not to laugh too hard. "Well, he heard right. She could never please my customers. They came running as soon as I opened my doors. The mercantile struggles to keep enough material in for me. They plan on doubling their order again next week."

"Wonderful, sis. I'm so proud of you."

Maude put her things away. "How is Penelope?"

"She's great. Dr. Johnson says he'll stop by next week and see her. He's already teasing me about filling up the house again."

Maude laughed. "I hope Dr. Johnson doesn't retire anytime soon so he can see it happen."

"I better get back and pick up Charlie. He wants to go back to his place when we get home. He's had enough of his mother."

Maude and Carla both laughed. "Poor Aunt Jesse

May. She does love her family."

Maude nodded. "Tell Charlie hello from us."

"Will do." Another hug, and he was out the door.

Charlie's splints were off, but he was to continue to use one crutch until his strength was back in his leg. Heading for Charlie's place, Jackson told him that he would drop off his clothes the following day. Jackson was sure they would be clean and folded on the bed by the time he got home. Charlie was sure of it. Charlie also reminded him to drop off some food when he brought his clothes back. Jackson saluted and headed home.

Charlie sat down in his chair. The previous owner left most of the furniture, and even though the house wasn't much to look at, it was comfortable. Once he and Jackson fixed the roof, it was tight from the weather.

He had a few canned items he could fix for supper, but first, he had to take a nap. He would never tell anyone that the trip to town had worn him out. He also had papers to read from the college Dr. Johnson had told him about. But right now, the nap won out. Charlie moved to the settee and laid back. With his sore leg propped on a pillow, he fell asleep a few minutes later.

Over supper, Charlie spread the papers out in front of him. He read and reread the information. The only thing stopping him was the tuition. He had no income of his own. Charlie tossed the papers aside, finished his meal, and hobbled out to the porch with his sore leg propped up on a railing. The sun was almost down, but it was Charlie's favorite time of day. Peaceful, nature settling in for the night, and no visitors. Charlie watched the horses as they headed into the corral for their nightly water and feed. Jackson or Charlie always left some out for them, but he knew his father was going to do it today since Jackson went to town. So, it surprised him to see his dad ride up to the barn so late to take care of the chores.

When he was done, he walked over and sat beside Charlie. William knew Charlie would talk when he was ready.

"Running a little late tonight, huh?"

"Yeah. Mark had a crisis."

"What? Did his frog die or something?"

"Something like that."

"I swear. He acts more like Ma all the time."

"Heaven forbid, son." Charlie chuckled. "Splints off, I see."

"Yip. Just have to get my strength built back up in my leg. It doesn't hurt, but it sure is weak. I'm supposed to use this one crutch until I'm sure my leg will hold me."

"Great." Charlie was quiet for a few minutes, debating with himself. William got up to leave, so Charlie got up, too, supporting himself with the crutch. "Do you have time to come inside a minute?"

"Sure."

Charlie lit a lamp and set it on the table. "I'd like you to read these and tell me what you think."

William sat down and pulled the lamp closer. He scanned the papers, then went back and read every line. "I've never heard of such a school. Where did you get these?" William waved the papers around in the air.

"Dr. Johnson."

"Dr. Johnson, huh? That man knows a little bit about everything, doesn't he?"

"I guess so." Charlie shrugged. "He says it's the only one in the country right now. They've been around for about twenty years. Doc thinks I'd be a good animal doctor."

"You would. So does everyone else around here. Why do you think they have you come over when they have a sick animal?"

"My good looks?"

William laughed. "Only if they have eligible daughters in the house."

"I don't see too many of them in the barns."

"So, do you want to go? I know you hated school."

"I'm thinking about it, but there's one drawback."

"What's that?"

Charlie found the paper that had the cost of the tuition. "I don't have any money of my own."

"I'm not sure you've noticed, but your parents aren't destitute. We learned back when we were your age how to handle money. We almost lost the farm that first year."

"I remember you telling us about that."

"I'll talk to your mother, but you know she will be just fine with your decision. Except you will be an awful long way from home."

"I'm the same age as Paul, and he's been gone for about a year already."

"Yes, but we're talking about your mother, not Aunt Maude."

"Oh, right."

William pushed the papers toward his son. "If you want to go, fill them out, and we'll provide the money."

"Yes, sir. I'll let you know my decision tomorrow."

His father left, and Charlie sat there long afterward looking at the papers. Several minutes later, he realized he didn't have a pencil. Charlie began laughing until he cried. Then, shaking his head, he decided he might as well go to bed. His leg was aching, and it had been a long, stressful day.

In the morning, Charlie had barely managed to get himself cleaned up and dressed when someone banged on the door. Jackson let himself in, and he had his hands full. Dropping it all on the table, he hollered at Charlie, who was just coming into the room.

"Beware! Mama Bear coming down. I've got to get

the horses some grain, and then I'm outta here."

"Thanks, Cousin. For bringing both my stuff and the warning."

Jackson high-tailed it out of the house and to the barn. Charlie was sitting down to a cup of coffee when his mother arrived. She knocked and hollered his name. He yelled at her to come on in.

"I see Jackson brought your clothes and some food."

"Yip. You want a cup of coffee?"

"I'll get it. Stay sitting." Charlie didn't move a muscle. He knew better. "May I see the papers?"

Charlie dug them out from under the stuff Jackson had dumped on the table and handed them over. He sat and drank his coffee as his mother read every word on the pages. Charlie knew he could stay silent forever, but instead, it was his mother that was astoundingly quiet for a change. She finally laid the papers down and looked at her oldest son.

"I wasn't sure I believed your father when he told me that we were sending you off to college. I honestly thought he had lost his mind. But he told me you had the papers to prove it." Charlie nodded. "Why haven't you filled them out yet?"

Charlie got up and poured himself another cup of coffee. His mother began to protest and offered to help, but he refused. "I'm fine." He sat back down. "No pencil."

"What?"

"To fill in the papers. I don't have a pencil."

"Oh. I'll bring you one back with me later. I'll bring your lunch today."

"Could you have Mary Ann do it?"

"Mary Ann?"

"Yes."

"I suppose so. Why?"

"I'd like to talk to her about the horses."

"Horses? Mary Ann?"

"Mother, please. Stop repeating me."

"Fine." She finished her coffee and headed home. Charlie chuckled. "Horses."

Mary Ann arrived just as confused as her mother was. "You want to discuss horses?" She set the food on the table and uncovered the dishes.

"So, here's the thing. Jackson is going to need help. I thought you could ride with him for a couple of days and learn what needs to be done. I won't be able to help for another week or two, and I figured Pa would be busy."

"I can do that, but why me and not Ma?"

"Seriously? I can't believe you had to ask that."

Mary Ann laughed. "I had to say it."

Charlie inhaled his lunch. He hadn't eaten much for two days. Mary Ann sat a big piece of apple pie in front of him.

"I made it fresh this morning, just for you."

"Thanks."

"What did you need a pencil for?" Charlie shoved the papers her way while he took a huge bit of pie. "You want some help? Your handwriting is terrible."

"Sure."

Mary Ann started filling out the papers, asking questions as she went. It wasn't long before the form was completed. "There. All done."

"Thank you."

"You're welcome. So. Horses. You better give me an idea of what I need to do to help. Mother will be quizzing me when I get home."

Charlie went over a few things, and then they walked out to the barn to look around. Mary Ann had never been there, so he took his time. She took a few moments to brush Charlie's horse. The horse was getting old and couldn't keep up with the young bucks in the pasture. But he tried. So, Charlie kept him in the barn. Mary Ann promised to walk him every day until Charlie could handle getting on the horse again. They put a halter on him, and Mary Ann hopped on bareback, her skirt hiked up.

"I'll ride him back tonight to help Jackson."

"Tell you what. You ride him back and forth for a few days. The horse will feel right at home in the big barn. Just put him in his old stall."

Mary Ann smiled and headed for home.

Charlie returned to the house and put his papers in an envelope. He would have Mary Ann take it to the house for someone to mail it. Then, all he had to do was wait to hear if he was accepted or not. Two months later, Charlie had his answer. He would be headed to college in the fall.

HARRIETT RAY and CECILY PARING

Harriett and Cecily dedicated themselves to the Turner and Walker children. They were both Grandma to all of them. It wasn't until the children were old enough to understand how the grandmothers were actually related, but it never mattered. Everyone was treated and spoiled equally. It was fate when the two families eventually intertwined.

The women had begun making trips back home to visit with friends. And they would occasionally go to California when Cecily's husband could still join them. On this trip, Harriett had business to attend to with her solicitor, Bertram Benjamin. Once all her holdings had sold, Bertram bought other investments for Harriett. He had done right by her all these years.

When Paul was ready to leave for Baltimore, Grandma Ray went with him. Mr. Paring's health was declining, and Cecily said she couldn't join them on this trip. Harriett didn't plan to stay as long this trip. It didn't seem quite right without Cecily. Maude didn't go either, as she didn't think she should leave her family for too long. Besides, she wouldn't want to leave Paul behind, even if it was college.

Harriett took her grandson around the city of Baltimore before taking him to Johns Hopkins. Once he was settled, Harriett made an appointment to see the dean in a few days. When she returned, Paul was doing fine and excited for classes to start. He had already begun to make friends and was familiarizing himself with the campus. She left him with some cash and hugged him tightly.

The dean of the college was waiting for her. They visited about Paul's scholarships and made sure all his needs were met. She left a substantial check with the dean and asked that she be contacted if Paul ever needed anything.

Harriett headed back to her old hometown. She met with Bertram, and they discussed her investments. He lost his wife in the last couple of years. He had begun to think about Harriett differently as they sat having a cocktail before supper.

The following day, she met with old friends and observed them. She always forgot how snobby she used to be, but after watching these women, Harriett was glad to have changed. At times, she found herself getting pulled into their gossip, but could hear her daughter and family enjoying themselves in the community without all the pretenses. Of course, they asked Harriett how she was doing out in the primitive West.

"I just dropped my grandson Paul off at Johns Hopkins engineering school. He has the prestige of being honored to be in the first class, due to the medical equipment he has already invented. He is the oldest of the grandchildren. Jackson and Carla are the twins. Jackson has involved himself in raising some of the finest horses in the area. People come for miles to buy from him. Carla is the finest seamstress that ever lived. She makes all my clothes. Jack, Maude's husband, owns the bank and is involved in its day-to-day activities." She conveniently left out Jesse May and William. "So, they are all doing quite well. The young ones are still in school."

"How did they buy a bank? I suppose you gave them the money after Herbert died?" The woman sneered at Harriett over her teacup.

"Actually, no. I wasn't aware of the purchase until afterward."

"Oh." The woman was put in her place, and Harriett soon excused herself from the group. Listening to all the gossip had been tiring, and she wondered if she had ever truly enjoyed it.

Before leaving for home, she and Bertram had another lovely evening out. Outside of mentioning that he had purchased some railroad stock for her, they didn't discuss business at all. Instead, he asked many a question about the area where she was living.

The trip back to Hastings was pleasant. Harriett thought back to her first trip out and shivered. It had been horrendous, and she thought she would freeze to death before landing on Cecily's doorstep. She still hated the freezing temperatures that were often accompanied by strong winds. The wind seemed to blow year-round.

It was a year later when Charlie decided to go to college. She knew William and Jesse May would do everything possible to make it happen. But, unlike Paul, the college didn't offer any scholarships. Harriett asked if she could accompany Charlie to Pennsylvania, as she had Paul the previous year. Mr. Paring had passed away last year, and Cecily agreed to go with her on this trip. Charlie thought it a grand idea, believing it would be easier than having his mother fuss over him the whole trip.

Soon, the three of them got on the train. Charlie sat by himself for most of the trip, but he would sit with his 'grandmothers' to eat and was polite company. He didn't want to admit he was scared.

As Paul before him, they had done a little sightseeing first. Harriett and Cecily made sure Charlie was settled in his dorm, gave him a little cash, and then went to the dean's office. A large donation later, Charlie would be taken care of for all his education expenses. In addition, his parents would be notified that a scholarship was offered, and they would no longer need to pay for his education.

Cecily was proud of Harriett. She had changed so much since moving to Hastings. She was much more selfless than selfish. It was nice to see her spend her fortune on someone who wasn't even actually related to her.

Cecily decided she needed to be more like Harriett for a change. It hadn't occurred to her to spend her money on anyone except Ada's family, even though she had 'adopted' the Turner family early on. Ada and Maude had been such good friends for years now. They both loved Jesse May, so it was an easy transition to love the William Turner family, too. Over the years, Cecily and Harriett had shown their love to the seventeen Turners and six Walkers. And what a family they were.

Harriett and Cecily returned to their humble beginnings and met with friends of Cecily's. Due to their financial circumstances, Cecily's friends were not necessarily Harriett's. However, her friends were more down-to-earth and not nearly as snobby. Harriett also arranged to visit with Bertram while Cecily attended a function with her friends.

The two stayed for several days longer than planned due to circumstances beyond Cecily's control. Harriett sent a wire home to Maude and explained she was bringing a friend home with her and would be delayed a few days. When Harriett and Cecily got off the train, a man accompanied them. Maude was waiting with the carriage.

After hugs from the women, Harriett said, "I'd like to introduce Bertram Benjamin."

"Nice to meet you. I've heard a lot about you over the years. I appreciate your taking care of my mother after my father passed away."

"The pleasure was all mine, and I was glad to handle her business."

"Maude, we married before coming home."

"You what?"

Harriett blushed, and Bertram cleared his throat. "Yes, Ma'am. I've always admired your mother. After my wife died, I've been quite alone. She stopped to see me last year, and I couldn't get her out of my mind. The West has done Harriett a world of good, and I wanted to be part of her life out here. So, when she returned, I asked if I could come back with her and be her husband. I believe we are well-suited to each other. I hope you can accept me into the family."

Maude stared at her mother, then Cecily. Cecily just shrugged her shoulders. Her mother blushed and looked very happy, but Maude knew her mother was worried about how she would take the marriage.

"Well. If Mother's happy, I'm happy." What else could she say? "Mother, you never cease to surprise me. Let's get your baggage loaded, shall we?"

They dropped Cecily off first, then went to Harriett's. Once the baggage was brought inside, Harriett had Bertram wait in the parlor while the two women talked.

"Maude, I know this is a shock, but I trust Bertram, much as you feel about Jack. He made out some papers that will keep all my assets in my name. He has his own wealth, which will go to his family. Another solicitor helped us handle all of the legal work. That's what took us so long to come home. We had to do all of that before we got married. It protects both his and my family. Not a common thing these days, as you know. But I refused to marry him unless you received all of my assets once I'm gone."

"Oh, Mother. Are you happy?"

"Very much, dear. The relationship is as much about companionship as it is about respect. His wife was lovely,

223

and I'm sure he misses her terribly. His children were unhappy with our marriage, but having the paperwork done ahead of time appeased them somewhat. Bertram has wanted to come West for some time, once I stayed here and relayed how much I enjoyed being out here with you. His wife refused to think about moving. So, I think it all worked out like it was supposed to."

"Come to the house in a couple of days so everyone can meet him. Rest up first. I'll tell Jack and the children they have a new grandfather."

"Thank you, Maude. And you're right. We're both tired. We'll be over in two days."

Maude left, shaking her head. If nothing else, her mother was full of surprises.

FINDING TROUBLE

The Harder boys were usually involved when things went wrong or something sneaky happened. Most the excitement in town had one or more of the Harders in the middle of things.

When the boys were smaller, their father never treated them well. In turn, the boys became bullies themselves. People stood up to them at times, but they grew so big so fast that they intimidated the smaller ones around them.

Mr. Harder sent the boys to school, not that they showed up all the time, but he wanted them to learn to read and write, which was something that he couldn't do himself. The farm wasn't much to look at and was never very productive. The land could probably produce more, but Mr. Harder was too lazy to work.

Mrs. Harder up and left one day. People say she was pretty bruised up when she left town and didn't blame her for running. But they felt sorry for the boys left behind.

When Mr. Harder died, the oldest boy was barely twenty. He was stuck with the farm and the other boys— the youngest was twelve. He sold the farm and moved them all to town. That's when most of the trouble in Hastings started. If it wasn't a bar fight, it might be just someone walking down the street getting shoved around. No one was safe with those boys around.

The youngest two were closing in on manhood, but they weren't turning out any better. Liam and Pete didn't appear to have many smarts between them. Even though they attended school off and on for several years, their reading and writing abilities were very limited. Their main goal in life was to be mischievous. They saw nothing wrong with lighting a trash can on fire or breaking someone's window.

The oldest three boys got into a scrape, and they

landed in jail for several months. After that, Liam and Pete ran out of food and had no money to buy some. So, they stole whatever they could and begged for the rest. That's when they got the great idea that they should start robbing shops.

When darkness arrived, the boys jimmied the back door locks and ransacked shops, looking for money. They took food or anything else they could use – a pair of boots, jeans, food, hats, pots and pans, blankets. After a few of these robberies over a couple of weeks, the sheriff walked the streets and notified owners to watch themselves, as whoever was doing it probably wouldn't quit.

One day, about closing time at the bank, Liam walked into the bank with a loaded shotgun and pointed it at the teller. Pete walked in right behind Liam with a sack to put money inside. They had kerchiefs over their faces, but there wasn't a person around town that didn't know who those two were. At least there were no customers, but Jack and Maude were in the back office. She had just arrived by the back door. Maude was out of the boy's line of sight, so Jack waved her to move to the corner and crouch down. She never hesitated.

Liam waved the shotgun around as the teller began pulling cash out of his money drawer. Jack reached under his desk and pulled out his pistol. Then, with a quick draw, he shot at Liam. Liam screamed and dropped to the floor. The teller dropped behind the window, and Pete stared at his brother writhing in pain. Then he ran out the door screaming.

"Someone shot my brother! I need help! Get the doctor and sheriff! Someone shot my brother!"

Pete had forgotten to take his kerchief off, and people stood around gaping before someone walked into the bank to see what was happening. Jack yelled from his office to get the sheriff. Liam lay there screaming in pain, and Pete ran around the streets, yelling for help.

Maude quickly left for home, and Jack waited for the sheriff to arrive. The teller put the money back in his drawer, took Jack's gun from him, and pointed it at Liam until someone came to relieve Liam of his shotgun.

The place was chaos soon enough. Pete came running back inside to be by his brother. Finally, the doctor arrived and treated the wound. Jack had shot the gun out of Liam's hand and didn't cause much damage to his arm. Once treated, the sheriff took both the boys to jail. It wouldn't be long before they would be joining the other brothers.

Pete told the sheriff that because Jack was in a wheelchair, they figured the bank would be easy pickings. Unfortunately, they hadn't realized that Jack was a crack shot and never missed what he was shooting at. Liam was lucky Jack didn't want to kill him.

THE THIRD GENERATION ARRIVES

Joseph and Effie May had the surprise of their life. Dr. Johnson and Bea helped deliver squalling twins a year after their wedding. Yes, twins. Their names were Elizabeth May and William.

Dr. Johnson knew early on there were two and let the couple know. He said it was in the Turner genes. They, in turn, kept it a secret but prepared the house for the additions to the family. Joseph worked hard to add on a large bedroom in time for the delivery.

Noreen agreed to live with them until Effie May was back on her feet. Cecily Paring was thrilled, and even though her husband had been ill, he lived long enough to meet his first of many great-grandchildren.

Several months later, Jackson and Penelope also delivered a set of twins. Jackson, having grown up a twin, was beside himself with pride. They named the boys Jackson III and Joshua.

Gary and his wife, who had married in between Joseph and Jackson, managed to have just one baby at a time, and his wife was just fine with that. Gary said he was glad he was a Walker and not a Turner.

Carla had met the son of one of her clients, and they were keeping company. She was being stubborn and refused to give up her shop, even if they had children. Maude wasn't surprised. She had raised her children to be independent people. Cecily Paring raised Ada that way, and Maude emulated that daily. The young man had his hands full if he thought he would change Carla's mind.

Mary Ann and Donna were also seeing young men, and there would be weddings in the near future. The youngest boys were all growing like weeds and helping William and Jackson on the ranch. Georgia, surrounded by boys growing up, was quite the tomboy and could keep up with the rest of them. She loved going to the ranch and riding horses.

Jack was hoping one of the boys would come to work at the bank, but none of them seemed interested in office work. They were still a little young, and there was always hope, but the ranch called to them.

Jack advertised back East for someone that wanted to manage the bank. His current employees either had no interest or would be retiring soon. After exchanging correspondence with a few young men, Jack invited two of them out to see the bank and the growing town of Hastings. After their arrival, one decided there was no way he could live in such a rough area. Jack appreciated his honesty –the prairie life wasn't for everyone. The other young man thought the West was just the beginning of the new frontier and practically begged to take the job. He was very young but showed promise. Jack hired him to train as a teller, and then he would see how things went from there. Robert was focused on his job, and was anxious to learn all he could about the bank and its customers.

One evening, Jack invited Robert to supper. Although Maude and Jack had entertained the young man previously, their children had all been out at the ranch that evening, and did not return until after Robert had gone home. It was the first time the young man had met the rest of the family. He was pretty impressed, but more so with Georgia. He was actually a little jealous of her. Active and vibrant, she didn't care what anyone thought about her riding horses in long pants. Georgia was only fourteen, but Robert told himself he would wait for the young lady. And wait, he did. Georgia had no idea what hit her a couple of years later when Robert asked her out on a date. Needless to say, Jack had finally found someone to take over the bank for him that would eventually turn out to be a family member after all.

When Dr. Johnson first met Bea at the Turners, he tried for several years to get her to work for him. She wouldn't agree to the deal until the Turners were done having children and they no longer needed a nursemaid. Both in their forties, they married soon after Bea moved to town. She had loved him from afar and hadn't realized the good doctor had mutual feelings for her; they wasted several good years by not expressing their feelings to one another. They never had their own children but delivered multiple babies over the years. They worked well into their eighties.

Noreen never married but helped wherever she was needed. After her mother died, she worked for Mrs. Ray, assisted at the doctor's office, and was often a nursemaid for the Turner and Walker children.

Paul married while he was living on the east coast. He remained there after college and became quite famous for his medical inventions. He recreated the wheelchair for his father, and it became the one most people would buy. He, his wife, and children would make trips to Hastings at least once a year or more, as time allowed.

Charlie returned home from college and was certainly glad to be out of the city once again. He was now a veterinarian and worked throughout the local counties. He brought with him a wife, who was just as quiet as he was. Charlie fixed up the old cabin and built on a few rooms for their growing family.

Cecily and Harriett lived long lives, happily encouraging a new generation of great-grandchildren. Harriett took Bertram back East when he became ill. She stayed several months and didn't return until after his death. They had been very happy in those last years. Harriett's money and investments were passed down to Maude after her death.

With extreme wealth, Maude said it was time to give some away. She and Jack had never had to touch her money over the years. Jack agreed she should make it available for her children and grandchildren now. After some consideration with a lawyer, Maude made several investments. All her girls were given a large amount of money, placed in their own accounts at the bank. Again, she was following her mother's example. Life was still a man's world, and she wanted to ensure the girls never had to depend on someone else for support.

Except for Paul, her boys were still ranching. She sent Paul a large check as an investment in his inventions. For Jackson, she bought him more land to expand his pastures for the horses. She included the money for a large stable. James and Thomas were more interested in raising bulls. She bought more land and built strong corrals and a large barn to help them succeed. James and Thomas built a smaller cabin close to their brothers. Neither one had found that special girl yet. They were too busy spending time at rodeos with their bulls – both supplying and riding them. Jackson had a string of horses that he sent on the rodeo circuit, too. And the big house that everyone loved so much was finally updated.

Jack was consumed by pneumonia one winter, and the loss was traumatic for all the Turners and Walkers. The accident from so many years ago had damaged a lung. When he became very ill, Jack couldn't fight off the infection. He had often said that he only lived as long as he did because of his wife's love and Paul's inventions to help him get and stay strong.

After Jack passed away, Maude sat with William, Jesse May, Greg, and Ada. She had given much thought to her suggestion, and with Jack gone, she wanted to see it happen. She and Jack had talked about it occasionally in the last few years but had never acted upon their idea.

With the families intertwined now, Maude thought it was past time for the families to be official partners. Maude wanted to buy up any available land for the three families so all their children and grandchildren would have enough land to operate. With some going back and forth over details, Ada suggested Greg take Cecily's money to add to the pot of funds to buy more land and become partners. They were getting too old for the day-to-day operations and needed to pass on their legacy to the children. After visiting with their lawyer, the Turner-Walker Ranch was developed. The families made an equitable split between the three, with Maude's family being the majority shareholder. There was enough land that it would support generations to come, no matter what.

Starting early in Jack's career as a banker, he saw the needs of many people. So, he had tried to help wherever he could. Paul had fixed up a small carriage for him to travel around the countryside. Jack would visit the farmer in trouble and see their land. If possible, Jack would make suggestions to try and save the farmer from going broke. Unfortunately, the settler was often ill-prepared for the harsh summers and wicked winters. Sometimes they would give up after a year or two. There were several plots of land in the area that, no matter how hard you tried, it wouldn't grow a decent crop of anything.

Word got around that Jack could help one way or the other. They knew from experience that if they couldn't make ends meet, Jack would help sell the land or buy it himself. Once the Turner-Walker Ranch was established, the offers continued. What made the difference in the transactions was that the farmer had the option to sell the land to their family, but remain in their home and get paid work for the Turner-Walker Ranch. It was a win-win for several, as the depression was just beginning.

Maude moved into her mother's house after Jack passed away. The staff at the banker's house had retired long ago, and no one thought to replace them. She aired out her mother's home and settled in. She couldn't handle living in the banker's house without Jack.

Carla, Donna, and Georgia were still living in the banker's house. Georgia had no plans to move out if and when she married Robert, but she did move into the master suite her parents had occupied. She told Carla and Donna they could still live there even when they married, if they wanted. Donna said absolutely no way, but Carla loved the upstairs part of the house and the big room she used for sewing. If she ever agreed to marry, that might be another demand she would make of her husband. Keep the shop and stay in the house. That wasn't too much to ask, was it?

When the depression hit hard in the thirties, so many people were affected. There were many bank failures, too. But Jack, followed by Robert, made sure the bank's money was secure. Maude still had so much money in the bank that she would never let it fail. Robert continued following Jack's ways and eventually bought three neighboring banks that were no longer solvent.

Even though cars began to dot the countryside, Jackson's horses remained an integral part of the ranch. Charlie started working with James and Thomas on a new bull breeding program. After a few years of using the lineage from King, ranchers from miles around were willing to buy young bulls for a hefty price.

Henry and Mark stayed at the ranch and continued to raise cattle. William watched his children all grow up and have children of their own. Just down the road, Mary Ann and Carrie had married brothers and had homes close to each other. Their husbands both worked for the Turner-Walker ranch.

Sarah Walker walked into Carla's shop one day and said she wanted to be a seamstress. Carla needed the help, and once Sarah had proved herself, she had her taking on additional customers. Several years earlier, the crabby drab seamstress down the block had closed her door within six months of Carla opening hers. She moved out of town in a huff.

The largest donation, using Harriet's money, went to building a hospital Dr. Johnson knew would benefit the whole area. He spent much of his later years recruiting doctors and nurses. Bea and the doctor also made sure that if anyone wanted to go to college, they went. Harriett, then Maude, made scholarships available to as many people as possible. It was all done secretly, but with Dr. Johnson's investigative abilities, he would find out what each young person wanted to do with their life. Then he would make it happen. He started with Paul and Charlie, and he never quit.

After the Turner-Walker consolidation, William and Jesse May moved to town and let the children decide who wanted to live in the big house. Greg and Ada moved into Cecily's house in town. That allowed their farmhouse to be used by their children, too.

Instead of building onto their cabin, Effie May and Joseph moved into the big Turner house. Now their twins would be raised alongside Jackson's twins. They felt it only right the two oldest (since Paul wasn't around) should fill the big house once again. Jackson, Charlie, and Joseph became the overseers of the ranch, with help from all the brothers, sisters, and cousins.

Who would have thought that three young girls that plopped down on the rough side of Omaha would one day be the co-owners of one of the largest ranches in the state? The city girls to the prairie girls had worked out just fine.

PART THREE

THE NEXT GENERATION

To the Future

LIST OF CHARACTERS
PART THREE

Elizabeth May and William Walker (twins) – children of Effie May Turner and Joseph Walker.

Gerald Moffit – soldier.

Jackson III and Joshua Turner (twins) – children of Jackson II Turner and Penelope Walker.

Jeannie Turner – daughter of Charlie Turner.

Pete Perkins – son of a shopkeeper in Hastings – in love with Elizabeth May Walker.

EIGHTEEN YEARS LATER

Elizabeth May Walker waited in front of the college for her favorite cousin, Jeannie Turner. She was in awe of the beautiful building and couldn't wait to enter. Standing there in her starched white pinafore and polished shoes, she daydreamed of the day she had received her acceptance letter into nursing school. She rushed over to Jeannie's house and found that she, too, had been accepted. The two were very close in age and had grown up together.

Jeannie rushed up to Elizabeth May and grabbed her arm, pulling her into the throng of people headed inside. They giggled and whispered as they entered the school. Stern matrons and professors stood inside the doors directing the students forward to the Ray Auditorium, named after their great-grandmother, Harriett Ray. They quieted as the crowd pushed forward. All you could hear was an occasional whisper and the rustle of clothing.

The girls were going to stay in Paring Hall, a dormitory named after their other great-grandmother, Cecily Paring. Cecily Paring and Harriett Ray donated much of their wealth to the hospital, and building the college soon followed. It was all started by Dr. Johnson and his wife, Bea. So, it was only natural that the college would offer a nursing school, along with courses for the men who wanted to become doctors.

The girls were directed toward one side of the auditorium and the boys to the other side. Getting situated, Elizabeth May looked around and saw a few more of their cousins and her twin brother, William. She pointed out Uncle Charlie's boys to Jeannie before being shushed by a matron.

Charlie had two boys close in age. One wanted to be a veterinarian like his father, and the other wasn't sure if he wanted to do the same or be a doctor, instead. They both decided to take classes close to home first, then head East to finish their education.

There were a couple of other cousins mixed in the crowd of students, and many more would eventually follow. Elizabeth May took a deep breath and realized her dream was finally coming true. Both she and Jeannie knew there would be a lot of hard work in the next three years, but they were looking forward to the reward of becoming nurses. Before the lecture started, Elizabeth May hoped that her friend Pete would wait for her. He promised he would. She had already decided she would break with tradition, and her first daughter would be named Sherri Wray. Grinning, she came to attention as the college dean began speaking.

The dean explained how the college came to be and pointed out various large portraits that were hung on a long wall. It was amazing to see relatives they hadn't known so prominently displayed. But what surprised Elizabeth May more was the portrait of her Aunt Maude Turner. She hadn't realized that the woman she so dearly loved had followed in her mother's footsteps.

The Turners and Walkers never discussed money in front of their children. They also didn't build big fancy houses or buy anything lavish. As a result, the children often forgot that their parents had enough money to send them to college or buy whatever they needed. Instead, they were all taught to help their neighbors and learn to read, write, and do their numbers.

Before their great-grandparents passed away, the grandchildren of all ages would sit at their feet and listen to stories of past struggles, or funny stories about how Grandma Jesse May would get worked up if she didn't know the details about something. They reminded them to all be careful around the cattle and told the story of how Grandpa Jackson was hurt.

Most of the great-grandchildren had never gotten to meet their great-grandparents. Elizabeth May was very small when they passed. She took one last look at the portraits, which brought up fleeting memories. The groups of students streamed out of the hall and onto their first class. She briefly closed her eyes and whispered a small prayer to her great-grandparents, promising to make them proud. Smiling, she took Jeannie's arm and marched proudly with her shoulders back, determination written on her face. Elizabeth May Walker was ready to take on the world.

ELIZABETH MAY

The last bell of the day rang, and the class erupted in joyous hollering heard across the campus. The women and men streamed out of doors and walked along the massive grounds. Graduation day had arrived, and families would be arriving tomorrow to congratulate their children. A few students had dropped out here and there over the years, or were excused for different reasons, but all the Turners and Walkers had made it through.

Eventually, the cousins all found each other and walked down the street to meet at what had always been known as the banker's house. Many of their other cousins would be waiting for them. From there, the whole group would head to the ranch for a family celebration. It was a joyous day, and everyone felt the excitement.

As the evening wore on, the cousins began returning home. The students had one more night in the dorm and had to be in their rooms by curfew. Once the graduation ceremony was over, everyone would pack their belongings and move out to make room for new students.

Elizabeth May would be moving into her parents' home. It was close to the hospital and would make it easier for her to come and go. Elizabeth's grandparents were more than happy to have more family close by once again. Jeannie would be staying in her mother's home for the same reasons.

William would move home for a few weeks before heading East to college. He had chosen to attend law school, and his parents were thrilled. Charlie's boys would be splitting up soon. One was headed to veterinarian college and the other to Johns Hopkins for medical school.

After the celebrations were over, Elizabeth May and Jeannie began working immediately at the hospital. They would be monitored for several weeks and given more tasks as they excelled. It was exhausting work, but the girls never wavered.

It was difficult for Elizabeth May to find time to meet and spend time with her friend, Pete. But, eventually, a routine was established at work, and they scheduled certain times of the week to see each other. Pete was easy to get along with and didn't mind taking his time courting Elizabeth May. In fact, he wasn't in any hurry to marry at all. But, of course, Elizabeth May didn't know that.

Pete was itching to do something other than work hard at his father's store. He wanted to travel and see the world. He also knew that Elizabeth May didn't see them doing any of that. As much as he loved her, Pete couldn't see himself stuck at home with children, working hard all day in the same place. Of course, he was afraid to mention it to Elizabeth May. Not wanting to disappoint her, Pete kept his thoughts to himself.

It was nineteen forty-one, and the war across the world stretched from country to country. The radio kept everyone informed by announcing the bombings and how Hitler was exterminating the Jews. Then, as everyone was thinking about the upcoming holidays and wishing for a white Christmas, the Japanese bombed Pearl Harbor. The United States soon declared war against Japan, and now young men were streaming to sign up to fight a war across the sea.

Elizabeth May and Pete were sitting on the front porch swing, bundled in a heavy blanket. It was early evening, and a light snow was falling. Elizabeth May expressed her thoughts about having a white Christmas and her family's plans to celebrate the season. But Pete couldn't wait any longer. He knew it was time to tell his beautiful girlfriend the truth.

"I'm going to help fight in the war."

Elizabeth May cried out, "No! Oh, no!"

"I'm sorry. I have to go. Will you wait for me?"

Elizabeth immediately had tears streaming down her cheeks. "I can't believe it. I thought…I don't know what I thought. The war is awful."

"Yes, it is. But I need to go. They need my help, and I'm afraid I won't come home again. But many of us from the area are planning on going together. Including some of your cousins."

Elizabeth May turned her head away, unable to stand the bad news. "My family. How can I stand it all?"

"Elizabeth May. I love you. But we have to do this. It's our duty. We are strong and capable, and the government needs our help. I'm sorry to be the one to tell you all of this, but your cousins thought it easier for me than them."

Elizabeth May laid her head on Pete's shoulder. "Promise me you will all come home."

"We will do our best, sweetheart."

The young men across the county got together and decided they would all leave as soon as they celebrated one last Christmas with their families. Pete took it upon himself to notify a government agency how many were willing to serve. The government promised to send out a bus to pick them up since there were so many. On December thirtieth, twenty-eight young men boarded the bus and headed for a training camp. Their families and friends waved goodbye, and the tears flowed freely. The weather was freezing cold, and faces were now icy from tears.

Elizabeth May was one of the last to leave the bus station. Her mother took her arm and led her home. It was going to be gut-wrenching for the whole town. The youngest boys of Maude Turner had never married. James and Thomas kissed their mother goodbye before they stepped onto the bus. Henry and Mark were from Jesse May's family, and they joined up, also. Jesse May was beside herself. So involved with traveling with their horses and bulls, none of the boys ever found the time to settle down with families. The four were the oldest on the bus, and they reassured everyone they would keep an eye on the group as long as possible. Greg and Ada were glad that their boys remained home. Those two were much older and stayed to work the ranch.

All the male great-grandchildren were still a bit too young to join, except for William and Charlie's boys. Everyone hoped they could continue their studies without the interruption of the war. William, George, and Howard were all off at college now. Howard knew that if the war were still going on when he graduated from medical school, he would probably have to help with the wounded.

Elizabeth May threw herself into her work to try and keep her mind from straying to the war. Sleep was elusive, no matter how tired she was, as her fear for her cousins and Pete continued to haunt her. She was beginning to lose weight, and her mother finally sat her down for a talk.

"Elizabeth May. What is going on? You have bags under your eyes, you aren't eating right, and I hear you pacing the floor in your room."

Elizabeth May burst out crying. "Oh, Mother! It's so awful!"

Effie May held her daughter and let her cry, soothing her with quiet words of comfort and rubbing her back until Elizabeth May began to relax. Then, handing her a dry handkerchief, she smiled at her daughter. "Now tell me, child, what is going on?"

"This war. It's awful. The things we hear. I worry so about Pete and the other boys."

"Oh, dear. I understand your worries because we are all worried about them. But you can't make yourself sick over this. I don't know what I can do to help you." Effie May felt just as helpless, knowing that no words could help her daughter.

Elizabeth May sat back and stared out the kitchen window. Her mother made some tea and sat a cup in front of her. "I must seem so silly carrying on like this. But I fear for all of our friends and family. I just know they won't return, and I can't help feeling helpless and hopeless. It overwhelms me."

Effie May drank some tea and encouraged her daughter to do the same. "Whether they come home or not won't depend on how much we worry about them. All we can do is wait. You realize I have brothers and cousins in the war, don't you?"

"Oh, yes, Mother. I'm sorry."

"Although they were much older than so many of the other boys, to me, they will always be my little brothers. Henry and Mark never seemed to grow up. And James and Thomas are just as bad. But they are also responsible and will keep an eye on Pete as long as possible. I don't know where they will be sent and what they will be doing, but I pray daily for them. Have you heard from Pete?"

Elizabeth May nodded and pulled an envelope from her pocket. It was worn from carrying it around. "He gave me the address where I can write to him and says he doesn't know how long it will take to catch up to him, but he will look forward to my letters. Have you heard from Uncle Henry and Uncle Mark?"

Effie May nodded. "They sent one letter, but both wrote a few lines. I know all the boys they trained with are ready to ship out. It's time for me to realize they are men, not boys. They have good heads on their shoulders, so I will just have to believe they will be alright. My mother is beside herself. I'm not sure your grandmother is handling this any better than you are."

That statement put a smile on Elizabeth May's face. "Grandma Jesse May always was a worrier."

"Yes, and I guess you got a good dose of that handed down to you. Maybe you two should cry on each other's shoulders."

"Oh, no. I'm not going over there. The last thing I need is to get us both worrying. She hasn't been feeling well, anyway."

"I know. I worry about both of my parents. Father often goes out to the ranch, but Mother hasn't been able to get around. She won't talk to me about it, though. Maybe she would talk to her nurse?" Effie May reached over and patted her daughter's face.

Elizabeth May smiled. "I'll stop and see her more often. I promise. Maybe I can help her."

"That would be great. I know she would love that. You have been working so hard lately. Take a few minutes to see your grandparents here and there."

"I will, Mother." Elizabeth May finished her tea, hugged her mother, and then went up to her room to take a nap. She was exhausted.

DISASTER STRIKES

It was six months before the bad news began coming to the families across the county. First one family, then another. Their sons wouldn't be coming home. It was fall before Pete's father came to the Walker home to let Elizabeth May know that Pete was missing in action and presumed dead. Elizabeth May went to her room and cried for hours. Her worst fears had come true.

It was difficult for her to return to work, but Elizabeth May knew that she would no longer have a job if she missed her days to work. Besides, her Aunt Maude was in the hospital right now, and Elizabeth May was assigned to help care for her. Aunt Maude was always the steady one compared to Grandmother Jesse May. It was she who Elizabeth May would go to when she needed sound advice. It was an honor to return the favor of caring for her. Unfortunately, her aunt was failing and would not recover from this latest illness.

Elizabeth May went to work and sat by her aunt's bedside. As she worked to cool the fever with a wet washcloth, Elizabeth May explained that Pete wouldn't be coming home.

"My dear child, you are suffering much at such a young age. I remember when I almost lost your Uncle Jack from his accident. It was awful. But you are strong and need to continue your life without him. Just as I will leave all my loved ones behind, I want you to remember that you have a future to look forward to. Maybe not with Pete, but someday you will look back and be surprised at how far you have come." Maude paused as she took some deep breaths so she could continue. "Do you remember the story about how we came to this area so many years ago?" Elizabeth May nodded as she rinsed the washcloth and continued wiping her aunt's sweaty brow. "Who knew that the three of us girls would end up here? Your grandmother and I made our way through many trials in our life. I know you can, too." Maude reached up to still Elizabeth May's hand. "I love you as my own. You will continue to grow into a fine young woman. Have faith in that, Elizabeth May Walker."

"I love you, Aunt Maude. I don't want to lose you." She reached down and hugged her aunt.

Maude tried to hug back but was very weak. "I love you, too. Take care of your grandmother for me."

"I promise. I'll do my best."

"Now go, child. I need to sleep. Tell everyone I love them, please."

Maude Turner passed away in her sleep that evening, with Elizabeth May and Jeannie on either side of her. As Elizabeth May walked home, she decided if she could handle losing her Aunt Maude, she could handle anything. Once again, she threw back her shoulders and marched home. She had made a promise to her aunt, and she planned to keep it. Opening the door, she found her mother and told Effie May the news. Then they both walked over to Grandma Jesse May's house to let her know. Jeannie would be notifying her family at the same time.

Several weeks later, Effie May heard from her brothers, Henry and Mark. They were still both safe, but the fighting was getting worse. They were going to be sent to Africa to fight and had no idea what that meant for them. They also mentioned they didn't know where James and Thomas were. Effie May walked to her parents' place and read the news to them.

Jesse May had been almost bed-bound since losing her best friend, Maude. Ada had come over frequently but was unable to console her friend. Maude and Ada had been best friends since they were youngsters, and the loss was devastating for her, too. But Ada had always handled stress much better than Jesse May. It was Ada that finally convinced Jesse May she needed a doctor to figure out what was wrong with her.

The doctor spent a long time visiting and checking several things out on his patient. His diagnosis was severe depression, and he told William to get her out into the sunshine and back to the ranch and family for visits. The more she holed-up in the house, the more depressed she became. Jesse May balked at the diagnosis. But William demanded she walk out to the buggy for a daily drive. Otherwise, he would have some of the boys come to town and physically pick her up and haul her outside to the buggy. Jesse May wasn't one for a scene and finally agreed to try. Almost three weeks later, she realized how much better she was doing. Seeing the boys off to the war had started the downward spiral, and Jesse May couldn't seem to stop. Effie May and Elizabeth May couldn't believe the difference.

Still refusing to invest in cars, the buggy and horses remained the family's choice of travel. After all, they raised horses. Now that there was a gas shortage due to the war, they were grateful that they still had horses available for traveling.

It was late summer when Maude's family received the news that Thomas had been killed in action. Three other families in the area were also notified that they had lost their sons, too. The whole county was devastated by the news. And the war raged on. More of the boys from the area were enlisting, and more tears were shed.

Elizabeth May hadn't heard from her twin brother, William, for several weeks. She had no idea if he was still planning on finishing his education or going to war. She was also afraid to ask him.

One day at work, Jeannie came up to Elizabeth May

and asked if she was able to take a break. Jeannie helped her finish the immediate tasks before they headed outside for a quick breath of fresh air. It was turning into a crisp fall day, and it felt good to walk around the grounds for a moment.

Jeannie waited a few moments before springing the news on her cousin. "I've signed up to help the war effort and work in the hospital wards for our injured boys."

Elizabeth May grabbed Jeannie's arms. "No. You can't go. What will I do without you?"

"I didn't tell you before now because I knew how worried you would be. I leave in a few days. I didn't know how to tell you." Jeannie took Elizabeth May's hands off her arms and held them tightly in her own.

"Where will you be?"

Jeannie turned to walk again, looping an arm through her cousin's arm. "Right now, they will send me for training in the bigger hospitals in New York or Boston. But I might end up going overseas. It will depend on how the war goes and where they need me."

"I couldn't bear it. All those boys with their war injuries."

"I know. That's why I didn't tell you or ask you to come with me. I knew it would be too much for you."

Elizabeth May stopped walking again. They were headed back inside the building. "You have always handled life and death much better than me. After all, I'm Jesse May's granddaughter, and you're from the saner side of the family."

Jeannie laughed. "Thank goodness for that."

They walked arm in arm into the building and were soon back to work. That would be Jeannie's last day working. She needed a couple of days to pack and say goodbye to her family. The hospital allowed Elizabeth a day off to say goodbye to Jeannie alongside her family. It just seemed to Elizabeth May that the skies refused to be anything but gray for her. She would have to remember her Aunt Maude's last words about staying strong and making a future for herself. It was difficult when the future looked so bleak for so many.

THE WAR CONTINUES

Elizabeth May came home after a difficult shift at the hospital. It had been six months since Jeannie left, and everyone at work still missed her. Faithfully, Jeannie sent a letter home every month to her parents and one to Elizabeth May. Her words to her cousin were much different than the ones to her parents. Only Elizabeth May would understand what she saw in the wards of the army hospital where she was stationed. Elizabeth May remained certain that she would never be able to handle the stress and devastation that was brought upon the men and their families, but she was mightily proud of Jeannie for helping wherever she was needed.

Opening the door to the house, she was surprised to see the living room filled with people. Then she realized her cousin James was home. She rushed over and hugged him tight before realizing that he was injured.

"Oh, James. Did I hurt you?"

James smiled. "I'm fine. My leg is busted up pretty bad, but all my other injuries are healed up okay."

"When did you get home?"

"I got off the train late this afternoon. Uncle Joseph picked me up. I didn't want to go to Mother's house."

Elizabeth May frowned. "Did you get our letter?"

James reached over to hold Elizabeth May's hand. "I did. Way too late to come home. I'm glad Thomas never knew."

Elizabeth May looked around the house at everyone. "I'll go change and clean up." She hugged James again before heading up the stairs to her room.

As Elizabeth May changed into her regular clothes, she wondered about James' injuries. He had said his other injuries were healed, but she doubted what he said. War injuries were very complicated, according to Jeannie's letters. There were always the after-effects of the war to consider. Depression and lingering health concerns seemed to bother the young boys the most. Jeannie cared for many young men with more mental injuries than physical ones. She wished Jeannie were home now to help James.

By the time she returned to the living room, James was being helped to a side room to rest. He had been on a long journey and was exhausted. Effie May placed some water by his bed. Joseph helped James into the bed. They closed the door and allowed him some privacy to rest.

The family members dispersed, leaving the house eerily quiet. Elizabeth May heard the grandfather clock chime the hour as she prepared some tea. Her mother joined her in the kitchen. Joseph remained in the living room reading the latest newspaper.

"Is he going to be alright?"

"I think so. He's much older than some of those boys who went to war. So many were still wet behind the ears."

"What is he going to do now?"

"Tomorrow, he needs to see a doctor, so your father will help him do that. After that, we will let him stay here if he wants to. Georgia and Donna said he could stay with them, too. But he needs to stay with someone until he can get around by himself."

"I bet he lives with Aunt Donna. She's pretty level-headed and reminds me of Aunt Maude."

"You might be right about that. He has his cabin out at the ranch, but there is no way he can get around with all of those steps."

"I bet he's anxious to get out there again, even if all he can do is look around."

Effie May nodded. "Your father promised to take him out tomorrow. His mother's rig would be perfect, and we can use one of our horses."

"Aunt Donna has a car. What about that?"

Effie May laughed. "All James talked about was getting reins in his hands again. I suppose the car would be quite a disappointment."

Elizabeth May laughed. "I didn't even think about how much he missed the horses."

"I haven't even started supper, and it's getting late. So, let's fix up some sandwiches. James is probably starving. He looks like he lost a lot of weight."

Elizabeth May nodded. "You'll fatten him up in no time."

By the time the dinner table was set, James was ready to get up. The hour was late, and everyone was starved. The meal was a quiet affair, but Joseph caught James up on what he had missed at the ranch in the last year or so. James knew it wouldn't be the same without Thomas around. And both Henry and Mark were still overseas somewhere. He guessed everyone had to make changes in their lives, and James hoped that the ability to ride again wouldn't be out of his reach. That was all he could think about, and he planned to do everything he could to get back in a saddle again.

James did decide to stay with his sister, Donna. She lived in the country, but her home was easy for him to get around. It was only a few weeks before he could move back into his cabin. There, he had to get used to being without Thomas. Someone had gone through the cabin and removed most of Thomas's personal belongings, but so much of the cabin was a mixture of the two. He was beginning to adapt to life on the ranch one step at a time.

Riding horses again was the best medicine he could have. If he had a nightmare, James would walk out to the barn and check the horses. Sometimes his brother Charlie, or one of his many cousins, would find him asleep on the hay bales. Everyone learned quickly to make plenty of noise as they entered the barn in case James was there.

Six months after James returned home, Henry and Mark returned physically unscathed. The men had made it through their time in Africa the year before and had been moved to the fierce fighting in Europe. Their regimen was all but decimated. Only a handful remained alive after a long and terrible fight. All the remaining men were sent home. It was now nineteen forty-four, and the war raged on.

EPILOGUE

Jeannie had written that she would be coming home soon. She had served her time well and had seen much more devastation to young men than she ever thought possible. There had been more than one opportunity for her to go overseas to assist, but she had decided to remain in the states to do what she could at home. After all, someone had to be there to do her job. Naturally, she was anxious to see her Uncle James again, but Elizabeth May kept her updated on his condition. Now that he was back at the ranch, Jeannie knew he would be in a much better place mentally.

As Jeannie penned a new letter for Elizabeth May, she mentioned that she would be bringing home gifts and surprises for everyone. When she knew more details about her arrival date, Jeannie would let Elizabeth May know. Elizabeth May and her mother planned to open-up Maude's house, air it out, and clean it from top to bottom in anticipation of Jeannie's arrival.

The hours at the hospital had continued to be long and arduous, but Jeannie loved it all, even though she was exhausted most of the time. Losing some of the soldiers was definitely the hardest part, but so was sitting with the boys that cried out in pain from what they went through.

There was a particular young man that Jeannie took care of that pulled at her heartstrings. He had been severely wounded, and no one thought he would pull through. So, Jeannie spent extra time by his bedside talking to him and holding his hand. She would sing, and the entire ward would always get quiet while she entertained her soldier.

Jeannie believed the man would come through after all as the young man began to respond to her touch and voice. She hoped so, as Jeannie had gotten quite attached.

The wounds were healing, and the doctors couldn't believe the soldier didn't have a raging infection by now. They told Jeannie to keep up the excellent work.

Several months later, the young man was sitting on the side of his bed looking out the window when Jeannie entered the ward. Smiling at each other, she went over and sat beside him. They held hands for a moment before Gerald gave her a quick kiss on the cheek. Gerald was ready to be discharged, and Jeannie was there to take him home.

Still a little weak from all those months of illness and recovery, Gerald walked slowly beside Jeannie as they said goodbye to several patients and staff members. Then, as they entered the fresh air and sunshine, Gerald stopped and smiled, took a deep breath, and hugged Jeannie. Smiling, they walked over to the taxi that was waiting for them and got in.

The first stop was the courthouse and the Justice of the Peace. The taxi waited as the couple got married, then took them to Jeannie's apartment. Gerald rested as she packed up the rest of her things. Jeannie turned in the keys, and the taxi soon arrived at the train station. There they were met by another man, and the trio waited for their train to arrive. Soon, they were on their way back to Hastings.

Jeannie sent a telegram earlier that morning to her Aunt Effie May to inform her of their arrival date and time. Since she had no idea what Elizabeth May's work schedule was, it was easier to make sure that Aunt Effie May was notified.

The trip lasted over two days, with all the stops that were made along the way. So, naturally, the men tried to rest as much as possible since they were both still weak. The dining car provided them with enough food to sustain the hungry men on board. In addition, there were several ex-soldiers headed for their homes. The men had lots to talk about on the trip, and Jeannie relaxed in her seat while the men conversed.

Jeannie was more than ready to get off the train when it pulled into Hastings. She and Gerald would be moving into her mother's house, and they were anxious to start their marriage. Gerald had no idea what he would do for a job, but Jeannie reassured him there was no hurry. The hospital would be happy to have her back for the time being. She hadn't even mentioned that her family was all well off. He would find out soon enough.

Joseph was waiting at the station for Jeannie's arrival. Alongside were the parents of the other man that arrived with them. Jeannie introduced her husband to her Uncle Joseph. Joseph got the luggage, and soon, they went to the Turner home to drop the couple off. It gave Jeannie time to explain a bit about Gerald and the other man. There were tears in his eyes as he dropped the couple off, instructing them to stop by for supper. Agreeing, the couple entered the house, and Joseph quickly went home to talk to Effie May.

When Elizabeth May got off work that evening, she was anxious to get home and see if Jeannie had arrived. She was excited to hear her voice as she walked through the door. They hugged and chatted excitedly before Elizabeth May noticed someone standing beside her.

Jeannie reached over and pulled Gerald closer. "This is my husband, Gerald Moffit. Gerald, my favorite and closest cousin, Elizabeth May Walker."

"Miss Walker, it's so good to finally meet you. Jeannie has talked about you incessantly." He took her hand and clasped it tightly.

"Oh, my. I wish I could say the same thing about you." She turned to her cousin. "This is the surprise you have for us?"

"One of them." Jeannie couldn't help but grin from ear to ear.

Elizabeth May laughed and looked back to Gerald. "It's wonderful to meet you. Welcome to the Walker-Turner family."

"Thank you." Gerald turned and went to sit back down.

Elizabeth May took Jeannie by the arm and pulled her along up the stairs. "You are going with me while I change." They ran into the bedroom, and Elizabeth May slammed the door and squealed, "Oh! Tell me all about Gerald!"

"I will. Go on ahead and wash up and change. Put on something nice for supper."

"Why? You're already married. I don't think I need to impress the young man."

"Do it for me, please?"

Elizabeth May shook her head and laughed. "Start talking."

It was several minutes before the cousins came back downstairs. Elizabeth May refused to move until Jeannie had answered all her questions. The story was quite moving, but she could tell they were quite smitten with each other.

"What is he going to do now?"

"I don't know. He still needs to rebuild his strength. I figure our families probably have something he could do somewhere. It doesn't matter right now. I have the Turner house to live in. It seems no one else wants it, and I can go back to work at the hospital until I'm in the family way."

"I'm so happy for you."

Elizabeth May gave her a long hug, and then they joined the family. They were getting ready to sit down to dinner when there was a knock on the door.

Effie May turned to her daughter. "Elizabeth May, would you go see who's at the door?"

"Certainly, Mother. Everyone, please have a seat. I'll be right back."

Elizabeth May smiled as she opened the door, expecting more family members arriving to see Jeannie. She wasn't expecting the man standing in front of her.

"Pete? Is that really you?"

A frail young man stood there holding his hat in his hands. He nodded. "Yes. It's me, beautiful."

Elizabeth May stood there shocked. Her hand went to her chest, and she found it difficult to breathe right. Then, feeling Jeannie's arm around her waist, she heard a whisper say, "Give him a hug, dear cousin." Then the arm moved to her back and gave Elizabeth May a little shove toward Pete. The two grasped each other, and both of them began to cry. Elizabeth May could hardly control herself and wept tubs of tears. Finally, they found their way to the porch swing and sat holding each other for what seemed like forever. The family had gone ahead and sat down for supper, leaving the couple alone.

"I don't understand. I thought you were dead."

"I was in a German prison camp. I thought many times I might as well be dead because I was in terrible shape. So many of my brothers didn't make it. Then I would think of you waiting for me, and I knew I had to come home someday. I was rescued a few months ago, and that's when I met Jeannie. I was trying to recover, and she was my nurse one day. I recognized her immediately, but I looked so pathetic it took her a minute or two. I'd lost a lot of weight and was pretty sick. She worked to make me strong enough to come home. I notified my parents when I returned to the States, but I told them not to say anything to you. My father came to see me once to make sure I was really alive. Honestly, it was still iffy for some time, but I wanted to surprise you once I found out you hadn't moved on."

"Oh, Pete. I would have come to see you, too, if I had known."

Pete shook his head. "I wasn't fit for man or beast. My father told my mother she couldn't come, either. I still have nightmares, but I hope things will get better now that I'm home and with you."

Elizabeth May's stomach growled, and they laughed. "Let's join the family and have supper. I'm sure there is plenty left."

"Alright, but we need to talk about our future afterward." Elizabeth May nodded her head, and they walked into the house hand-in-hand.

"Jeannie, you are such a sneak." The women were washing the dishes and catching up.

"It was all I could do not to tell you about Pete, but he threatened me within an inch of my life if I said a word about him coming home."

"Besides that, you brought home a husband we didn't know about."

"Well, he wasn't my husband until we left the hospital to come home. Speaking of which, I'm taking my new husband home right now." Jeannie threw her towel at Elizabeth May and quickly left the kitchen, hollering for Gerald.

Elizabeth May followed, looking for Pete. He was waiting for her, and she stopped walking and smiled at him. He was so gaunt and frail, but she knew she could help him get stronger. Once Gerald and Jeannie left the house, Effie May and Joseph excused themselves to leave the young couple alone.

"I have missed you so much, my beautiful lady. I had forgotten how pretty you were. Unfortunately, I lost my picture of you." Pete paused. "I have to confess something."

"What?" Elizabeth May looked worried.

"Before I left for the war, I didn't tell you that I wasn't in any hurry to get married because I wanted to travel and see the world. I knew you were a homebody and wouldn't be interested. I didn't know how to tell you. Then, when Pearl Harbor was bombed, I thought it was an excellent opportunity to see the world and that I wouldn't have to pay for the trip."

"That was a stupid reason to join. You could have been killed." Elizabeth May was incensed at Pete's reasoning.

He patted her hand. "I know that now, but you have to remember I've never been too bright." He let out a sigh. "I saw the world alright. But it was ugly, dirty, and I never want to leave home again."

"So, you're staying home and going to help your father?"

"Stay home, yes. Helping my father? I don't know. I'm too weak to do anything right now. Mother will feed me, and I'll keep walking and building my strength. I have brothers that are helping Father in the store. I haven't been home long enough to decide on much of anything. But there is one decision I made long ago, and I'd like to stick with that."

"Really? What is it?"

Pete got down in front of Elizabeth May and held out a ring. "Will you marry me, my sweet, beautiful lady?"

Elizabeth May looked at the ring and reached over to help Pete sit back beside her. "Yes. A thousand times, yes. We have lost so much time. I'm ready whenever you are."

"Wonderful. I'd love to get married like Jeannie and Gerald, unless you want a big wedding. After all, you have a huge family."

She laughed. "You don't know the half of it. No, let's do the courthouse."

"Oh. I forgot."

"What?"

"We don't have a place to live by ourselves, and I certainly can't afford to buy a house right now."

Elizabeth smiled. "You leave that to me. With our family, someone always has room in their house for another couple."

"Meaning?"

"Have you ever been in the Turner house where Jeannie is living?"

"I can't say that I have."

"It's huge. My Aunt Maude always had family staying at one time or another. I bet Jeannie and Gerald would let us move into the guest wing for now."

Pete smiled. "You Walkers sure know how to live."

"Ah. The Walker-Turners know how to live. And you are marrying into the nicest family in the region."

"I don't care where we live, as long as I'm with you. I love you so much, Elizabeth May."

"I love you, too, Pete Perkins."

A few days later, Pete and Elizabeth May were married at the courthouse with the parents looking on. That afternoon, the couple moved into the Turner home, making the guest wing their own private space for the time being. However, when the children began to arrive, Elizabeth May hoped to have their own home by then. Preferably close to Jeannie and Gerald. She wanted to raise their children together as her parents and their parents before them did.

The following year, the war was over when the atomic bombs were dropped on Japan. Up to fifty million people perished in World War II. So many were left homeless and wounded throughout Europe and East Asia. A few young men returned to Hastings, but many never returned. Pete, Gerald, James, Henry, and Mark tried to put the war behind them as they returned to their daily lives. It was never far from their thoughts, but they never discussed the war with their family members. Occasionally, they might discuss it amongst themselves, but it was easier to leave the past in the past.

Maude, Jesse May, and Ada left a great legacy behind. The generations that came after forever tried to live up to the proud Walker-Turner names.

About The Author

Diane Winters is from Southwest Nebraska and is an avid reader of all genres. She came from a large family and grew up in a farming community. She was blessed with two children and has four grandchildren of her own. Diane has been a nurse for many years and held various positions in the healthcare field over time. She appreciates the sunsets, rainstorms and rainbows, and views from the mountain tops. She and her husband enjoy traveling, and the drive time gives Diane the opportunity to work out new storylines. You may wish to keep a watch for her next book release on her Facebook and web page:

www.facebook.com/DianeLWinters
webpage: **www.DianeWinters-author.org**

www.blossomspringpublishing.com

Made in the USA
Monee, IL
04 February 2023

26324714R00156